Stepping into the Flames

By Charles L. Foti
Copyright 2022

For Robin

Who rescued me…and believes in me

My muse, my editor, my inspiration…

1

1982

Pia had no future, so she lived in the past. She focused on her happy childhood living with Nonna, her beloved grandmother, in a small village in Ulster County, New York. When Nonna died, twelve-year-old Pia was sent to the county orphanage since she had no other living relatives. She was alone.

She continually attempts to block out all thoughts of the six years she spent in the orphanage, watching younger children greet their new parents, knowing no one *wanted* her. She was a teenager soon after her arrival and all the folks who frequented the bleak institution were looking for babies or toddlers or prepubescent children. She gave up all hope by the time she turned fourteen and accepted the fact that she would never again have a family.

Her parents died in a fire a few weeks after her fourth birthday. Gaetano, her baby brother, was not quite two when the fire broke out in the kitchen. Flames swept through the house like a hungry, crazed demon in search of kindling to fuel its fury. The firemen later told her grandmother that her parents and Gaetano died from smoke inhalation. Nonna was thankful they did not die of painful burns.

Pia had been spending the night with Nonna when finger-like flames engulfed her parents' house shortly after midnight, strangling and suffocating Pia's family, pocketing their oxygen without mercy or shame. The firemen said faulty wiring caused the humble home to burst into a ruthless blaze on that cold March night that foreshadowed a late spring. Pia loved to spend Saturday nights with Nonna, who loved to roll on the floor with her granddaughter and pepper her belly with kisses and giggles.

When Pia woke that Sunday morning, Nonna sat on the side of her little bed and kissed her gently on the cheek. She calmly whispered that Gaetano and her mommy and daddy had gone to Heaven. Pia wept often over the months that followed, as her grief weighed on her heart like shadows clinging to the walls, but her love for Nonna kept hope alive. It was just the two of them now.

They nearly skipped the following Christmas, since fire not only burns flesh, but also freezes the hearts and souls of the grieving survivors, paralyzing their ability to feel joy. But as the spring crocuses and daffodils ushered in the shamrock-green summer grass, Nonna discovered her smile again and infected Pia with laughter and an appreciation of what remained. They had each other and the empty spaces began to fill up again as Nonna taught Pia to prepare Italian delicacies in her humble kitchen and food not only sustained their bodies, but awakened their hearts. It was a quiet Christmas that year, but it was enough of a diversion to allow them to smile a bit and find solace in simple blessings.

Pia clung to the notion that she was profoundly loved by her grandmother as she became disabused of her belief that her life was more miserable than most because of the tragedy that haunted her dreams. She studied Nonna's old photographs in order to create precious, invisible watermarks in her memory so that she would never forget sweet Gaetano or her loving parents. She had celebrated her fourth birthday exactly four weeks before the world she knew was scuttled by faulty electrical wiring.

She would never forget her fourth birthday party where Nonna led the family in song as they serenaded her with a joyous rendition of *Happy Birthday* and showered her with priceless, humble gifts. How was she to know that it would be her last birthday with her parents as Gaetano licked chocolate cake icing from his lips and pleaded relentlessly for another small slice?

Nonna gave Pia a comfortable life and they found many reasons to laugh as the years elapsed and Pia grew to be taller than her beloved grandmother. Seven months after Pia's twelfth birthday, during her second week of 7th grade, Nonna's heart stopped while she was stirring a marinara sauce on a Sunday morning. Pia was still asleep when it happened. She would discover her grandmother on the recently-mopped, gray linoleum about an hour after Nonna closed her warm, nurturing eyes for the final time. Pia instantly knew Nonna had gone to Heaven to join her daughter, her son-in-law, and her precious grandson. Young Pia was now completely alone in the world as she began to wall off her heart.

As a fledgling adult she is comforted by dreams that dwell on the joyful years, the years when she and Nonna laughed and danced around the kitchen together, sliding across the shiny, gray linoleum in worn, white cotton socks. Nonna was partial to the Beatles and Pia knew the words to most of their songs by the time she was nine. Whenever she hears a Lennon/McCartney tune on an elevator or in a restaurant, her thoughts immediately run to Nonna. She can picture herself as that nine-year-old child, twirling around and around with her grandmother, giggling to the point of nearly peeing her panties as they sing into their Italian breadsticks.

During the six years in the orphanage, she focused on her happy memories with Nonna until she drifted off to sleep each night, hoping for pleasant dreams. But sometimes, she dreamt of the demon fire that felt no mercy, not even for a child who would never taste birthday icing again, a boy who was not yet two years of age. She had *not* experienced the horrific heat from the horror and she hardly remembered her parents or her baby brother, but her imagination often ran wild and turned her dreams to nightmares that caused her to wake on saturated sheets, covered with sweat and sorrow.

Pia grew up with a conflicted personality. Part of her was still that happy child who adored her life with Nonna. But then there was the dark side, the part of her that feared fire and wallowed in her paralyzing pain. She had lost her entire family by the time she turned twelve and a half and her only living relatives were in Italy, far, far away from the world she knew. But no one bothered to track them down and Pia was simply cast aside as a ward of the state of New York.

She married Arty three months after her twentieth birthday. He was the only man she had ever known in that way. He wasn't actually a boyfriend as she had never had one of those. Arty used to buy his groceries in a little store where Pia was employed. Her work responsibilities included keeping the floors clean and tidying up the shelves and produce. She got the job when she left the orphanage a few months after her eighteenth birthday. The county set her up in a halfway house where she had her own room, but she shared a bleak, communal bathroom with a chipped porcelain sink and a temperamental toilet seat that was loosely secured by a single, rusty bolt.

Arty would flirt with her when he picked out a melon, asking her to help him pick out a good one, not too ripe, but not too soft. Pia did not know many boys very well as the orphanage kept the children segregated by gender. The county even sent her to an all girl's Catholic school, where there were no boys to interfere with her education, and scratchy, woolen uniforms were mandatory. When she graduated, she gave both of her school uniforms to charity and closed that chapter of her austere life.

Arty was sweet at first and when he finally took her on that first date, her head was spinning with delight. Two months later, they were married by a justice of the peace and she lost her virginity that evening. Arty promised he would be gentle, knowing she lacked experience, but his lovemaking was hasty and quite perfunctory. He wasn't much older at twenty-two and he had had limited experience with affairs of the heart or of the flesh. Pia thought marital relations would be anchored by a tender *sharing*, but she discovered Arty's perception of making love was all about *taking* without *giving* as he reached his peak of pleasure with little regard for his partner.

The sex was accomplished more from mutual persistence, than from true desire, but Pia believed it would get better over time. She did not climax on her wedding night, but when Arty had reached satisfaction, he merely rolled over and quickly dozed off. She remembered thinking that sex was disappointing at best and demeaning to the point of her suffering a damp pillow case that was stained with her tears. Arty seemed to be masturbating and merely using her body as a mechanical device that enabled him to reach his carnal objective. But she was too diffident and totally inexperienced to express an opinion and when Arty asked her if she liked it, she nodded, shyly, as she served him his morning coffee.

He never beat her during their four nights at Niagara Falls, not physically at least, but his moody disposition caused her to feel emotionally abused when she returned from the dull, humble honeymoon feeling forlorn and empty. Pia kept trying to please him in the bedroom over the months that followed, but it became apparent that Arty had grown bored with her body and her inability to arouse him when he was sober and distracted by life. Everything in life is but a diversion, and for Arty that was all their lovemaking was, a diversion from taxes and aching feet, a distraction from mundane conversation and mindless television. But as the sex became as humdrum and routine as the dialogue, he started to search for pleasure elsewhere.

He began to ignore her as he focused on watching a game on the television or tinkering with the engine of his 1977 Chevy El Camino that he kept parked on the street. Pia waited for an opportunity to flee from Arty's apathetic ambivalence, to run away from a marriage that had barely just begun. She quickly realized that he was smitten with her prior to the wedding, but from that day forward, he gradually lost interest in her thoughts, her flesh, or her sanguine aspirations. She didn't understand what happened between them, but she lacked the courage to discover how to repair the stagnant relationship. She simply wanted out.

And finally, the moment arrived when Arty had to go upstate for a family funeral. His great-uncle passed away and it was rumored that Arty was in the will. The possibility of sharing in his rather large estate was not something that Arty took lightly. Naturally, he would attend the services and show his respect.

"Shall I go with you?" Pia asked, innocently.

"No, you stay here. Keep working and don't spend any of your next paycheck. The rent will be due soon," Arty mumbled as he shaved his chin, carefully, so as not to nick himself. Pia nodded and left the cramped bathroom with hope in her heart.

Arty worked nights as a bartender and Pia worked days. She loved being alone with their small television that was wired to an old rusty antenna. They got ten channels on a good day, but Pia never complained. She loved the solitude where she could lose herself in happier times, when Nonna would serenade her with a ballad like *Michelle* or *Yesterday*. Paul McCartney's sweet voice lived in her head, along with Nonna's mezzo-soprano renditions. She *had* been happy once upon a time, she still remembered.

But she feared Arty would begin to become physically abusive on the nights when he came home from work with a few drinks in him. He had never raised a hand to her, not yet, but she sensed he was growing more impatient with everything she did and she refused to hang around long enough to find out where the marriage was heading. Every time she asked her husband if he was happy, he would laugh and tell her he had never met a truly happy individual.

On the day Arty left for the out-of-town funeral, Pia packed her two suitcases and boarded a Greyhound in the opposite direction. She had been secretly saving every dime she could and she left town with nearly two hundred dollars tucked into a dainty money belt. She said goodbye to New York State and headed south to Wheaton, Maryland.

Pia knew a woman in Wheaton. They lived in the orphanage together for four of the six years Pia lived there. Portia was older and she had moved to Wheaton two years before Pia left the orphanage, but she wrote letters to her every month or two. Pia kept the letters hidden from Arty and she never spoke of her friend from the orphanage. As far as Arty knew, Pia had no friends and no family. Perhaps that was the appeal, the reason why he convinced her to marry him so quickly, she was alone in the world. In his mind, she would never leave him, despite the emotional abuse that seemed to give him a deranged kind of sadistic pleasure. He seemed to enjoy mocking her if she burned the toast and ridiculing her when she struggled to iron all the wrinkles out of his dress shirts. They were apparently not a match made in heaven, and she feared their marriage would turn her life into a lonely, unfulfilled hell.

As the bus crossed the state line into New Jersey, Pia breathed a sigh of relief. She had scoured the apartment, making sure she left no clues behind. She counted the letters twice before she tucked them into her larger suitcase. There were twenty-eight letters. She had them all. She called Portia from a payphone on the day she learned about Arty's plan to attend the funeral.

"Have you mailed any letters recently?" she had asked.

"No, sorry about that. Been so busy with the new job in DC," Portia told her.

"Good. Don't send anymore. I'm leaving Arty and I don't want him to know about you. Can I stay with you for a few weeks?"

"You can stay as long as you want."

"Thank you, Portia. You just saved my life." Portia suspected the emotional abuse, but Pia had never actually told her much about her lonely marriage. She just knew Pia was unhappy and she was glad her old friend was leaving the bastard. Portia knew Arty was not a good man. The signs were all there.

"Arty doesn't know anything about me?" Portia whispered into the phone as if the creep might somehow be listening in the muddy shadows.

"No, he thinks I have no friends, no family, just him. I'm not sure he knows how to love someone. I think he married me so he didn't have to be alone anymore. He wants a maid to cook and clean and iron his clothes. He isn't interested in getting to know me, the real me."

"I'm so sorry, kid. Did he hit you?"

"No, he has never raised a hand to me, but the apathy and sarcasm are worse. A bruise would heal, but he has been destroying what little self-confidence I have. I need to run away from him. I guess I never loved him, but I thought I could learn to love him if he loved me. But I seem to constantly annoy him. I just can't seem to do anything right."

"I'd like to pay the coward a visit. I have two uncles who would be happy to come along and bring their baseball bats with them." Orphaned at fourteen, she didn't know until recently she actually had kin living in Virginia.

"I just want to disappear."

"What about the marriage?"

"Someday, I'll try to get it annulled. But for now, I just need to hide from him."

"Come, stay with me for a year if you want. I'll help you find a good job. DC has lots of opportunities for women. The government jobs pay a lot better than that grocery store."

"Thank you. I'll see you on Thursday. I'll call you when I get close."

"OK, just be careful. I love you, Pia."

"I love you too."

And so it was decided. Pia would be living with Portia and starting over. But as the bus moved through New Jersey and then Delaware, she kept worrying. Could Arty find her? Was she making the right decision to cut and run? Was she giving up on her marriage vows too easily? She was so conflicted, but she just couldn't stay with Arty a minute longer. She was suffocating inside. She needed oxygen and Portia was her only salvation.

2

Pia now believes she *has* a future. Forgetting Arty was easy, she simply pretended it was all a mere nightmare. But she is awake now, living with Portia, ready to begin her life.

Her memories of her parents and baby brother are faint, blurry and distant. Her memories of Nonna are the foundation that provided the strength to leave Arty and take that first step towards a life worth living, far away from her sadness.

Her memories of the orphanage, as sad as they are, provide her with resolve and pluck. Portia continually reminds her of the happy moments when the two of them pulled pranks on the adults at the orphanage and broke a few of their ridiculous rules, sneaking outside at midnight, pajama-clad and giddy, as Portia sneaked a smoke and Pia gazed at the ebony sky and the noble stars that she felt were also orphans in the night. Portia has spunk and Pia is now evolving as she imitates her friend's optimistic attitude towards life and basks in her sisterly warmth.

Portia sashayed into Pia's life wearing a threadbare frock and a mischievous grin shortly after she arrived at the orphanage, and after that the two of them became inseparable. But when Portia aged out Pia slipped into an abyss of sorrow. That was when the dark side of her fragile personality began to fester. Her nightmares focused on the demon-fire that took away her family and she refused to befriend another orphan to console her shattered heart after Portia moved far away.

She loved Portia and when the older girl left the orphanage, Pia shut down. She barely spoke to anyone during her last two years before she too aged out. She had become a recluse, living among other orphans, mostly younger than her. She simply stopped talking and soon the others ignored her and whispered behind her back, calling her a backward weirdo or a stunted odd duck.

Her teachers noticed the change in her personality, but most of them were penguin-like nuns, and they simply told her to pray to eradicate her soul of whatever demons had possessed her. But Pia was not very religious, despite Nonna's influence. Nonna attended mass every Sunday morning and Pia was at her side. But after Nonna died Pia's faith began to waver and the stoic nuns gave her no comfort, no answers.

"I think I may be a lesbian," Pia blurts out, casually, one evening as they devour a mushroom pizza together.

"Really," Portia comments. "Maybe you've just never known any nice guys." Portia has a boyfriend, and Pia knows he is one of the good guys.

"I know. It's easy to think all guys are like Arty. I know Ben is a good man."

"He's the best. I think one of his friends just broke up with his girlfriend. I should get Ben to set you up." Pia has not dated since she arrived in Wheaton two months ago. It is time. She is officially still married, but she tossed her simple wedding band into the bottom drawer of her dresser in the guestroom, buried under a slouchy, shamrock-green shirt that she seldom wears. One day she will try to sell it, but she doubts it is worth much.

"I'm not ready to date anyone, especially a guy who is on the rebound."

"OK, no rush. But I doubt you are gay. I know you better than anyone and I've never seen any signs that you are a lesbian."

"Do you have any lesbian friends?" Pia asks.

"Sure, I mean not close friends, just work friends. I know at least three or maybe four. Not sure about one of them. Why, do you want me to set you up with one of them?"

"Not set me up, just invite them over for dinner. I want to get to know some lesbians. How else can I figure this all out? I've never known any lesbians to my knowledge."

Pia works in a small office with three married men and two married women. She is the only single employee, not counting Marie, their supervisor, who was married twice. The seven of them spend forty hours a week, putting data into a computer, and trying to make sense of their purpose. But the job pays well and it is right on the subway route.

Portia told her she would invite a bunch of her coworkers to a house party soon. The apartment isn't large, but they can cram a couple of dozen guests into the living room and kitchen. It will be fun. Hopefully the lesbians will show, but if not, they will still have a good time. Pia is excited about the prospect of meeting some actual gay women because she really doesn't know what she wants. She only knows she never wants to lay eyes on Arty again.

She often lies in bed at night, wide awake, suffering from her usual insomnia and attempting to suppress the dark side of her personality. Pia has one friend in this scary world and had it not been for Portia, she surely would have gone mad by now and leaped off of a bridge or walked straight into traffic.

She is used to having no family since none of the girls at the orphanage had relatives, but after Nonna died, she lived in a place where hugs were few and affection was rare. Portia would hug her goodnight on random nights…until she aged out. After that, Pia withdrew and became more paralyzed with loneliness. She could never hug any of the others as she felt she would be giving away a part of her heart, a part that would never be returned to her.

All the people in her life died or were taken from her and she no longer wished to risk the pain of needing another human being again. Is it possible to feel completely alone while living with fifty other girls in a dormitory? It wouldn't have mattered if there had been 500 girls, once Portia left Pia would have felt just as alone.

The party was on. But in order to accommodate everyone's busy schedules, it would not occur for five weeks. The party would be on February 19th, a week after Pia's 21st birthday. It would feel like a belated birthday celebration, even if the guest list was comprised mostly of strangers. She would only know Portia and Ben. Thank heavens for Ben. She was comfortable around him and their conversations were never guarded or trivial. Pia liked talking to Ben as he was nothing like Arty. He was the antithesis of her husband and she envied Portia.

Pia would just have to wait a little longer to meet some lesbians. She could have searched for a bar where gay women frequent, but she was underage and she had never frequented a place like that before, not even a neighborhood pub or a family tavern. She considered trying to find a social group where she would meet lesbians, but she was far too shy and intimidated by the prospect of walking into a room of complete strangers.

She asked Portia if she would accompany her to such an event and her only friend told her she would look into it. So Pia waited, she waited to begin her life. She really wasn't at all sure of her sexual preference, she only knew she loved Portia. Did she fantasize about Portia in that way? Not really. Perhaps she was asexual or frigid. She was poorly schooled in such matters and she was confused about the allure of sex since she had never actually experienced an orgasm. The only intimacy she had known was shrouded in apathy and abuse. Arty had introduced her to sex, but he had poisoned her ability to find any joy in it and now she was slipping deeper into the darkness that had numbed her heart.

When Portia hugged her goodnight a few days ago, she froze up, feeling her muscles tense as if it had been the first time anyone hugged her. But this was Portia, the person who had hugged her hundreds of times during her childhood. Why would she suddenly feel so uncomfortable? She feared she was regressing into the kind of individual who was repulsed by human touch, even a hug from her only friend, the only person she now loved.

It was a mystery to her. And then it happened again last night. When Portia hugged her, she pulled away and surprised her friend with a wrinkled look of despair on her face.

"Is something wrong?" Portia asked, jokingly, but then she saw the look on Pia's face and she knew something was up.

"I don't like to be touched. After what Arty did to me, I think I have become frigid or something."

"You should have said something earlier. I won't touch you until you initiate. If you want to be hugged, just give me a sign. I think you will get over this in time. You were mistreated and abused by a troubled man, but he is gone from your life. He'll never find you."

"I hope not. Sometimes, I think I should move further away. He's only seven hours from here."

"Don't worry. I still have my two uncles with the baseball bats. If Arty ever bothers you again, you won't have to face him alone."

"I'm sorry about the hug," Pia muttered as tears threatened her dark eyes.

"It's fine. I've hugged you a thousand times. It's me, remember? You don't need to feel threatened by my touch, but I realize you have no control over what you are feeling. No more touching for the time being."

"What about when all those people come to the party?"

"No one will hug you. You are a stranger to them all. Would you have a problem shaking hands with a few of them if they reach out?"

"I don't know."

"Well, let's give you some time. Most of my coworkers will just say hello. It will be fine."

"Don't tell them I don't like being touched. They'll all think I'm a crazy person."

"I won't say a word to anyone, not even Ben. This is just between you and me. You know I love you, right?"

"I love you too," Pia said as she nodded. It would have been a perfect moment for her to fall into Portia's arms, but both of them knew that was not going to occur.

On Saturday mornings, Pia goes grocery shopping. It is a small establishment, bigger than a gas station convenience store, but much smaller than the huge supermarkets. Portia hardly ever goes there because the prices are higher than the bigger stores, but Pia prefers the quiet. There are always plenty of parking places and the checkout lines are rarely very long. Of course, Pia doesn't drive and she simply enjoys the walk as she hauls her small wire cart. The aisles are never filled with rowdy children or crammed with grocery carts filled with junk food and beer. Pia can meander through the store, lost in her thoughts, and take her time. She is seldom in a hurry as she has no social life on weekends.

"Do you know how to tell if a melon is almost ready to be cut?" a voice asks. She freezes up because his words remind her of Arty. That's how he wormed his way into her life.

"Push on the part where the stem used to be and see if it is a little soft," she responds, politely.

"Like this?" he asks as he steps closer. He is inches away and she tenses up. She nearly screams out in distress, but she suppresses her impulse to panic.

"Yes, like that."

"Can you press it to tell me what you think?"

She reaches out to press on the correct spot while he holds the melon. Their forearms touch for an instant and she pulls away. He notices her alarm and he steps back.

"I'm sorry…I don't like to be touched," she admits, frantically. She is trembling, but she notices the compassion in his warm, green eyes. He has beautiful eyes and for a second she finds herself attracted to him. But her emotions force such thoughts from her mind and she continues to back away, to look away. Then she stops and stares at her own feet in complete embarrassment.

"It's OK. I really know exactly what you are feeling. I used to be the same way. My stepfather sometimes beat me when I was young. By the time I left the house, I was so afraid of being touched that I didn't date for a couple of years. I'm 22 years old and I'm still a virgin. I don't know why I told you that. Now I'm embarrassed."

"You don't have to be embarrassed." She looks up and realizes he is grinning. He is the handsomest man she has ever seen and thoughts of lesbian women begin to evaporate as she finds herself staring. She makes sure her shopping cart is between them and he makes no sudden moves. He understands she is afraid.

"I have dated girls, and touched them, and allowed them to touch me, but I'm still afraid of complete intimacy. Maybe I'm waiting until I find the right girl. There's no hurry. It's just that you know how guys are. A 22-year-old virgin would be ridiculed by other guys."

"If they made fun of you, then they aren't your friends," she mutters. A part of her wants to get away from this man, to continue her shopping, and yet, another part of her is mesmerized by his warm, perfect smile and hypnotized by the cadence of his words.

"That's true. I have a few buddies I've known forever. I grew up in Silver Spring and we still shoot hoops on Saturday mornings. They all talk about the women they have had sex with and I pretend I'm a player, but it's all a lie."

"They may be lying as well," she responds without looking him in the eye. She wants to walk away, but her feet feel glued to the floor and she is paralyzed by this sudden interaction with another human being.

"That's true, I mean if I'm lying, they must be embellishing at the very least. But I doubt any of them are virgins. I'm the baby of the group. They're all 23 or 24 years old. One of them is actually divorced. Sam married young after high school. They were together since 8th grade. But it didn't work out."

"I would guess Sam has had sex," she says with an awkward grin.

"He claimed they were doing it in 9th grade. I guess they just burned out. I mean they would always remember one another from 8th grade when they were still evolving. Sam had terrible acne in 8th grade and we were all surprised he was such a ladies man. Kids change and I guess Sam and Marnie grew apart."

"I like that name…Marnie," she says as she shifts her weight from her right foot to her left and then back again. Why is she continuing this conversation that began over a melon and evolved into her panicking when their elbows touched? Is it because she has felt such loneliness during so much of her life? For some odd reason, she is more comfortable with this complete stranger than she is with any of her coworkers at the office.

"Yes, I agree, and Marnie is as pretty as her name. She's probably already married again. I lost track of her."

"I should finish my shopping."

"Can I introduce myself?"

"I guess."

"I'm Jake, Jake McGuire."

"Hi Jake."

"And you are?"

"Marnie," she lies.

"You're joking?"

"I am."

"So you won't tell me your real name?"

"I could tell you anything, how would you know if it was the truth?"

"I wouldn't, unless you show me a driver's license or something with your name on it…"

"I don't drive."

"I could teach you."

"I'll tell you my name, but you'll just have to trust me."

"I trust you."

"My name is Pia."

"That's a beautiful name, even prettier than Marnie."

"I don't know, it's just my name."

"Any last name?"

"That's for another day. We *are* still strangers."

"True, if I knew your surname, I could stalk you by looking you up in the white pages."

"I'm not in the phone book, but you're right. Girls shouldn't give out their last names or phone numbers to strangers."

"I agree. You are very wise. A lot of guys are animals. I assure you I am a gentleman."

"Only time will prove that to me."

"Do you shop here often?"

"On Saturdays…why aren't you shooting hoops?"

"The guys cancelled, one of them twisted his ankle and another one was really hung over after a big night at the bars."

"Then you aren't here on Saturdays in general?"

"No, I actually tend to hit the bigger places where there's a better selection of melons. I eat a lot of fruit. Plus this place is a little pricey for me. I'm saving up to buy a house. I share an apartment with Sam right now, you know the guy with all the pimples in 8th grade."

"The ladies' man who married Marnie and then divorced her?"

"You were paying attention."

"I was…he claimed to have had sex with her in 9th grade."

"He did, but guys do embellish and lie, like you said."

"They do."

"It was nice to meet you, Pia." He extends his hand and she stares at him, but keeps her hands firmly on the handle of her shopping cart. "Sorry, that was just a reflex." He waves and she turns her cart away. She wanted to buy some fruit, but right now she needs to leave some distance between them. She thought Arty was nice at first too, and that was a huge error in judgment.

"Bye Jake," she calls out. She wants to turn her head and look back. She is certain he is smiling, but she does not dare to look. She simply keeps moving her feet as her mind drifts back to his penetrating green eyes and his perfect teeth. His smile could light up a dark room, but she is suspicious of men, of all men.

When she gets home, she pulls the perishables from her bags and moves a few things around in the fridge to make room for them. Portia is on the phone with Ben and she can overhear their conversation. It doesn't sound good.

"Look, if that's how you feel, we should just break up now," Portia yells. Pia tenses up as she closes the fridge door and focuses on her task. She places a box of cereal in an upper cabinet and then opens the doors under the sink so she can put away the glass cleaner and liquid soap.

"Fuck you, Ben. Go to Hell." Portia slams the receiver on the kitchen wall phone and storms off. She walks towards the bathroom in a trance, ignoring the presence of her roommate and shuts the door with a bang. The stereo is on low and Pia turns off the music and listens. She can hear Portia sobbing. She taps lightly on the bathroom door.

"Do you want to talk?" she utters. There is no response. "I'm here if you need me." Silence. She goes to her bedroom and lies down. She is worried about Portia who apparently just broke up with Ben. She wishes there was something she could do. But her mind keeps drifting back to the produce department where a very handsome guy smiled at her. Not all men are like Arty, she continues to remind herself.

Jake probably thought she is a virgin since she told him she doesn't like to be touched. She is almost 21 years old, but she looks young. She could pass for 18. He probably assumes she has never been with a man. Some guys are attracted to that. Portia says every guy is on the hunt for a virgin. But she is no virgin. She has experienced meaningless, perfunctory sex, but she never enjoyed any of it. How could she? She never came close to climaxing and now she is uncertain if she is even capable of an orgasm.

Of course she knows he could have been lying about having never had sex. Why would a stranger even mention to her that he is a virgin? It had to be a line. He must have been trying to win her over with his boyish charm. She shouldn't trust him. She doubts she'll ever see him again. He usually plays basketball on Saturdays and he doesn't shop in the small store very often. She is safe. He will not cross her path again. Or will he?

3

Pia fears she has lost her only friend. Portia told her that Ben asked for an open relationship where each of them would be free to date other people…to sleep with other people. Portia was stunned by the suggestion, but at first she believed Ben was merely joking and she laughed at the prospect. She actually asked him if he wanted to sleep with Pia and Ben went silent for a moment.

"Yes, I think I would like to sleep with Pia. I find her very attractive. I'm 24 years old and I'm just not ready to limit myself to one person anymore. But I do love you, Portia."

That's when Portia realized this was not a joke. That's when she broke into tears which were followed by rage and utter disappointment. Then she told Ben to go to Hell and she disconnected the call, nearly knocking the old yellow phone from the wall. When she told Pia about the conversation, Pia was comforting and supportive. But as the days evaporated, Portia became more distant. She cancelled the party in February and she told Pia is was time for her to look for an apartment of her own.

"I would never date Ben and I would certainly never have sex with him," Pia protests.

"I know you like him," Portia replies with a sarcastic tone.

"I did like him. I thought he was a great guy, but now I no longer hold him in high regard. He hurt you and you are my best friend, my only real friend. I'm loyal to you. Will you ever speak to him again?"

"I don't know. He left me a few messages, but I am screening my calls, here and at work. I just delete his messages without even listening to them. He made himself crystal clear that he wants to sleep with other women and I am a monogamous person. I thought we were in love. I was such a fool."

"You're not a fool. Maybe he's just going through something. I'll bet he feels terrible about how it ended. I still believe he loves you very much."

"But he fantasizes about jumping your bones, apparently," Portia declares with anger in her voice. But she is not angry with Pia. Ben is the one she wants to strangle.

"Do you still want me to move out?" Pia asks as tears threaten her eyes.

"I think you should start to look. This place is pretty small and I really wanted to make the extra bedroom into a den. I kind of need an office at home with work stuff piling up. I can't get it all done during the workday and right now I have piles of files cluttering up my dresser."

The apartment is small. There is a galley kitchen and a small combination sitting and dining area. Both bedrooms are just over a hundred square feet and the bathroom is cramped. Portia had offered Pia a year if she needed it, but she now realizes she yearns for space, for privacy.

"I'll start looking tomorrow," Pia mumbles.

"Thanks. We'll still hang out. I'm still your friend." Portia considers hugging Pia at that moment, but she stops herself, fully realizing Pia is still suffering from her recent phobia.

It took Pia a few weeks to find a small apartment. At least it is much closer to work and she can actually walk rather than deal with the Metro. She moves in on March 1st. It is her birthday tomorrow and Portia agreed to go out to dinner with her this weekend. Their relationship has been strained ever since Ben admitted he desires Pia. Pia thinks Ben is smart, handsome, funny, and very sweet. Under different circumstances, she could see herself falling for the guy, but she will never betray Portia. Dating Ben would break her only friend's heart and she will never do that.

But thoughts of Ben and Jake McGuire have invaded her dreams and made her once again question her sexual preference. She is not thinking about women at the moment, but she is starting to believe she could be asexual since she has never experienced an orgasm. It troubles her and she made an appointment to consult with a psychologist, Dr. Danielle Forte.

Her health insurance finally starts on March 1st and her appointments with Dr. Forte will be covered with a small copay. The first appointment is Friday, March 4th at 4pm. She will go to work early that day, so she can leave at 3:45. The psychologist's office is very close to work. It is something she has thought about for over a year now. Her six-months under Arty's roof made her question her future and relive much of her past.

Ben's sudden thirst for an open relationship has sullied the friendship between Pia and Portia, causing the older woman's self-esteem to plunge. Portia has descended into lethargic languor where she has lost much of the momentum that had once fueled her passion for life. Ben had defined who she thought she was, she was Ben's girlfriend, his one true love. Now she has morphed into a diffident shadow of her former self and she no longer continues to give Pia inspiration or encouragement.

The birthday dinner is quiet as they chose to make reservations on Sunday, one day after Pia's actual 21st birthday. Restaurants in the metropolitan area are always overbrimming with crowds of festive folks who are celebrating life. On Sundays, the crowds thin out. Portia and Pia are able to commemorate the birthday quietly in a laconic, laid-back fashion with guarded conversation.

"Have you spoken to him?" Pia asks while the waiter fetches two lime-flavored margaritas.

"No, but I finally listened to one of his pathetic apologies on the machine."

"What did he say?" Pia asks.

"He told me he would always love me and maybe someday we can put all this behind us and start anew. I guess he wants to have casual sex with random women for a few years before he settles down. He'll probably get AIDS or syphilis. He's such a fool. He blew the best thing that ever happened to him."

"So, will you be able to move on, start dating again?"

"Not yet, I hate men at the moment. Maybe I should invite those lesbians from work over. Maybe you and I are both a pair of dykes. At the moment I can't see myself ever trusting a man again."

"I've actually been thinking about a man I met at the grocery store a few weeks ago. I haven't seen him since and he said he doesn't go to that store very often, so I'll probably never see him again."

"You liked him?"

"I did, but I was a real basket case. I told him I didn't like to be touched."

"I'll bet that went over like a lead balloon."

"He was actually really nice about it. He said his stepfather used to beat him and for years he felt the same way. He also told me something very personal."

"What did he say?" Portia asks as her eyes widen and the margaritas arrive. They wait for the waiter to disappear, telling him they will order in a few minutes, before they continue the delicate conversation.

"He is 22 years old and he's still a virgin. He's waiting for the right woman."

"I think that was a line, sweetie," Portia says as she sips her drink. "Let's toast to you, happy belated 21st birthday."

"To me, to our friendship." They clink glasses and then peruse the simple menu, narrowing it down to halibut or salmon for Pia and pork chops or lamb for Portia.

"Are you excited about the new digs?" Portia finally asks.

"I am. I hope I don't get lonely. The only time I ever lived alone was at the half-way house when I left the orphanage, but I wasn't totally alone since I shared the bathroom with a few other women."

"It will be good for you. Maybe you can learn to masturbate with all that privacy. You have to figure out what gets you off. You're 21 now and you still haven't ever had an orgasm."

"But I'm not technically a virgin at least," Pia mumbles.

"I feel bad for you, you don't know what you're missing."

"I read some women never reach a full climax. I guess everyone is different."

The waiter returns and the discussion on orgasms is halted as Pia orders the salmon and Portia opts for the lamb. When he vanishes into the kitchen, Portia returns to the subject at hand.

"I was going to buy you a vibrator for your birthday, but I chickened out. I didn't want to upset you in case you felt that was weird. So I went with a Joni Mitchell album."

"And I love it, I'm glad you didn't buy me a vibrator," Pia laughs. "But if I ever do own one, I think I would like to pick it out myself." Portia begins to giggle and Pia smiles to see her friend step out of the shadows of her ire and gloom.

"There's a bric-a-brac shop around the corner. We should see if they are open when we leave," Pia says.

"I doubt it, it is Sunday evening. Looking for something special?"

"I just thought I might see something I like for the new apartment. Something I can afford."

"Well, if they are open, we can take a look. I'll chip in if you need a little cash."

"You're already buying dinner."

"And I make twice as much as you. Will you be OK paying the rent by yourself?"

"I think so. Some of my coworkers are donating some furniture. When everyone found out I was getting my own place, a few of them told me they are sitting on a bunch of old furniture. The stuff is just cluttering up their attics. One of them owns a van and he offered to bring it all over."

"Is he sweet on you?"

"He's married."

"He could still be sweet on you."

"He's old enough to be my grandfather."

"He could still have the hots for you."

"Can you drop it?"

"Sorry."

"Actually, it's good to see your feisty personality surfacing again. You are too smart and accomplished to allow Ben to define you. You'll find another boyfriend when you are ready."

"Or a girlfriend."

"Are you really considering that?"

"Hey, you were the one who wanted to meet some actual lesbians."

"I kind of changed my mind on that. It was just a whim."

"Well, I'm not gay. But at the moment, I'm off the market."

"Let's go dancing next Saturday night, just the two of us."

"I'll think about it."

"I do love you, Portia, I always will. You kept my heart alive at the orphanage, but when you left, I became a real introvert. I guess that's why I married Arty so fast. I just wanted to start living some kind of life. Turns out, that was a huge mistake."

"I love you too."

"So we're still solid? I was so afraid I was going to lose you after what Ben said."

"Ben wants to sleep with everything that moves at the moment. We're still good. You didn't do anything wrong."

Pia smiles and the salads arrive. While they pick on their first course, Pia thinks about Nonna. Food always reminds her of her dear grandmother, the one person in the world who completely adored her. She wishes she had clearer memories of her parents, especially her mother, but it's all so fuzzy.

She thinks about her baby brother, Gaetano, who never saw his second birthday. It was a life unlived and it breaks her heart to ponder all the wonderful experiences he is missing. Had he lived, he would be turning 19 next month. Her father, her mother, her brother…they all died so young. They live in her dreams like relentless shadows from her childhood. Had it not been for Nonna, she would have been orphaned at four. She is grateful for the years she spent with her grandmother, the person who taught her how to feel joy, how to feel love, how to create Italian delights like melanzana or manicotti. She knows her parents loved her, but she remembers so very little. Nonna's love will always live in her heart.

4

Pia moved into her apartment on Sunday, February 27th, two days ahead of schedule. The previous tenant left on Friday and the landlord sent in cleaners on Saturday morning. He made her an offer. He could give the place a fresh coat of paint on Monday, the 28th, or she could move in early and paint the place herself. She opted for the latter so that she didn't need to miss a day of work for the move. She wanted to think about paint colors and the current paint wasn't in bad shape. The place was clean and that's all she cared about.

She got to move in two days early, rent-free, and the landlord would pay for the paint when she was ready. A coworker provided her with a couch, a table and chairs, and a stuffed side chair. A second coworker had a bedroom set she no longer needed, but Pia purchased a new mattress and box spring. Everything except for the mattress was delivered that Sunday morning and Pia slept on the sofa that night. On Monday morning, February 28th, the mattress and box spring arrived. She was at work, but her chubby landlord, who lives downstairs, accepted the delivery.

Life is coming together at last. She will be meeting with Dr. Forte on Friday and she and Portia are in a good place. She knows she couldn't stay with Portia indefinitely and she is glad she finally moved on with her life. But she still needs Portia's friendship as much as she needs oxygen or food.

Dr. Forte looks young for a psychologist, but her degrees, which cover one of her office walls, reflect her years of experience and expertise. Pia is anxious, but she knows this is the first step towards healing, towards having any kind of a real, meaningful future. There is an old canard that claims any decent bartender is as good at listening to someone's problems as a high-priced shrink, but Pia is trying to be open-minded and hopeful as she waits for the woman to speak. Arty is a bartender and he wasn't much of a listener.

"So, Pia, what led you to make this appointment today?" she asks in a nonthreatening voice that is devoid of judgment.

"I'm not sure. There are so many things bothering me."

"Let's start with the one thing in your life that you would most like to change," she says calmly.

"I feel like I'm at a critical turning point in my life. I've had moments when I found a man in a grocery store attractive while I pondered the possibility that I might be a lesbian. I'm also probably frigid and I told the man in the store I do not like to be touched."

"You said that to a complete stranger?" she asks.

"Yes, he got too close to me. He was asking me to help him pick out a melon. I sort of liked him, but when he got close, I froze up."

"How did he react?"

"He was very nice about it. He said he used to feel the same way after years of living with an abusive stepfather."

"I see, did you grow up with abuse?"

"Oh, no, the complete opposite, at least until I was twelve. My parents loved me according to my grandmother. They died when I was four and I hardly remember them. I want to remember, but it has been hard."

"I may be able to help you remember, Pia. We can generally reach back to about age two and a half in our recollection of our childhood. But let's get back to your parents for a moment. How did they die?"

"There was a fire. My baby brother was a month away from turning two. They all died. I was at my grandmother's. I used to stay with Nonna on Saturday nights. We would have so much fun together. It's my fault they all died."

"Why do you blame yourself for the fire?"

"I don't know, I just do. I should have been there. I might have smelled the smoke and woken them up."

"You were only four."

"I was, I turned four a month before the fire."

"You should not blame yourself. It was a tragedy of course. Did your grandmother take you in?"

"Yes, I lived with her until I was twelve and a half."

"Then what happened?"

"She died suddenly. They thought her heart failed. I found her on the kitchen floor. I knew she was dead. I'm not sure how I knew, but I had no doubt."

"That had to be awful for you. I'm sure you loved her very much."

"I did. She was great. We would sing Beatles songs together, using breadsticks as microphones, and we would dance for hours. She called it her aerobic workouts, but it was so much fun."

"What happened to you after that?"

"Social services put me in an orphanage. They may have tried to locate other relatives, they're all in Italy, but I don't know any of them. When that didn't pan out, I just stayed there until I was 18. At first, I thought I might be adopted, but by the time I turned 14, I gave up."

"It had to have been lonely for you."

"I made one close friend. But she aged out when I was 16 and moved to Wheaton. I moved here a few months ago. I stayed with her at first, but I just moved into my own apartment."

"How is that working out?"

"It's all pretty new. So far, it's OK."

"Where did you move from?"

"Upstate New York."

"And you kept in touch with your friend after she left the orphanage?"

"Yes, we wrote letters."

"Do you have other close friends?"

"No, just Portia."

"So back to my original question, if I could wave a magic wand and unburden you of one of the things that is troubling you, what would you choose?"

"I would like to be divorced and never see him again."

"You're married?"

"Yes, but I ran away from him."

"How long were you together?"

"I was working in a grocery store after I left the orphanage and he used to flirt with me when he shopped. He finally asked me out. We dated for two months and he was sweet. Then we got married and everything changed. I left him six months after the wedding."

"What changed?"

"I was a virgin on my wedding night and he promised to be gentle."

"Was he?"

"Yes and no, he never beat me or anything. He is probably what you might call a selfish lover. He had no interest in helping me enjoy sex. He just satisfied himself and then went to sleep. He asked me once if I liked it and I nodded, but I was lying. After the honeymoon, we didn't talk much. He worked nights and I worked days. We had sex once or twice a week, but it was always the same. He showed no real interest in me. He didn't care what I thought about things or what I dreamed about."

"Have you ever reached an orgasm?"

"No, not even close. I found myself wondering why people thinks sex is so great."

"That's not as unusual as you think. But it doesn't mean you won't be able to reach multiple orgasms in the future. You said you don't like to be touched, did your husband's touch disturb you?"

"Not when we were dating. We held hands and kissed and it was fine. I trusted him. No one had hugged me in years before I met him. The last time anyone hugged me before I met Arty, was the day Portia left the orphanage. I hugged her so hard I nearly squeezed the breath right out of her. They had to pry us apart. We were both crying and she promised to write to me every few weeks."

"And she kept her promise?"

"She did."

"So when you started having sex, is that when Arty's touch began to bother you?"

"Not right away, but over time. I kept thinking the sex would get better, but I found myself praying he would come home from work and just fall asleep."

"And he never raised a hand to you?"

"No, but he mocked me when I made mistakes. If I overcooked dinner, he wouldn't just tease me, he would…belittle me…and call me names like moron or idiot. He could be mean sometimes, especially when he drank. But he never hit me. I decided I wasn't going to hang around any longer because I believed his mean behavior might escalate. I wasn't going to wait for that first punch."

"So you disappeared?"

"Yes, no one knows where I am, except for Portia and Ben."

"Who is Ben?"

"Portia's boyfriend, except they just broke up."

"Was he a good guy?"

"I thought so. He kind of broke Portia's heart. He suddenly wanted an open relationship. She asked him if he wanted to have sex with me and he said yes. That caused Portia to pull away from me, but she knows I would never go out with Ben. I could never hurt her. After they broke up, she asked me to find a place of my own."

"But you are still friends?"

"We are, we went out for my birthday last month. Then we went dancing a week later. She doesn't blame me for what Ben said. The guy seems to want to sow his wild oats all of a sudden. I still think he loves her, but she is very angry and hurt right now. She thought he was her one true love."

"Back to Arty, do you plan to hire an attorney to begin divorce proceedings?"

"Eventually, I can't afford it right now. My health insurance is paying for this visit, except for the copay."

"Don't worry about the copay. I'll just take what the insurance company pays me. I don't want you to stop coming because it is a financial burden. I think I can help you."

"Would I have to come here for years?"

"No, maybe one year, probably six to nine months. It depends on what other issues are bothering you. You most likely feel you are frigid, but when you find the right relationship with a man or a woman, you will be able to work through that. You just need the right partner and a strong desire to get past some of your phobias. Not wanting to be touched is likely rooted in many things. The fact that Arty was mean and selfish caused you to likely pull away from him emotionally. The trauma of losing your family and spending your teen years in an orphanage has caused you to withdraw. Do you still hug Portia?"

"I asked her to stop hugging me in January. I told her I no longer liked to be touched. Then I also asked her to invite some lesbian coworkers to a party. I was thinking I was done with men after Arty."

"I assume you haven't dated other men?"

"No. I left the orphanage a few months after my 18th birthday and I didn't even know any boys up until then, not since I was twelve. I met Arty and we got married after only two months. There have been no other guys. No women either. The party got cancelled."

"Why do you think you rushed the wedding?"

"It was all Arty. He knew I wanted to keep my virginity until we got married. He pushed me and I hated living in the halfway house where I shared a bathroom with a bunch of other girls. So I moved into his place after the wedding. I guess he just wanted sex, but he got bored with me after a while. I wouldn't be surprised if he was cheating on me. It was never love, not on my part. It was just the closest thing I have ever had to a real relationship with a man."

"And you just turned 21?"

"Yes."

"You are very young. You have your entire life ahead of you. Your childhood was difficult, but you have many happy memories with your grandmother and I will help you rediscover some of the happy times you shared with your parents and your baby brother. Are you suicidal?"

"A little, but not as much as I was. I felt trapped with Arty, but then I started saving money. That kept me going. I saved almost $200 and then Arty had to go away for a few days. His great-uncle died and he went to the funeral, hoping he is in the will. I asked him if he wanted me to go and he said no. I knew that was my chance. So after he left, I hopped on a bus and headed south. I made sure I had all the letters from Portia. I never told him about her. I called her and told her I was coming and asked her if she had sent any letters recently. I didn't want to risk Arty finding out about her. When she told me she hadn't sent any, I said I was on my way."

"If he should find you, he has no right to drag you back. We aren't living in the 19th century. Would he get violent?"

"It's possible. I don't want to find out."

"Well, it appears you are safe. I wish I could wave that magic wand and hand you a divorce, but I will see if I can get you a lawyer to handle that for you, pro bono. I know a few lawyers who owe me a favor or two."

"You would do that for me?"

"Of course. Women need to stand with other women. So what would be your second wish?"

"I hate the fact that I cringe when people get too close. It started right after the honeymoon. It's getting worse. A work colleague brushed against me yesterday and I freaked out. I didn't make a scene, I just ran to the bathroom."

"Did people hug you in the orphanage or touch you in any way?"

"Only Portia. And I liked her hugs."

"And now you don't?"

"No, I don't want to touch anyone. I tend to go to grocery stores that are not crowded so I don't run into people. The prices are higher, but I can't deal with the chaotic supermarkets."

"I want you try something. Do you trust me?"

"I think so."

"I want you to consider shaking my hand when you leave. It will be entirely up to you. I won't initiate it. It will be your call. I won't squeeze hard and it will be quick. But you need to make the first move."

"Is the session over already?"

"Not yet. Just ponder what I just said."

"OK."

"So the orgasms are something we can deal with later, once you find a new relationship. You could be a lesbian, I have no way to be certain. When you meet your next lover, male or female, you will know if it's what you want. I'm going to write down a few book titles for you to explore both your sexuality and your inability to climax. It actually isn't surprising at all if Arty was a selfish lover. Feeling frigid may simply be a reflection on what a bad lover your husband was. I wouldn't worry about that right now. Have you ever tried to pleasure yourself?"

"No."

"You may wish to explore that. The books I am recommending will address that. Now that you live alone, you will have the privacy to explore your own body."

"It's true. I've never actually lived alone before. It's only been a few days and I'm still getting settled. But I guess I can do whatever I want now."

"Even if you simply massage your own breasts at first. Touch your legs and arms. Get used to touch. People cannot tickle themselves and you will not have problems touching yourself. Wait until you are completely relaxed before attempting to pleasure yourself. Have a glass of wine, have two," she laughs.

"OK, Doc. I'll try."

"The next time you come in, we'll try to recapture some of the happy memories when you were two or three years old. They are in there, hiding away. Is there any other reason why you blame yourself for the fire, other than the fact that you were not at home to help alert your parents?"

"Yes, I have one memory of that morning."

"What happened?"

"I was trying to be a big girl and make myself some toast while my mom was giving Gaetano a bath. Dad was in the basement. I plugged in the toaster and put in the bread. I had seen my parents do in lots of times. I even knew to adjust the knob. But I think I turned it too high because the toast got burnt. One of the pieces got stuck and it was smelly and smoky. I panicked and stuck a butter knife into the slot. I think I screamed, but no one heard. Then I yanked on the electric cord and the toaster fell off the counter. I remember sparks. My father came running. I remember the lights flickered. I was crying and he held me. I didn't get into trouble, but then the next morning, Nonna sat on the bed and woke me to tell me about the fire."

"Do you think you caused the fire accidently?"

"When I was older, Nonna told me it was an electrical fire that started in the kitchen. I never told anyone about the toaster, but I started thinking it was all related."

"Or it was a convergence of coincidences. Perhaps, what happened with the toaster had nothing to do with the fire. It may have all been a sad coincidence."

"It's my only clear memory of living with my parents. If I did cause the house fire, then it's just not fair that they all died and I got to live. My brother wasn't even two years old." Pia begins to cry hysterically and Dr. Forte comforts her without touch. She wants to hold her client in her arms, but she knows that could further upset her. She uses words to sooth her tears and then she tells her the session is over.

But Dr. Forte does not rush Pia to leave. There is finally a break in the silence as Pia stands to say goodbye. She starts to walk out the door, but then she turns, wiping away some tears with her left hand while she extends her right hand.

"Are you sure?" Dr. Forte asks. Pia nods, she is trembling, but she continues to extend her arm. Dr. Forte shakes her hand briefly, gently, with a comforting smile.

"I'll see you next time, Doc," Pia sobs. She did not pull away when their hands touched. It is a beginning.

5

Pia bought two books that were recommended by
Dr. Forte. She devoured them in a weekend and came to the
conclusion that she is asexual. She has little interest in men at the
moment, but she also internalized the fact that she is not sexually
attracted to other woman. She likes women and she feels more
comfortable around Portia than any human being on the planet. She
purposely chose a female psychologist because she would have been
mortified if a man had asked her about her inability to have an
orgasm.

But she searched her soul and came to the conclusion that she
has never thought about other girls in a sexual way. She was
surrounded by girls in the orphanage and even when she had crushes
on movie stars or famous musicians, they were always men or boys.
Still, now that she has given up her virginity to Arty, she is
beginning to question her ability to enjoy making love to anyone.
The thought of living an asexual life disturbs her as she assumes it
will lead to a lonely existence. It seems pathetic to live a life without
passion like a nun in a convent, but that appears to be her reality.

She is lying on her bed in a semi-darkened room as she peers through the open curtains and gazes up at the moon. The moon only shows us one face, hiding the others from sight. She begins to speak to the moon, silently, but with definite purpose. Humans are quite similar as they wear different faces. At her job she attempts to be cordial and focused on the work at hand, but she assumes they all see her as a kid, a weirdo who cringes when another human tries to get too close, physically or emotionally. She is 21 and they are all older and probably wiser.

Her diffidence is rooted in her guilt and her loneliness. Did she cause the fire? Why did she try to make toast all by herself? Did she cause her grandmother's heart to weaken after Nonna was forced to bury her only daughter and her baby grandson? Was she responsible for Nonna's suffering, for the deaths of her mommy and her daddy and her beloved Gaetano? She barely remembers her baby brother, but she grew up studying the few family photographs that escaped the fire, those that Nonna kept tucked away in albums. She knew every inch of Gaetano's face as he haunted her dreams and invaded her thoughts when she least expected.

Whenever she hears a child cry in a grocery store, she thinks of her brother, whenever a baby giggles or coos in public, Gaetano appears in her flustered mind and the guilt pours into her tormented soul. She should not have stuck that knife into the toaster and she should have been home to smell the smoke before it filled her baby brother's lungs. She failed her family and she turned Nonna's life into utter turmoil.

Nonna cooked and cleaned for her, helped her learn how to take her first shower alone, danced with her, sang to her, and provided her with a deep sense of family. But she heard her, she heard Nonna sobbing into her pillow late at night. The walls were thin and Nonna's despair often woke her from her own nightmares. She didn't tell Dr. Forte how much she fears fire, but that will need to be addressed at some point.

Nonna didn't just cry in the days and weeks that followed, she cried for years and Pia's guilt hung around her neck like an albatross of remorse and culpability. She blamed herself for all the sorrow that had fallen upon Nonna, for all the lives unlived, her mommy's life, her daddy's life, and Gaetano's life. The baby never got to experience the taste of a chocolate brownie or the rush of the wind through his hair when he flew through the air on a big-boy swing.

He never got to blow out the candles on his second birthday or experience the wonders of his third Christmas.

She has no memory of her first two Christmases, but she does have one recollection of her third Christmas in 1964. She was less than two months from her third birthday and Dr. Forte told her she could tap into memories after age two and a half. She remembers one thing. She remembers Gaetano, at nine months of age, trying to eat a piece of the wrapping paper. He showed no interest in the presents or the empty boxes, but her mommy kept taking small, spit-soaked chunks of red and green paper from her brother's mouth. She remembers laughing about it.

It's Saturday, grocery shopping day. She has looked for Jake McGuire at the grocery store, but he has not resurfaced and she assumes he is playing basketball somewhere. Today, she is going to confront her fears and enter a supermarket near her new apartment. It is both conveniently located and cheaper than the smaller stores. She has to pay the rent now. She was giving Portia a few hundred dollars a month, but now her rent is $600. Her expenses have more than doubled and she needs to save for a lawyer in case Dr. Forte is unsuccessful in her attempt to procure her free legal services.

She needs to file the divorce papers, she needs to put it all behind her, the unfortunate marriage and the loneliness of living in a loveless relationship. She assumes Arty realized he was never in love, he was merely lusting to have sex with a young virgin. He seemed so indifferent after the humdrum honeymoon and she quickly realized she had jumped into marriage without thinking it through.

She is living alone now, without a pet or a roommate, but she feels less alone. Pia had never felt more alone than when she was living with Arty during the last months of their brief marriage. Now she needs to make it official so they can both move on. She would like to send him a letter, but she would need to have it postmarked in Virginia or maybe even in North Carolina. She is considering taking a bus trip since she doesn't own a car so that she can mail such a letter. But what would she say?

The store is crowded and Pia gasps and nearly turns around, but she takes a deep breath and forces her feet to move forward towards the piled up shopping carts. She brought her small folding wagon and she slides it under one of the shopping carts. It can hold three or four bags of groceries and she can pull it with one hand should she need to carry some of the groceries in her free hand. She is going to do this. She must face the crowds and search for bargains in order to fill her refrigerator and cupboards with healthy food. She promises herself to avoid the junk food aisle and focus on food that is more budget friendly and easier on the waistline.

She has no problem maintaining her 115 pound figure, but she did notice Portia has been putting on weight ever since Ben broke her heart. Portia has a weak spot for ice cream, but Pia knows it would melt on the walk home if she indulged herself. It is still March, but it warms up quickly in Maryland and the cherry blossoms are already about to pop.

She avoids the aisles where many other people are perusing the canned goods or the meats on sale and heads for the less traveled areas, darting around the store in a haphazard manner in order to avoid other humans. It is less efficient compared with her usual routine where she begins in produce and works her way towards the dairy department, stopping at breads and proteins along the way. But she has her list and she is unfamiliar with the store anyway. Her goal is to avoid being touched while scouting for sale items.

Her list says fruit, but she is not fussy and is quite content opting for whatever is marked down so long as it still looks fresh. Just as she approaches the grapes, her eyes fixated on a red sale sign over the purple ones, a familiar voice captures her attention. He is a few yards away, but she knows it is him. She turns and maneuvers her cart for protection as she spies his warm smile.

"So, I still don't know which melons are ready to eat," he laughs.

"Oh, hi, again," she utters as her heart begins to race and she wonders if her laconic response will appear to show indifference or distrust.

"Funny running into you again in a produce department. I thought you hated these crowded supermarkets."

"I…I…do. I do. But this place is close to my new apartment and I'm putting myself on a budget to afford the rent."

"Makes sense…and the selection is much better here."

"Jake, right?" she asks, pretending she has forgotten, but of course, it is a lie. She has fantasized about his eyes and his smile and considered attempting to pleasure herself with images of his face and his broad shoulders.

He traipses towards her, but keeps his cart between them and holds out a melon. She takes it and nods. It's ready to be cut open.

He thanks her and flashes a smile that would knock a horny, old, blue-haired lady right off her feet. She laughs at her own silly thoughts and begins to turn away, but he continues to engage.

"Do you have a boyfriend?" he prompts as he shuffles his feet like a schoolboy of 12 who is attempting to ask a girl in braids to dance with him.

"No, no boyfriend," she replies. It is the truth. She has no boyfriend, but of course she does still have a husband somewhere. She assumes Arty is back in Ulster County, serving cocktails to pretty women, flirting, and wondering where the hell she is.

"I kind of figured since you don't like to be touched and all."

"Right."

"I was wondering if I could invite you to dinner. My treat. We would meet at the restaurant and I know a place where we could get a quiet corner table where you would feel safe. I promise there will be no touching, no expectations, just conversation and maybe a few laughs."

"Why do you want to go out with me?" she asks in a befuddled tone, trying not to encourage him, but still considering his sweet proposal. He is cute and he seems so nice, but so did Arty at first.

"I like you. I know you have your issues and I'm not looking for romance right now. I just want to spend time together and get to know one another. I promise you I am one of the good guys," he declares with an undaunted air of confidence and a boyish charm.

"Why do you like me so much? We are pretty much strangers."

"I never said I like you so much," he laughs. His laughter is contagious and Pia breaks into a suppressed chuckle.

"You're right…you didn't say so much," she giggles. "But I don't understand why you want to get to know me better."

"I really need to have a friend in my life who can differentiate between a ripe melon and one that needs to sit on the counter for a week."

"I thought I taught you how to do that by yourself."

"I'm a slow learner."

"And a virgin," she teases to see how he responds.

"Now I told you that in strict confidence. I hope you haven't been spreading it around."

"Oh, yes, I told everyone at work that Jake McGuire is challenged in the produce department and he is still a virgin," she teases.

"So you remember my last name," he responds with a hearty laugh.

"I remember…unlike you, I am a fast learner."

"What are you doing for dinner tonight?" he pleads.

"Why are men so persistent?" she asks with a hint of a smile as she clings to the handle of her cart as if it is her life preserver and she is about to fall overboard.

"I think it's in our DNA, we are hunters, and we love the chase."

"I agree and when you catch a girl, you begin to lose interest and move onto the next conquest."

"I'm not like that. Meet me for dinner."

"You are relentless. I don't even think you're a virgin. I think it's a line which makes me distrust you."

"I swear it's not a line. I'm not sure how to prove it to you, but I have been waiting all my life for the right girl. I'm not saying you are her, but I really want to have dinner with you. I want to get to know you."

"Why waste your time on a girl who hates being touched? This store is probably filled with eligible girls who would love to go to dinner with a cute guy like you."

"So, you think I'm cute?"

"You know the answer to that. You do own a mirror, don't you?"

"You're funny."

"I'm just saying you know you can get a girl to go out with you with your charm and your smile. I think you are probably quite the player."

"I swear I'm not. I'll tell you what. I'll invite my mother to join us for dinner…or even better yet, my grandmother. They both adore me, but especially Nana."

"You call your grandmother Nana?" she asks.

"I do. Is that strange?"

"No, not at all. I called my grandmother Nonna."

"Is she still alive? You said you *called* her Nonna?"

"She reared me for most of my childhood. She died when I was 12."

"I'm so sorry. Are your folks deceased as well?"

"Yes, they died when I was four."

"I am very sorry. Where did you live after your grandmother died?"

"In an orphanage."

"I feel badly for you. I thought my stepfather was bad, but at least I had Mom and Nana."

"Is your stepfather still in the picture?"

"Don't spread it around, but I murdered him when I was fourteen," he jokes. She hesitates, but his smile tells her he is not serious.

"So he's dead? I promise I won't tell a soul."

"Nah, he's probably slapping some other woman's kids around down in Florida. He moved down there after he split up with my mom. I was seventeen when he finally moved out, but I did think about murdering him a few hundred times."

"Whenever he beat you?"

"No, whenever he slapped my mother."

"How long did he live with you?"

"Five years."

"So your mom is alone now?"

"She has me. I still live with Sam, but I have dinner with Mom and Nana at least once a week."

"Right, Sam, the guy who married Marnie."

"You do have a good memory."

"I really need to get going," she says.

"No dinner?" he pleads as he squints his lime-green eyes and puffs out his lower lip.

"Not tonight."

"Not ever?"

"No, just not tonight."

"That gives me hope."

"There is always hope," she jests as she turns away.

"Can I get your number?"

"Not yet, we are still strangers."

"Can I give you my card?"

"You have a card?" she teases.

"Yes, I'm a salesman, I sell cars. Take my card, just in case you ever need a good deal on a used car."

"I don't own a car. I don't even have a driver's license."

"I remember. How will you get your groceries home?"

"I have my cart," she replies as she points to the folded contraption that is lying underneath her hamburger meat and chicken thighs.

"But it may rain soon."

"I won't melt."

"You are tough."

"I'm a survivor. I survived six years in an orphanage."

"I'll miss you."

"Bye Jake."

As she turns the corner and heads towards the bread aisle, she can feel his eyes on her, watching her movements, but she does not turn. Instead she hums a Beatles tune under her breath and thinks about him, *I once had a girl or should I say she once had me...*

She knows he likes her, but why? She is frigid, she doesn't drive, which means she may be poor, and she is simply not that special. A guy like him can do so much better. The only reason he is pursuing her in her mind is because she is saying no. Men love a challenge. As soon as she said yes to Arty, he became a tad less interested and after the honeymoon he became indifferent and almost hostile.

She feels she disappointed her husband in bed. He knew she was completely inexperienced, but he seemed to expect so much more. It seems men want a virgin, but they want her to be a whore in the bedroom. It puzzles her. A good man, a less selfish man, would have concerned himself with teaching her to enjoy sex by educating her and attempting to please her rather than just satisfying his own carnal needs. Arty just wanted a quick release and then he would roll over and hug the side of the bed while he feel into a raucous, restless sleep. The man snored. He was a disappointment, but not all men are Arty.

She suspects Jake is a better man. She wonders if he would really have brought his mom or his grandmother to dinner to vouch for him. If she runs into him again and he persists, maybe she will hold him to his word and tell him to bring his grandmother to dinner. If he shows up alone, she will turn and walk away. But then again, she'll probably never run into him again. What are the odds?

Pia is still clutching his card in her left hand. She pulls her cart over by the pudding and places the card inside her wallet. She'll hold onto it for now. It has his work number on it. Who knows, she might be in the market for a car someday, but she'll have to find a way to increase her income first, and of course she will need to learn how to drive an automobile.

Pia grew up without a dad to teach her to drive, without a mom to teach her about the opposite sex, without a baby brother to tease her and idolize her at the same time, and without a family to share Thanksgiving dinners and festive Christmas mornings. It was just her and Nonna for such a long time. There were no other relatives living in America as far as her grandmother knew, and the two of them tended to celebrate holidays alone.

She used to resent people with large families until Nonna died and she landed in the county orphanage. She shared her holidays with a bunch of waifs and even though it could be rowdy and unruly during their Thanksgiving dinners, she felt completely alone, missing Nonna so much. Had it not been for Portia, she feels she would have simply vanished into an abyss of melancholy and gloom. Once Portia left the orphanage, she withdrew into a shell of her former self and she grew to fully realize how lucky she was when she and Nonna once celebrated holidays together.

The unlived lives of her parents and her brother would continue to haunt her during those dark days when she was missing Portia and feeling depressed and alone. But Pia wants to confront her demons and move forward. Dr. Forte told her she is just beginning her life at 21 and she wants to believe that, but she still can't see herself going out to dinner with Jake, even if she does find him attractive. She still doesn't want to be touched and Jake would soon grow impatient with her if she dated him. It is best to forget about Jake McGuire and focus on her new apartment and her job. She still has Portia. She is not alone.

6

The next few months seemed to evaporate and before she knew it, Pia was suffering through her first summer in Maryland with its sweltering weather. The heat index made it feel like 110 degrees on most days and the actual temperature hit 100 degrees for the past several days. A person could roast in such heat and brown like a chicken in an oven that was about to be devoured by hungry children.

She has not heard from Arty and she assumes he has no idea where she is. She met with Dr. Forte a dozen times, but then the doctor went on a long vacation to Europe and gave her the number of a colleague whom Pia could reach out to in a crisis. The sessions with the psychologist were fruitful as Pia was able to recall her last two Christmases in the old house, the one where baby Gaetano kept attempting to eat scraps of wrapping paper and her final holiday with her family gathered around the tree.

When she was two months shy of her 4th birthday, Santa brought her a special doll that could talk if you pulled on a small ring as if she were a lawnmower that needed to be started. She named the doll Sara, but she had forgotten all about her.

Sara burned in the fire along with most of Pia's toys and books. But Dr. Forte was able to bring her back to the morning of December 25th, 1965, as Pia squealed with delight when she opened the box and discovered Sara. The doll's eyes blinked like an actual human and her lips were painted bright pink. She loved Sara, but her memory had blocked out the existence of the doll. She thanked Dr. Forte for helping her relive that special moment when she first laid eyes on Sara.

She remembered Gaetano opening a toy where he stacked multicolored plastic donuts on a stem that looked like something men use when they toss around metal horseshoes. Each of the colorful donuts was a different size and she remembered helping her baby brother place them in the proper sequence from the largest to the smallest. In the recesses of her mind, she could still hear him giggling with joy as he said her name. He called her Pi, leaving off the last letter. She had completely forgotten all about that. Gaetano called her Pi and she called him Guy. It all came back to her after Dr. Forte used some kind of hypnosis to help stir her memories. She wasn't sure why it was so important to her to remember those last two Christmases with her family, but it filled her with a sense of belonging, a feeling of history, her history.

They all left this earth far too young, and the tragedy of the kitchen fire would forever haunt her dreams, but she was comforted by her ability to reach back into her memory bank and relive a few happy moments in time. Dr. Forte taught her a few simple tricks to continue her search for childhood memories. It was easier to relive Christmas Day, but far more difficult to remember an average Sunday morning breakfast where Gaetano might be throwing broken cheerios off his highchair tray or her mom might be browning a few blueberry pancakes on a skillet. She wanted to remember it all. She needed to remember.

She returned to the supermarket many more times, always on Saturday mornings, when she didn't have to go to work. If she needed a quart of milk or an onion during the week, she didn't mind paying nearly double at the corner store near her new apartment. Each time she walked into the supermarket, she froze for a few seconds and braced herself as she confronted the hustle and bustle of the crowd.

Pia also can't help but keep an eye out for Jake each time she approaches the produce aisle, but he never reappears. She assumes he has fallen in love by now and moved out of Sam's apartment and in with his lover. She imagines him having a torrid affair with a seductive goddess and she doubts she could ever compete.

She still has not enjoyed an orgasm, but with the help of Dr. Forte, she has begun to read another book about erogenous zones and self-awareness when it comes to carnal needs. She has touched herself down there a few times, but she never climaxes despite her attempts to fantasize. She always thinks about the same thing when she tries to pleasure herself. She thinks about Jake McGuire, the guy who struggled to pick out a melon, but never failed to dazzle her with his penetrating green eyes, his winning smile, and his witty comments. She has only spoken to him on two occasions, but he continues to haunt her thoughts, especially when she attempts to reach an orgasm.

Dr. Forte told her it would take time. She recommended simple things like a long hot bath and dim lightening with scented candles illuminating the tiny bathroom. Pia told her she hates candles. She suggested partaking in a bit of wine and even slipping into something sexy like a lace nightie or silky, bikini panties. Dr. Forte's book recommendations encouraged her to caress her own breasts, paying special attention to each of her tender nipples and areolas.

Pia feels she is getting closer to reaching a sexual climax, that she is making progress. She is also trying to face her recent phobia by allowing Portia to hug her again, fully internalizing that Portia is certainly not a threat to her. She finds comfort in Portia's arms and that tells her the day may come when she can feel a similar pleasure in the arms of a man. Thoughts of getting to know some lesbians has left her mind, but she is still not ready to date men, not yet.

It has been over three months since she last saw him. So why does she think about Jake so often? She wakes with thoughts of him, wondering what he is up to. She forgot to even ask him why he wasn't shooting hoops when they had their second encounter. As she drifts off to sleep each evening, her final thoughts are always the same. She even started praying again and she prays for her lost family, praying for their souls. She also prays for Portia, that she will find a new boyfriend and regain her self-esteem since Ben seems to have vanished. And finally, she prays for Jake McGuire. She prays he is well and she hopes he is thinking about her still. She has her doubts about him, questioning his tale about being a 22-year-old virgin. But she wants to believe he is a good guy.

She is not a virgin, not technically, since she lived with Arty for six months and allowed him to penetrate most of her orifices. But she never enjoyed the sex and sometimes it hurt, so the fact that she is no longer a virgin gives her little consolation. Life with Arty had been bleak at best and shadowed by a different kind of loneliness than the kind she felt in the orphanage. That's why she ran, she could no longer tolerate the loneliness of living with a man who had become so apathetic and cantankerous.

All she had wanted was a little pleasant conversation around the dinner table, or a bit of romance like bringing home a small bunch of daisies wrapped in tissue paper and tied with a simple ribbon. On one occasion, when the rent was due and Arty had blown his own paycheck on beer and cigarettes along with a few car parts, he asked her to consider selling her engagement ring. He said their simple, matching, gold wedding bands would suffice and the diamond, while small, could still fetch a few hundred dollars. When she refused to sell the diamond, he stole it while she was asleep and she never saw it again. But she knew, she knew he had pawned it and squandered the proceeds on some bourbon and scotch. When he brought the expensive liquor home, after she had torn apart the house in search of the missing ring, she knew.

But she said nothing. Instead, she started to skimp at the grocery store, searching for sales, so she could save her pennies, her runaway money. She would buy him food that was near its expiration date in order to save a dollar or two and on one occasion she even made a casserole with tuna that was canned for a cat. When she opted not to partake, telling Arty she wasn't hungry, he simply replied, "More for me."

She spiked the casserole with cat food about a week after her diamond engagement ring vanished. It was the beginning of the end for her. She even contemplated suicide for a while, but then she thought about Portia and she decided she would simply disappear, just like that diamond ring.

Portia saved her life when they were in the orphanage, providing her with friendship and warmth, allowing her to enjoy laughter again and even dip her toes in a bit of devilish behavior. They were a team for a few years, but when Portia left, she slipped into a funk and Arty was the first person to help her climb back out of her sadness. But it had simply been a lapse in good judgment and she had moved on.

Dr. Forte has not yet given her the name of an attorney who might help her secure a simple divorce without breaking the bank.

Her savings account has a balance of just over $300 and she knows lawyers are expensive. She needs to remind Dr. Forte about her suggestion to find a lawyer who might take her case for free, but the psychologist is probably sitting in a gondola in Venice, enjoying the wonders of Italy, and she does envy her. Pia was born in America, unlike Nonna who was born in Naples, but she longs to visit the land of her ancestors and partake in the culinary delights of authentic lasagna or melanzana Parmigiano. Her time will come. She is still 21 years old and she has a future after all.

7

It's July 1ˢᵗ, Friday afternoon. Pia left work early to run some errands and she's excited about the three day weekend ahead. She plans to relax on Saturday and Sunday and then she and Portia will attend the Washington, DC July 4ᵗʰ extravaganza at the National Mall. The Beach Boys are performing, and while they aren't the Beatles, she does love their music. The fact that Portia is still single has given Pia a sidekick when she wants to see a movie or attend a concert. There are advantages to having Ben out of the picture.

Neither of them has seen Ben in months and the rumor mill claims he has a new girlfriend, but it's unclear whether or not they are monogamous. Portia's heart is healing. She is a strong person and a survivor after spending four long years at the orphanage. Pia was there for six years and she doesn't know how she would have kept from going mad had she not met Portia. They both arrived within a few weeks of each other and instantly bonded, quickly becoming utterly inseparable. Portia's past life is even sadder than Pia's story, but she tends not to dwell on it very much.

Pia lost her parents and her baby brother to a tragic accident, even if Pia continues to carry some of the blame. Portia's father left her mother when she was a toddler and she has no memory of him. As far as she knows he is dead since she has never attempted to locate him, not even after her mother died of an overdose. Portia's mother wasn't a lifelong drug addict, but she did experiment on occasion, especially when she was feeling anxious or particularly low. She died when Portia was nearly 14 and a cousin took in the teenaged waif for about six months. But she eventually moved away and left Portia with the county.

Pia arrived first. She kept to herself and grieved for Nonna. Her grandmother's sudden death paralyzed her heart and took away her appetite and her will to live. Nonna was a fabulous cook and the food in the orphanage wasn't fit for barnyard critters in Pia's mind. Since the food was tasteless and often disgusting, and Pia was severely depressed, she existed on crackers and water for a few weeks. She refused to touch the meat or fish, which were impossible to tell apart, and the vegetables were canned and so overcooked that they fell apart when a child poked them with a fork.

On the day that Portia arrived, Pia's life began to evolve. The younger girl had been there for about a month at that point and she was friendless and miserable. But then she noticed the new girl who seemed to bond with a few of the others within hours of her arrival. Portia strolled into the dining room at dinner while Pia sat in the corner, hunched over and staring at her untouched plate of meatloaf and green beans. She thought the beans smelled sour and the meatloaf had specks of purple and cobalt in it that Pia was fairly certain were not edible. She wasn't even interested in the chocolate pudding for dessert and she simply nibbled on a cracker as she stared at the plate in order to avoid eye contact with the other girls at her table.

She didn't actually see Portia enter the room, but she heard her laughter as she explained to her two followers that the way to improve the food was to either organize a protest or go on a hunger strike. Pia heard little of the conversation, but she slowly looked up when she heard Portia's laugh. She was drawn to the new girl instantly and when Portia walked past her table, the newcomer smiled at Pia as if to say, "Help has arrived, no reason to be so sad any longer."

Within days, the two began to eat together and Portia convinced Pia to try everything since crackers and water were not enough to keep her body fueled with energy for much longer. So Pia promised her new friend she would taste everything the cafeteria had to offer. Most of the time, Pia spit it out instantly and made comical noises and even funnier comments. Her commentary on the cuisine caused Portia to break into hysterical laughter and Pia's mood began to shift from self-pity to sarcasm and joy. It was now the two of them against the institution.

Portia was a natural born leader and the orphanage staff seemed to respect her. She was taller than most of the girls and her smile was contagious. The cafeteria staff displayed empathetic forbearance and curiosity when Portia complained about the food and over time the administration widened the selection by adding raw vegetables, sliced and diced, and fresh fruit to selection of edible creations.

Pia began to add fruit and crunchy carrot sticks to her diet and Portia convinced her to take a few mouthfuls of the tasteless roast beef or the overcooked dry chicken. Pia would hold her nose and swallow a few bites of the protein in order to please her mentor and ally. It was the combination of vegetables, fruit, and protein that kept her from shriveling up and falling ill. Portia kept her body alive by convincing Pia to eat a healthier diet and she kept her soul alive with laughter and the occasional hug.

When Portia aged out and moved to Maryland, she stayed with the same cousin who had cast her aside when she was a 14-year-old waif. The cousin was elderly and frail and she took Portia in so that the 18-year-old would now be her caretaker. Portia cleaned and cooked and even changed the cousin's diapers for over a year. The woman had never married or had children of her own and she had no one else to look after her in her declining years.

When Portia turned 20, she wrote a letter to Pia. She had written her several since leaving the orphanage, but this one provided Pia with hope should she ever decide to head south once she aged out. Pia was months away from leaving the orphanage and she almost took Portia up on her offer, but then she met Arty and her trajectory shifted once again. Portia's letter continued to provide her with a life preserver in case her relationship with Arty turned ugly. Pia often thought about moving south, but she needed to save some money first. When she met Arty, he was the first guy to give her any real attention and she was naïve and foolish for believing he was her one true love, her destiny. She continued to reread Portia's letter every few days during her young marriage.

Dear Pia,

I turned 20 today and I am no longer a teenager. I'm an official grown up. My cousin died a few months ago and she left me the house, the creepy furnishings, and a small bank account. I sold the house right away and moved to Wheaton where I'm renting a really cute apartment that is filled with sunshine in the morning. I sold the house as is, furniture and all, and as far as I know, they set the whole pile of wood and dust on fire and built something new on the land. The land had value, I suppose, but the house was damp, decrepit, and smelly.

I spent over a year and a half taking care of the old bat, even changing her diapers, but in the end, I grew up a lot. I'm on my own now and I have a guest room. You are welcome to visit anytime and if you decide to move here, you can stay with me for as long as you need. I love you Pia and I apologize for not writing for a few months. My cousin's last days on earth were pretty tough and I was depressed and exhausted from playing nurse and continually washing her soiled sheets. I felt like it was never going to end. But for all things there is a season and now it's my turn to blossom. Come visit me. Come find me. I am here and I am your friend, now and always.

Love,

Portia

There is a new restaurant that opened right around the corner from Pia's apartment and she is dying to try it, but Portia is on a diet at the moment. When she finishes her errands, she intends to stop by and check out the menu, maybe grab some takeout for her Friday night dinner. The air is stale and she is hoping for a welcome breeze to wander in tonight since her AC window unit is on the fritz again. Her aging landlord promised her he would bring her a new unit tomorrow morning, so she won't need to suffer for much longer. The rent is due today and she did not pay it yet. Instead, she left the landlord an envelope with the following:

I know today is the 1ˢᵗ and the rent is due. I have it, but I'm paying in cash this month, instead of my usual check. I'll give it to you tomorrow when you come up to install the new air conditioner. I'm excited to be getting a new unit. Thanks for taking care of it so quickly.

Pia

The landlord has actually been dragging his feet for over a month, but Pia knows she can get further with honey than with vinegar. Still, she is no fool, and she intends to hold the July rent hostage until the AC unit is installed.

The restaurant isn't crowded since it's still early for a Friday night and the place is brand new. Pia places her takeout order after quickly perusing the menu and they tell her it will be ready in fifteen minutes. She could take a walk or even run home for a bit, but she opts to stay.

"Where is your restroom?" she asks the hostess. The young woman is about her age and Pia can tell she is inexperienced and a bit flustered as she points in the direction of the ladies room. Pia slips past the wait staff, weaving to the right and back in order to avoid the bustle of the busboys who are clearing away dirty dishes. She still has her phobia about people touching her, but she feels like she is getting better. Still, she makes sure she doesn't bump into anyone as she approaches the restroom.

She washes her hands and pats down a stray strand of hair before heading back to the lobby to await her dinner. She can smell the aromas emanating from the kitchen and she fully anticipates the takeout will be delicious. As she moves left to avoid a waiter who is carrying a tray of colorful cocktails, she bumps into a table and apologizes to the two patrons who are sipping on tropical drinks.

"So sorry," she mutters as she makes eye contact with the man.

"Pia?" he exclaims with a smile. She looks up and realizes she knows this man, even if she hasn't seen him in a while.

"Oh, hi," she mumbles as she glances at the exotic looking woman who is also staring at her with unfriendly curiosity.

"Claire, this is Pia. Pia, this is Claire." He is a gentleman, of course, and he immediately introduces the two strangers.

"Hi," Pia says with a forced smile.

"Hello, how do you two know each other, Jake?"

"Oh, we go way back, don't we, Pia?" he laughs.

"Not really," she whispers under her breath as she attempts to flee and find her takeout.

"It's actually a funny story," he continues. "Pia helped me pick out a melon in a market on two separate occasions. I gave her my card in case she ever needs a good deal on a used car. But we haven't seen each other in a few months."

"And yet, you still remember her name," Claire declares, sarcastically.

"You know us car salesmen, we never forget a name or a face," Jake laughs.

"Nice meeting you, Claire. I have takeout waiting. Bye Jake, good to see you again." Pia walks away and Jake excuses himself and pursues her.

"Hey, wait up. Do you need a lift home?" he asks.

"I live around the corner," she replies as she avoids eye contact. She grabs her bag and hurries out the door as he watches. He sees her turn right and he makes a mental note.

"Bye, pretty lady," Jake mutters under his breath as he stares into space for a moment. Then he returns to his date. He will have a bit of explaining to do for chasing after her, but he couldn't help himself. He is smitten.

8

The next morning, Pia wakes to a loud banging on her door. She throws on a chenille robe and rubs her eyes as she exits her bedroom and turns the knob with a yawn. She greets the jolly, bald landlord who is standing next to a rather large cardboard box. She smiles and ensures the belt to her robe is fastened as she presses down her hair with the flat of her hands and puts on a pretense that she has been up for hours. He can see she overslept. It was challenging to sleep in the heat and she found herself tossing and turning in a sweaty frenzy as her usual nightmares tormented her heart and invaded her dreams.

"Did I wake you?" he asks with a grin.

"No, I'm up, I'm up," she laughs as she beckons him to enter. He gets right to it while she puts on the kettle. She offers him a cup of tea and he wrinkles his nose.

"Too hot," he laughs.

"Ice tea?" she offers.

"You got ice?"

"I think so."

"OK, this won't take long."

She brews a ceramic pot of Earl Grey and plops five cubes into a tall, highball tumbler before pouring his tea. The ice melts rapidly and she empties some of his tea into the sink before adding more ice. She finds him a paper straw and adds a wedge of lemon. He has already removed the old unit and he is unpacking the new one.

"I'm going to jump in the shower," she proclaims with a smile. "Your rent envelope is on the coffee table in case you finish before I come back. Thanks again for being so prompt."

While she soaps her slender body, she is thinking about Jake and Claire. She wonders if she is his girlfriend as she certainly wasn't his mother or his grandmother. She was very pretty, almost exotic, with her straight, jet-black hair that kissed the floral seat cushion and her matching ebony eyes, crowned with extended lashes. The tight black dress flattered her figure and clung to her as if she had been dipped in dark dye.

Pia knows Jake is about 22 years old, but Claire looked closer to 30. Her voice was sexy, like Lauren Bacall's, but Jake is no Humphrey Bogart. Jake is handsome, whereas she always thought Bogie was a bit weathered and rough looking in the old black and white flicks she used to enjoy with Nonna. It was apparent that Claire was annoyed by the intrusion. As far as Pia knows, Jake was just about to propose marriage when she accidently bumped into the corner of their table, causing both water glasses to spill a few drops on the white linen cloth.

When she returns to the living room, her landlord is already gone. The empty glass with a lone single ice cube, the squeezed lemon wedge and flattened paper straw, is sitting on the counter. The new unit is humming away and the apartment is cooling down rapidly. She smiles. He is gone and so is the cardboard box and the rent envelope. She is alone with her thoughts and she decides to run to the bakery to pick up a chocolate croissant to enjoy with her second cup of tea. She grabs an apple to munch on during her walk.

As she exits the building and turns the corner, her eye fixates on an olive-green bench across the street. She lives near a small park and the benches are often filled with pedestrians who are simply enjoying a bit of fresh air or taking a load off their tired feet. There is a man perched casually on the green wooden slats. She knows him.

She approaches with caution and asks him why he is sitting there and he laughs. He tells her he has been stalking her and she may as well submit to his desires. She wrinkles her nose a bit and plops down beside him, leaving a suitable distance between their bodies.

"Really, Jake, why are you here?"

"I got here a few hours ago. I've been waiting to catch you walking on the street. I knew you lived in one of these buildings."

"Why?"

"Why not?"

"What about Claire?"

"It was just a date. She bought a car from me. She actually asked me out. It's not a relationship if that's what you were thinking. I'm still flying solo."

"And now you are stalking a girl you met twice in a grocery store?"

"I have run into you four times now. That must mean something. I think they call it *kismet*."

Well, the fourth time is hardly a coincidence. You tracked me down."

"I figure after three chance encounters, it's time we had a deeper conversation."

"What now? On this bench?"

"Why not?"

"I'm hungry."

"You're eating an apple."

"I need more. I was going to buy a chocolate croissant."

"Well lead on, I'll join you."

"OK, I guess I'm stuck with you for a little while."

"You could do worse."

"I figured you were still in bed with Claire on a Saturday morning."

"I do have a confession."

"What?"

"I am no longer a 22-year-old virgin," he laughs.

"So, you did sleep with Claire last night?"

"Nope." She gives him a puzzled look as they both stand to head for the bakery. She turns to him and takes another bite from her apple.

"So, who took away your virginity?" she mumbles as she chews on a rather large chunk, puffing up one cheek, attempting to be nonchalant.

"No one."

"You just said you are no longer a virgin."

"I said I am no longer a 22-year-old virgin."

"You had a birthday?" she laughs.

"Yup, two days ago. I spent it alone. Isn't that pitiful? That's why I went out with Claire, to have a belated birthday dinner."

"So you are still a virgin?"

"I am…I'm a 23-year-old virgin…which is even more pathetic, I suppose," he laughs as they walk. She finds a trash receptacle and drops the core of her apple inside. Then she turns to him.

"I do *not* think you are pathetic."

"Are you a virgin?" he asks.

"That's a pretty personal question."

"I told you."

"If you must know, I'm married. So, no, I'm not a virgin."

"You have a husband?" he prompts with sudden alarm and obvious disappointment.

"Yup."

"When did you get married?"

"Fourteen months ago."

"So, where is he?"

"I left him after six months. I wasn't happy. He's in another state."

"Does he know where you are?"

"I don't think so. I'm saving up for a divorce attorney."

"I can't say I'm sorry. I want you to be single."

"Why?"

"So there is hope for me, hope for us."

"You are such a flirt."

"Not really, I'm just smitten, smitten with the girl who knows about melons."

"And doesn't like to be touched," she reminds him.

"Did he hurt you?"

"Not physically, just emotionally."

"Did he cheat on you?"

"Probably, I'm not sure. He mostly ignored me and mocked me."

"I want to kill him."

"Get in line. My friend, Portia has two uncles with baseball bats. She didn't even know they were her uncles until about a year ago. They're her father's brothers and her dad vanished when she was two. They happen to both be living in Virginia and she tracked them down recently. Now they want to make up for lost time and be part of her life. She and I spent years together in an orphanage."

"And they want to beat up your husband?"

"No, but she offered to recruit their help if needed."

"It's good to have friends who own baseball bats."

"Or friends with uncles who own baseball bats."

"I remember you telling me you were in an orphanage. Is that part of the reason you don't like to be touched?"

"Probably…that and my painful marriage to Arty."

"Your husband's name is Arty?"

"Yup."

"I hate that name."

"Why?"

"Because he hurt you."

"Not physically. I left before that happened. I was afraid it would lead to that."

"I'm glad you left him."

"Me too."

"And you moved here because of your friend?"

"Yes, we're still close. We're both flying solo like you."

"Well, if you won't date me, maybe you could introduce us."

"I think she has sworn off men for a while."

"She got hurt?"

"Yes, her ex wanted to have an open relationship."

"I never got that. If you were my girl, I wouldn't want you dating other guys."

"So, you're a monogamous virgin?"

"Definitely. I hope to do something about that virgin thing before my next birthday."

"You have a year."

"A year minus two days."

"I think you should find a girl who likes to be touched. Why are you wasting time on me? I'm obviously frigid or something."

"Have you done anything about that?"

"I'm seeing a psychologist, a woman doctor. She's great, but she's on a long summer vacation. I'll see her in September."

"Any progress with the touching thing?"

"A little."

"I am a patient man. I've waited this long to have sex. I could wait a few more years. I just like talking to you."

"I don't even want to hold hands."

"I know. And that's the hard part. I can wait on the sex, but I really want to hold your hand."

"Are you making fun of me?"

"I'm dead serious. I'm kind of old-fashioned, holding a special girl's hand makes me giddy."

"And you think I'm special?"

"I do, I really do."

"You're a pretty handsome guy. You could get lots of girls to hold your hand. I'll bet you meet lots of women at the car lot."

"I seem to mostly meet men or men with their wives."

"You met Claire."

"I think she has a boyfriend."

"So why was she on a date with you last night?"

"Search me, maybe they have one of those open relationships."

"Did she hit on you?"

"She tried. She said she would spend the night with me at my place, but I told her I had a roommate and she got the hint. I think she wanted a one-night-stand. I don't want to lose my virginity that way."

"How do you want to lose it?"

"With someone special, where there will be a second night and a third night….and maybe a lifetime of nights. I want to grow old with someone and rock with her on a farmer's porch while the sun sets on a cool evening."

"You're a romantic."

"Most definitely."

"And you think I could be that girl on the farmer's porch?"

"I think it's a possibility. I think about you a lot, ever since we met."

"Maybe it's because I don't like to be touched. Men like a challenge."

"It's not that. I think I like the way you smell. You know, they say we are subliminally attracted to other people's pheromones. People think it's love at first sight."

"But it's really love at first smell?" she laughs.

"I think so."

"So I smell good to you?"

"Like a ripe cantaloupe."

"Suppose I don't like the way you smell?" she teases.

"Is that true?"

"I don't know. I haven't thought about it."

"You never get close enough to smell me."

"I don't let you get close to me either."

"I notice you are keeping your distance as we walk."

"And you are being very respectful of my space."

"I'm a respectful kind of guy."

"How can you smell me from so far away?"

"Maybe I have a superpower, the power to smell from a distance."

"Or maybe you are *super* horny after 23 years."

"I could have had sex with Claire last night and I turned her down."

"She was very pretty."

"She's gorgeous."

"Shut up."

"Are you jealous?"

"Why would I be?"

"Well, she is a fine looking woman, but she didn't do it for me. She was kind of pissed that I practically chased you out of the restaurant. But she got over it. I told her it was business and that I was telling you about a new car on the lot."

"Did she buy it?"

"I think so."

"Do you lie often?"

"Never to you. I tend to stretch the truth or recite alternative facts when I'm trying to move a car out the door. But that's the nature of sales. But I do have scruples and I never screw my customers. That's why I get lots of repeat business."

"Promise me you'll never lie to me."

"I promise."

"OK, then I'll give you a chance, I'll go to dinner with you."

"You will?"

"Well, depending."

"Depending on what?"

"On how our croissant breakfast goes. I thought we could eat them on a bench. There's another little park right by the bakery."

"How far is this place?"

"We're almost there."

"And if I pass the breakfast test in the park, you'll go out to dinner with me tonight?"

"I will."

"I think you just made me the happiest 23-year-old virgin on the planet."

"Well, at least the happiest 23-year-old virgin on this street."

"You make me laugh."

"So you like my smell and quirky sense of humor."

"You have a nice ass, too."

"I didn't know you checked me out."

"Oh, I checked you out the moment we first met. I said to myself, so this is where she's been hiding all my life. I tend to go to bigger supermarkets and I discovered you in one of the smaller establishments."

"But you never returned."

"Basketball got in the way."

"I'm glad we ran into each other again."

"Me too."

"But I still won't hold your hand."

"I can wait. I'll wait for as long as it takes."

"We're here."

"Where?"

"At the bakery, silly."

"Oh, I didn't notice."

"Can't you smell the warm bread?"

"I can only smell you. And I like what I smell."

"Hurry up, the chocolate croissants sell out early."

"I'm right behind you."

"Are you staring at my ass?" she calls out over her shoulder.

"I'll never tell."

9

Breakfast in the park was divine, she thought. Pia made him laugh and each time he cracked up over one of her stories about living in the orphanage and raising Cain with Portia, she became more and more relaxed. At one moment, their fingers touched for an instant, but she didn't pull away. It was just their pinky fingers. They sat on opposite ends of the olive-green bench with the bag of croissants between them. Jake reached for a piece of croissant at the same moment when Pia was searching for a bit of loose chocolate. Her finger felt soft and warm and his heart leapt into his throat when he first realized what was happening.

When their pinkies first touched, he froze and waited for her to react, fearing she would become frightened or upset. She didn't move a muscle and their fingers continued to rub slightly against each other for several seconds before she scooped up her renegade chocolate droppings and stuffed them into her mouth. He smiled, but he said nothing. As he had told her, he is a patient man. He is smitten and he is willing to wait for her to completely trust him, to surrender her heart and willingly allow their fingers to intermingle in an act of pleasure and complete acceptance. He will wait.

He wanted to slowly move his index finger towards her delicious lips and wipe away a smidgeon of chocolate that was nestled in the corner of her mouth, but he dared not. Instead, he pointed to his own lips and she took the hint and, using her paper napkin, dabbed at both corners and then wiped her upper and lower lips. For some reason, he found this to be erotic and he tensed up slightly to suppress his own state of arousal.

They talked for hours and then he walked her home. He would return to pick her up at 6pm. They were going out for Italian and he knew a place that prepared authentic dishes from the old country. She told him she would be able to tell the difference and he hoped she would be pleased. Pia had still not revealed her last name or her ethnicity, but he may have suspected she knew more about Italian cuisine than he as he waved goodbye.

She had given him her phone number and now he knew where she lived. This was a huge step for her as she was trusting him and even though she was far from certain she was interested in romance, she wasn't afraid to take this small step. She thought about Arty and wondered if having dinner with a man is a betrayal of their marriage vows, but since she never intended to see her husband again, she dismissed such concerns and called Portia.

"Hey you, are you excited about the 4th?" Portia asks as she chomps down on an English muffin that is smeared with peanut butter, the crunchy kind.

"What are you eating?" Pia laughs.

"Breakfast, I slept in."

"Well, I had my breakfast at the crack of dawn. Oh, and I got my new air conditioner."

"Did you blackmail the landlord like I told you to do?"

"I did, I paid the rent a day late, but only after he came inside to pick it up and brought the new a/c unit with him. It is so much better than the old one. I swear the other one pushed out warm air most of the time. The only time it felt cool was on cold days when I hardly needed it."

"This is Maryland, and you definitely need a good air conditioner."

"Tell me about it, I woke up in such a sweat. While the landlord was installing it, I jumped into the shower. You know how I hate cold showers, but I took a pretty cool one this morning. He actually woke me up. I forgot to set an alarm. Then I went out to my favorite bakery to buy chocolate croissants."

"You devil. You ate more than one, just one of those things is like a thousand calories!" Portia teases.

"I bought two, but I only ate one," she giggles.

"You bought one for me?" Portia pleads in a high-pitched squeal that reflects both gratitude and envy.

"Sorry, Jake ate the other one."

"What? Who is Jake?"

"Remember I told you about the guy I met twice at the grocery store?"

"Mr. melon-guy?"

"That's him."

"The 22-year-old virgin, right?"

"Well, that's no longer true."

"You had sex with him?" Portia shrieks.

"No, we just ate croissants on a park bench."

"That wouldn't make him no longer a virgin. I think I need to give you some lessons about virginity."

"I may not know much about sex, but I am married," she laughs.

"So who did Jake get lucky with?"

"No one, he had a birthday two days ago…so he's now a 23-year-old virgin."

"Funny, and you believe all this?"

"I think he is telling the truth."

"So, how did you run into him?"

"I had takeout last night at that new place and he was eating dinner with a beautiful, exotic woman. I went to the bathroom while I was waiting for my food and practically fell into his lap when I bumped into his table because I was avoiding a waiter with a tray full of drinks."

"I'll bet his date just loved that."

"Her name was Claire and I could tell she hated me on first sight. Then after a quick hello, I left with my food, but Jake chased me to the door."

"Why?"

"He offered me a lift home. He knows I don't have a car."

"I'll bet that would have gone over really great with Claire."

"I told him I lived around the corner and I figured I would never see him again."

"But you saw him this morning, how?"

"He got up early and headed for the park by the restaurant and watched for me. He didn't know which building I live in. When I was heading for the bakery, chewing on an apple, he was seated on a bench and he saw me coming. He just waved and I had to say hello."

"I guess he didn't get lucky with Claire?"

"She was up for it. She bought a car from him recently and he thinks she has a boyfriend."

"Another open relationship," Portia grumbles as thoughts of Ben run through her mind.

"I guess it's the latest fad. Anyway, he turned her down and I'm telling you she was gorgeous. If I was a lesbian, I would have had trouble turning her down."

"But now you think you're not a lesbian?"

"Yeah, I talked to Dr. Forte about it. She thinks I'm heterosexual. Arty was just a terrible lover. But I had nothing to compare him with."

"So, this Jake is stalking you now?"

"I think he likes me."

"You think?" she laughs. "He got up at the crack of dawn and sat on a bench, just hoping to catch a glimpse of you."

"Even worse, he had to call in sick. Saturdays are good days to sell cars and he took the day off. He usually plays basketball in the morning and then works in the afternoon. He gave all of that up with the hope of saying hello to me again."

"You have to at least buy the guy dinner after all that."

"I bought him breakfast instead."

"And how long did you hang out with him?"

"Over two hours. We walked to the bakery and talked. Then we ate the croissants and talked some more and he walked me home."

"And that's it?" she teases.

"And I gave him my phone number."

"You didn't invite him in and steal his virginity or at least show him your lovely new air conditioner."

"No, but he asked me to dinner tonight."

"And I suppose you turned him down," she moans.

"I actually said yes, we're going out for Italian."

"Oh, my God, you have a date! I was beginning to think it would never happen."

"Well, I am still married."

"Oh, screw Arty. You'll be divorced soon enough. You know, I can afford to loan you money for that."

"Let's wait until the fall. Dr. Forte will be back in September and she said she might be able to get a lawyer friend of hers to do it for free."

"I think they call it pro bono, they love to use their Greek words, those lawyers. That's why they charge a fortune."

"I think it's actually Latin." Pia laughs.

"Sounds Italian. Does he know you are first generation?"

"I haven't even told him my last name or my real first name."

"But he has your phone number and your address?"

"Yes, and I am pretty sure he has a crush on me, but I can't figure out why. I mean he knows I have my issues about touching. I'm a mess."

"Hey, you're getting better. You let me hug you last week."

"I know, but you're the only person I ever hug."

"Does he know about Arty?"

"Yes, I told him."

"And he's still interested?"

"He is."

"But are you attracted to him? We don't need another Arty where you just go out with any guy that shows interest."

"I liked him the second I first laid eyes on him. It's hard to explain. He said he likes my pheromones. I may like his too."

"What?"

"People emit odors that others can detect. People are attracted to other people's smell, it's called pheromones."

"Well, for me it's all about hormones. And I am horny as hell."

"Have you heard from him?" Pia asks.

"Funny you should ask. He called me last night around midnight. He knows I stay up late on Friday nights. I wanted to call you after we hung up, but we talked until after three."

"No wonder you slept in."

"I was just about to call you to tell you about it, but I had to eat something first. My stomach was growling. You know how I get."

"So, you talked for three hours?"

"Yup, he apologized for hurting me about twenty different times. He told me he hasn't been with any other girls. He went on a few dates, but all he thought about was me. Two of them wanted sex on the first date and Ben claims he turned them down. He told them he was still hung up on me."

"So, are you getting back together?"

"I invited him to join us for the concert on the 4th. I want you to chaperone. I'm going to make him work for it if he thinks he's getting back into my pants again anytime soon. Hey, you should invite Jake too," she suggests with glee in her voice.

"Let's see how tonight goes. Maybe. I am happy for you, Portia. Absence can make the heart grow fonder."

"But it can also make the horny boys wander."

"Well, I have a bunch of stuff to do before my big date with Jake. I'll call you Sunday morning and let you know how it went."

"OK, but if it's awful, go to a payphone and call me. I'll come rescue you."

"Deal…but it won't be awful. We had two fun conversations in produce aisles and a quick hello last night. But today was special. He got me to open up and he completely respects my touching issues. I still think he can do so much better than me."

"Hey, don't sell yourself short. You are pretty and smart and fun and honest."

"Keep going," Pia laughs.

"And sexy and mysterious and clever…"

"OK, you can stop now," Pia giggles.

"Look, just take it slow. If you really fall in love, the touching will come naturally and then you may learn how wonderful sex can really be. If you can hug me, you can hug the man you love."

"We'll see. The thought of Arty ever touching me again makes me cringe."

"You're done with that part of your life. You only married the guy because you were lonely and you wanted to get out of that dump the orphanage stuck you in. He felt like a step up, but he was a mistake. I could tell you weren't in love with him. I mean I never met the guy. You didn't even invite me to the wedding. But your letters made it seem like you married him out of desperation."

"I didn't invite anyone to the wedding. And you're right. I never loved Arty. I kept you a secret so I would have a place to run away to. I was actually thinking of leaving him as early as the day we got home from the honeymoon."

"That's sad. But you've grown so much in a year. A year ago, you were miserable and writing to me about it. I was so glad you finally left the guy in November."

"Marrying him was the dumbest thing I've ever done and leaving him may be the smartest. I love you Portia. If I was a lesbian, I would be hot for you."

"Of course you would. I'm gorgeous."

"I guess I should have realized I was never a lesbian since I had no desire to jump your bones."

"Well, for what it's worth, if I was a lesbian, I would be hot for you too."

"I guess we can end this conversation on that note," Pia laughs.

"OK, call me around ten tomorrow morning."

"I will. Thanks for being such a great friend. You are really all I have in this crazy world. You're my family."

"Well, we orphans have to stick together. I love you."

"Bye."

"Bye, Pia. Have a great time with Jake, the 23-year-old virgin."

10

Jake arrives promptly at 6pm. The dinner reservation is for seven and she invites him in to see her new air conditioner. He is impressed, or so he claims, and she laughs at his accolades and compliments to the landlord's workmanship. The unit is screwed to the window frame to keep if from falling on some poor shmuck's head and the insulation is neatly tucked in to keep out the sweltering Maryland heat or pesky moths.

"Would you like a glass of Cabernet?" she asks.

"I would love one, thank you. We should head out in about twenty minutes. I parked a block away and the restaurant isn't far, but you know the traffic around here."

"I don't even know how to drive a car and if I ever learn, I still think I'll be intimidated by the traffic."

"I'll teach you. You'll be fine."

"You expect to be around for a while," she comments playfully as she pours the wine.

"Only for about a century. I told you I'm looking for someone to grow old with."

"And rock the night away with on that farmer's porch."

"And bask in the memories of a life well lived."

"You definitely are a romantic."

"And proud of it too." He takes the glass and thanks her as she sits on the sofa with him. He makes sure he gives her plenty of room.

"So, I should tell you I am a first generation Italian girl," she says after taking a sip of her wine.

"You must know a lot about Italian food?"

"I do, Nonna was an amazing cook."

"Well, I guess I won't be able to dazzle you with my command of the menu. I was hoping to impress you."

"It's OK. You already impress me."

"I do?"

"You do."

"Tell me more."

"You are sweet and clever, and most of all, I feel like I can trust you."

"You can, Pia. I swear I would never hurt you. When I think about your husband mocking you, I just want to punch the guy's lights out."

"Are you violent?"

"Only when I have to defend someone I love."

"And you love me?" she teases.

"I'm not sure, but I think I *could* love you. I love lots of things about you."

"Like my smell?" she laughs.

"I think that is subliminal, but I am definitely drawn to you like a moth to a flame."

"I'm kind of afraid of moths too. They just creep me out," she admits.

"OK, then I'm drawn to you like you're drawn to chocolate croissants," he laughs.

"So, you want to eat me up?" she teases.

"Something like that," he comments with a twinkle in his eye. "I knew it the moment I first saw you in that produce aisle. The following Saturday, I missed a bunch of easy shots during our game. I mean I couldn't make a layup if my life depended on it. I was just awful."

"Why?"

"All I could think about was you. I wanted to walk off the court and head for that grocery store to find you."

"This sounds like a line."

"It's not. Somehow I'll find a way to prove it to you. I'll prove to you I am not a player. I speak from the heart."

"But you're a car salesmen. Everyone knows you guys can spin words to close a deal."

"I'm the worst salesman on the lot. I refuse to push a car on someone if they have any doubts."

"So, you're one of the good car salesmen?"

"Which is why I'm poor compared to most."

"But you have your integrity."

"I do."

"And I respect you for that."

"You never told me your last name. The first time we met you said that was information for another time. But I'm here, in your home, so can we introduce ourselves properly? I'm Jacobus Sean McGuire. I'm named for my Dutch grandfather on my mother's side. My father's grandparents were born in Scotland. I've been going by Jake all my life and very few people know my real name is Jacobus."

"Nice to meet you, Jacobus. I am privileged to know your real given name."

"And?"

"And Pia is not my given name, not my first name anyway."

"You are mysterious."

"Not really. I was baptized Francesca Pia Petrocelli."

"Very pretty name. Wow. Sounds like the name of an Italian movie star."

"Hardly. Nonna always called me Pia. She said my father called me Francesca and my mother called me baby girl or figlia."

"What does figlia mean?"

"Daughter."

"May I call you Francesca sometimes?"

"Only when I call you Jacobus," she teases.

"Deal. But never call me late for dinner," he laughs.

"You mean on those summer evenings on our farmer's porch when we are 88 years old?"

"I think you said you're 21, so you'll only be 86 when I'm 88."

"I'll still be a spring chicken."

"And I'll be hobbling along with my walker, but I'll still like checking out your perfect ass."

"I'm sure it will be far less perfect when I'm 86."

"Not to me. That's why God allows our eyesight to weaken with age. I'll still see you just as you are tonight."

"Are we flirting?" she asks

"Just a tad."

"Are you religious? You mention God now and then."

"I was reared a Methodist, but I'm not really anything anymore. I believe in kismet, karma and true love. I think it was kismet that led me to that grocery store. I think by not screwing over customers, it gives me good karma which led me to you. And you know I am searching for true love."

"So you can finally lose your virginity?"

"Precisely. Why would a guy want his first time to be with a Claire or a one-night-stand when he could learn about real lovemaking with his one true love?"

"So you think there's only one person for each of us out there?"

"No, that would be too random. But I believe there are only a precious few. I think many people marry the wrong person because they are impatient. Like I keep telling you, I am a patient fellow."

"I agree. I married for all the wrong reasons. I was never in love with Arty. I don't think he even knows what love is."

"Have you ever been head over heels in love?" he asks as he finishes his wine and places the empty glass carefully on the coaster. She appreciates his manners even though the coffee table is second hand and covered in scratches.

"I don't think so. I had crushes on movie stars as a kid, but that's not the same. I've never been around the opposite sex much. Nonna and I lived a cloistered existence and when she died, I was only twelve. They put me in that county orphanage and I lived with a bunch of girls. They sent me to all girl's schools, Catholic schools. It actually turned me off to religion."

"I would love to see you in your Catholic school uniform," he jokes.

"Men and their fantasies," she laughs. "That was the first thing I got rid of when I left the orphanage."

"Pity. So, now you aren't religious?"

"Not really. I think there may be a God up there, but I've been angry with Him for most of my life."

"Because he took away your family?"

"Yes."

"You were baptized Catholic?"

"I was. Most Italians are."

"So, we both believe in God, sort of, but neither of us goes to church. I told you I believe in kismet and karma."

"And true love," she adds.

"What do you believe in?"

"Family, friendship, and…maybe true love. I just haven't ever found it."

"We are both looking for the same thing. Maybe we could find it in each other."

"Anything is possible. Shouldn't we be going?"

"Yes," he says as he stands and picks up his empty glass. He walks to the kitchen and rinses it in the sink. She tells him to leave it and gulps down her final sip. They head out into the heat. He wants to take her hand in the worst way, but he knows his boundaries. She leaves the air conditioner on low.

They walk towards his car and continue discussing religion, love, family and farmer's porches. She laughs at his small jokes and he smiles warmly each time she makes a comment. He is mesmerized by her, but he is uncertain if she has any feelings for him. Still, she is with him, she said yes to dinner, he is making progress. Jake has never pursued a girl like this. He usually falls into short-term relationships without much effort. His friends introduce him to women, he meets them in public places, or they pick him up in the car lot. He never has trouble meeting women, but he also gets bored easily.

Pia doesn't bore him. Every syllable that falls from her lips intrigues him and fills him with a newfound energy, a desire to be a better man. Sam suggested Jake might be gay a few months ago due to his lack of interest in dating. Sam also knows Jake is a virgin, but he is sworn to secrecy because he knows the other guys would be relentless with their teasing.

But Jake is not ashamed of his virginity. Some of his friends see the opposite sex as notches on their belt. They like to count how many women they have slept with, but Jake finds that notion to be juvenile and selfish. He refuses to use someone for a carnal release as he could simply masturbate and skip the idle conversation. He does worry about AIDS and other STDs and he certainly doesn't want to get a random woman pregnant.

He wants the first time to be special and he is willing to wait, but he does feel uncomfortable with his inexperience as he continues to age. But 23 is still young, and he is certain that once he finds her, it will have been worth the wait. He could have had sex with Claire, but the attraction was purely physical. He found her to be shallow and self-centered, and even worse, he thought she was the most boring conversationalist he had ever dated.

Claire made it clear she just wanted a roll in the hay. She has a boyfriend, but occasionally she likes to sample something else from life's buffet of sexual treats. Jake refused to be someone's one-night-stand, knowing it would merely be mutual masturbation in his eyes. He is proud to have no notches on his belt as he respects people and women are not notches.

Arty is a fool in his eyes. He was able to convince Pia to marry him, but he completely blew it. She ran away from him, away from his emotional abuse. He obviously didn't appreciate what he had stumbled into, but Jake is determined to make sure he never makes such a mistake.

The restaurant is crowded as it is Saturday night at the peak dinner hour. They arrive two minutes early and their table is still occupied with an elderly couple who arrived when the restaurant opened at 5 pm.

"I'm sorry, but it will be a few more minutes. The people at your table already paid their check, but they're still talking at the table. As soon as they leave, a busboy will clean the table at once. You can wait in the bar if you like." The hostess is chatty and bubbly and Jake cannot help himself. He needs to tease her.

"Just point to the table and I'll get them to leave," he grumbles. The hostess looks shocked as her eyes widen and her jaw drops. She is speechless, but Pia comes to her rescue.

"He's teasing you. Thank you, we'll be in the bar."

"The name is McGuire," Jake reminds the hostess.

"Yes, Mr. McGuire, I have it," the young hostess replies with a forced smile.

"You shouldn't tease perfect strangers like that," she says.

"I thought it was funny," he laughs.

"You're right, the expression on her face was priceless. I think she was afraid for a moment."

"Afraid I'd pick up the people at our table and toss them out the door?"

The elderly couple in question walk slowly past the hostess and say goodnight. The man stops to grab a half dozen of the free mints, wrapped individually in cellophane, and his wife reminds him he should only take one. Jake notices them from his barstool and giggles to himself as he swivels in their direction.

"They may be the people who were squatting on our table."

"They look like they're over 100 years old," she laughs.

"I definitely could have kicked their asses and tossed them out the door."

"But would you have done such a thing?" she asks as if she is testing him.

"Of course not, I'm the guy who would jump the mugger in the street who tried to hurt those sweet, old people. Remember I want to be like them someday."

"On your farmer's porch," she reminds him.

"On *our* farmer's porch," he replies.

The hostess tells them their table is being cleaned and it will be ready in a few minutes. Jake pays the bartender and leaves the man a generous tip. Pia is impressed, he may be the poorest of the car salesmen, but he is no tightwad. They begin to wander towards the hostess who is busy with a takeout order.

"Now, don't tease her again," Pia whispers with a smirk on her face. He nods.

They wait patiently for the hostess to complete her call. Pia is inches away and he wants to place his arm around her soft shoulders and give her a friendly hug, but he remembers the rules…no touching, not until she is comfortable. She looks beautiful in her little black dress with matching low heels. She wears no jewelry except for a pair of dainty gold hoops in her pierced ears. Her hair is long and straight, almost black, like her eyes, and her arms are tanned from the sun, making her look like a native from her parents' homeland.

"Hello again," she says. "Right this way." The hostess leads them to their table and pulls out Pia's chair. When they are seated, she hands them each a menu and tells them their waiter will be right over. She sees they each have a full glass of wine and she stops herself as she is about to ask them if they need a cocktail. Just before she walks away, Jake speaks.

"The elderly couple that left a few minutes ago, were they the ones who were at this table?" The hostess flinches and nods.

"I believe so. They did linger at the table for a long time, but it's not our policy to ask people to leave when they are done eating."

"No, it's fine. We didn't mind waiting. I just wanted to say they were a cute couple. I hope to grow old with someone like that someday." She smiles at him and then she turns to Pia and tells them both to enjoy their dinner.

"You scare her," Pia whispers with a tad of delight.

"I was nice."

"You were. She's probably wondering if I'm the woman you want to grow old with. She looked at me with a weird expression."

"Like telling you to run for your life while you still can?" he jokes.

"Something like that."

"Good evening folks," the waiter proclaims as if he loves his job. "I see you brought your drinks from the bar."

"No, we actually sneaked them in from home," Jake teases.

"Jake, be good," she scolds with a smirk.

The waiter smiles politely. "Any questions about the menu?"

"How is the melanzana?" Pia asks, politely.

"It's absolutely divine," he declares. "We're famous for it, at least in this part of the country." She nods and smiles.

"She's a *real* Italian. You can't fool her with imitation Italian food," Jake announces in a nonthreatening voice.

"I think you will find all of our meals to be quite authentic. The owner and his father before him are both from Italy. The chef is also a native-born Italian."

"Good to know," Jake says. "Actually, I've been here before. I'm just playing with you. This place is the best in Maryland, maybe in the whole country."

"Grazie," the waiter says. "My name is Carlo, shall I give you a few more minutes to look over the menu?"

"Please," Pia responds before Jake makes another joke. Jake nods and smiles at Carlo and the waiter walks away.

"So, you've taken other women here?" she probes.

"Thousands, sometimes more than one on the same night," he teases.

"I guess you had time for multiple dates on one night since you never sleep with these thousands of women," she jokes.

"Precisely, I just eat dinner with one, enjoy a little small talk, and take them home by nine. Then I can have a second late night supper with the next one. It's like a revolving door of women and dinners."

"I'm surprised you aren't fat."

"Basketball, it makes you sweat it all off."

"Good to know."

"I think I may have the veal piccata with a side of their fabulous, famous melanzana," he says.

"That sounds good. I think I'll just go with the melanzana dinner and a side salad with the house dressing."

"I'll have a salad as well." He waves and Carlo comes running.

"Ready to order?" he asks.

"Yes, the lady will have the melanzana dinner with a side salad."

"House dressing?" She nods. "And the gentleman?"

"Veal piccata with a side order of the melanzana. Otherwise, I'll be stealing some of hers and she doesn't like that." The waiter nods and asks if Jake also wants a side salad. "Yes please, with the house dressing as well."

The busboy brings hot garlic bread and soft, creamy butter to the table as the waiter takes the menus and disappears. They are finally alone again.

"Have you actually been in fights?" she asks, remembering how he wanted to punch out Arty's lights or defend the old couple against a potential mugger.

"My last fight was about ten years ago. I was thirteen years old."

"Tell me about it."

"Not much to tell. I was at the bus stop and a younger girl was being teased. She was eleven or twelve."

"And you defended her?"

"I did. She wore braces and thick glasses. Her hair was in tight braids which made her look even younger. Three bullies were calling her four eyes and teasing her about the hardware in her mouth. One of them pulled on one of her braids and that's when I saw red. I tried to mind my own business, but that was the last straw when he pulled her braid and made her cry. I think she was more upset about being mocked than having her hair pulled."

"What happened?"

"The bus pulled up. I whispered to her to sit up front with me while the three assholes piled into seats in the back. I made her feel safe and we chatted on the way to school. I told her to ignore ignorant kids and I reminded her that when the braces came off, she would have beautifully, straight teeth while the boy who pulled her braid looked like one of those rednecks who will likely marry his first cousin. She laughed at my joke."

"She probably had a huge crush on you."

"Probably."

"But you said you were in a fight?"

"Well after school, she got a ride home. She told me her mother was picking her up early to go for one of her orthodontist appointments. When I got on the bus those three jerks were teasing another girl. That was it for me. My stepfather had slapped me around a few times and I wasn't really afraid of pain. They got off the bus one stop early. I heard them saying something about meeting a fourth kid at his house. The other kid skipped school and they were apparently up to no good."

"What happened?"

"I got off when they did and I waited for the bus to pull away. I began to follow them. They were all smaller than me, just three runts with a mean streak. My stepfather was tough on me, but I didn't go around taking it out on girls or smaller kids."

"What did you do?"

"I called out to them. They turned and faced me. I told them they had better stop bothering girls on the bus or they would answer to me. The biggest one of the three pumped up his chest like an ape and took a step real close to intimidate me. I didn't hesitate, I jabbed him hard in the gut with my left fist and landed a second blow with my right."

"Where did your right fist land?" she asks.

"Right smack-dab in the middle of his fat nose. Blood gushed all over his shirt. I stepped back with my fists in the air. He was on his knees crying like a baby and the other two backed up. I waited for them to attack, two on one, but they were cowards like most bullies. I stepped towards them and they ran like hell. I actually helped the bloody kid to his feet and sent him on his way. It wasn't much of a fight. I just hit him twice and he bled a lot."

"Did you get in trouble?"

"Nope, but the next morning, at the bus stop, they ignored me and they didn't bother any of the other kids."

"And that was the end of it?"

"A few weeks later, one of them came up to me in gym. Gym classes were huge, about 100 boys running around in shorts and trying to sink a basket. I didn't even recognize him at first. He actually apologized for the kid I hit. The kid I bloodied was the one who pulled on the girl's braids. He said he stopped hanging out with him because he was tired of the crap. He wasn't a bad kid, but his buddy had some real issues."

"And you never dealt with the kid you hit again?"

"No, it was over pretty fast. But I never saw him torment any other kids, not in front of me anyway. I was glad one of his pals stopped hanging out with him. Maybe it taught him a lesson."

"He's probably in prison by now," she says with a sly smile.

"No, he probably owns a car dealership and has a house bigger than this restaurant," Jake laughs.

The busboy returns and attempts to light the fat, jar candle on their table. Pia does not realize what is happening at first since she is lost in Jake's story about the bullies. But then she sees the flame.

"No, no fire. Please don't light the candle!" she shrieks and the teenager backs off and apologizes.

"I'm sorry. Should I take the candle off the table?"

"Yes, take it away," Jake exclaims in a protective manner as if he is Pia's father and she was just bullied by the busboy. The lad takes away the candle and walks off. Every instinct in Jake's body is telling him to place one of his hands on Pia's trembling fingers, to comfort her and assure her that everything is fine. But he resists. He knows it is not what she wants…not what she needs.

"Are you OK?" he whispers.

"Yes, I'm OK. I don't like being near a flame."

"No problem. I understand."

"You must think I'm crazy."

"I don't, sorry about the moth to a flame crack earlier. I guess you don't like moths or flames."

The salads arrive and the waiter asks if everything is OK. They nod. "You don't have a candle. I'll go get one."

"No, we asked the busboy to remove it. We don't like a crowded table," Jake insists. "Please take away the salt and pepper too." The waiter obeys and smiles.

"I don't use salt and pepper anyway," she comments.

"Well, I do," he giggles.

"Then why did you have the waiter take them away?"

"I don't know. It's the first thing that came to me. It doesn't matter."

They pick at the mixed greens in silence. She cuts the tomato wedges in small chunks and then she attacks the cucumber slice with the same precision. Jake grabs the entire slice of cucumber and stuffs it in his mouth. He does cut the tomato wedge in half before sticking in his fork. The waiter had sprinkled a bit of Parmesan on their salads before telling them to enjoy their food. Jake soaks his salad in dressing, but Pia keeps hers in the tiny, stainless steel cup and merely dabs her forkful of greens into the dressing as if she is attempting to keep it somewhat dry. Finally, he breaks the silence.

"So, have you been in any fights?" he jests.

"Not like yours. I had some verbal fights with girls at the orphanage. Portia would always stand up for me and threaten any girls who bothered me. She was like my big sister until I was 16 and she aged out."

"She is a good friend. Do you want to tell me about the candle?"

"I don't know where to begin."

"Just start at the beginning."

"I told you I went to live with Nonna when I was four."

"I remember."

"I used to stay at her house on Saturday nights."

"You must have loved her very much," he says.

"I did love her. I still love her. One Sunday morning, she woke me up early and told me there had been a fire at my house. My parents and my baby brother went to Heaven while I was asleep. That's what she told me. I never forgot her words. I kept asking her when they would be back and she would frown and try to explain. This went on for months. We drove by the remains of the house about three months later. That's when my phobia started. I've been afraid of fire since I was very young."

"That's terrible. I am so sorry. How old was your brother?"

"Gaetano was weeks away from his second birthday. He wanted a toy truck and Mama promised him one. For some reason I still remember that. Mama was twenty-nine and Papa was thirty-six. They all died of smoke inhalation."

"The lives that go unlived..." Jake whispers as he puts down his fork and fidgets with a bit of garlic bread, trying to find the words. "I am so, so sorry. So sorry." There are tears in his eyes and she notices. She does not allow tears to threaten her own eyes, but she is overwhelmed by the glow of the moisture that is beginning to drizzle down his cheeks.

"I made you cry," she utters with a bit of remorse.

"It's OK, I'm a wimp, I cry easily, in movies, even when I read a sad novel."

"I like wimps, I've been searching for a wimp all my life." she comments, sweetly as she plays with her salad.

"I wish I knew what to say about your family dying so suddenly."

"There isn't much to say. It was tragic. But over time, Nonna and I made a good life for one another. She adored me and I adored her right back. She was my mother's mama. She died at age sixty-four. She was stirring her marinara sauce on a Sunday morning. I found her. I knew. I knew she was gone. I cried and held her in my arms. I knew I was alone. Whatever relatives I have in Italy have never been in my life. I am alone."

"You have me," he says sweetly.

"Yes, I have a new friend name Jacobus."

"And I have a new friend named Francesca."

The waiter takes away the salads and plops two large meals down on the table. Then he returns with the side order of melanzana for Jake. He sprinkles more grated cheese on their meals and asks if there is anything else he can get for them.

"A little pepper?" Jake asks, sheepishly.

"Of course," Carlo replies with a puzzled look on his face. He brings both the salt and pepper back to the table and Jake tells him to just leave the pepper. He doesn't like a crowded table.

The food is piping hot and they agree to allow it to cool. He wants to kiss her so much, he has never wanted to kiss a woman so badly, but he cannot. He knows this. They look into one another's eyes and allow the break in conversation to float in the air like a cotton cloud. He is thinking about the fire that destroyed her world and she is thinking that he is a very special man, nothing like Arty.

"I like you Jake."

"I think I like you even more," he responds with a slight smile.

"You're flirting again."

"Always…even when I use a walker to get to that farmer's porch, I'll be flirting with you…and checking out your ass."

"Or it will be another woman…not me…"

"I want it to be you."

"You hardly know me."

"I know enough. I knew enough after our first conversation about melons and my friends."

"Sam and Marnie?"

"You remember…oh, Marnie got married to a guy named Jackson. That's his first name. Sam didn't take it well. She was his first love."

"I'm sorry for Sam, but happy for Marnie."

"As I was saying, I knew enough about you when you told me how to pick out a melon. I just knew."

"Maybe those pheromones kicked in," she jests.

"Maybe."

"I know I have a husband somewhere, but I am really very inexperienced. He was my first boyfriend. I was fresh out of the orphanage, lonely, living in a halfway house and sharing a communal bathroom with strangers. He flirted with me over a melon too. He got me to go out on a date. He was sweet and attentive. We got married after two months. I was still a virgin on our wedding night. It wasn't awful, but I did bleed and it did hurt. He seemed oblivious. He finished quickly and rolled over and went to sleep. I just laid there thinking that sex is not such a big deal after all. We did it twice a day during the four day honeymoon. It was always the same, but it hurt less."

"What happened after the honeymoon?"

"He started ignoring me. I felt more like his maid. He worked nights as a bartender. I worked days in a grocery store."

"It must have been lonely."

"It was, but I was used to being alone. I preferred it most of the time. His conversations were all about his car and sports. If I talked about fixing up the apartment, buying new curtains, he would shrug and say it was a waste of money. He squandered money on cigarettes and booze, but he wouldn't let me spend a dime of my own paycheck. He was a bully. He never hit me, but he pushed me around. When he stopped asking for sex for an entire week, I was relieved. I didn't care if we ever did it again."

"Have you dated anyone since you left him?"

"Just one guy."

"Who?" he asks, defensively. "I hate him already."

"You, silly, just you," she laughs.

"Oh, then I guess I don't have to hate him."

"Not unless you want to hate the guy you see in the mirror when you shave that handsome face of yours."

"Are you flirting now?"

"A little."

"Do you find me handsome?"

"I think every woman in the restaurant finds you handsome. I noticed a few women in the bar checking you out, probably wondering what you are doing with me."

"That's not true. Guys were checking you out for sure. I noticed. You're drop-dead gorgeous, don't you know that?"

"Claire was drop-dead gorgeous, not me."

"Claire was an empty vessel in a tight dress. You are real. You are natural. I think you are the prettiest girl on the planet, but more importantly, I love your heart and your mind. You do it for me, Pia, I can't deny it. I won't touch you until you ask me to. I won't light any candles, not even on your birthday cake, not unless you ask. I would do anything for you. Anything."

"You want to protect me, like the girl with braids and braces at the bus stop," she comments.

"I do, but it's far more than that. I want to love you."

"We are still strangers."

"Not really. This is our fourth date. I don't count the hello with Claire."

"Fourth?" she laughs.

"Yup, the two short dates in the produce aisles, the croissants in the park, and tonight. I am crazy about you and I can't hide it anymore. I'll give you time, all the time you need, to see if you could feel the same about me. And if I just don't rock your boat, I'll still be honored to be considered a friend."

"So this has been your way of hiding your feelings?" she teases.

"I guess I'm pretty transparent."

"You are a good guy, aren't you?"

"I've been trying to convince you of that for months. Meeting you over a melon was the best thing that ever happened to me. I may have to remain a virgin for my entire life. I may have to become a celibate priest or something if you don't want me. I can't imagine making love to someone who doesn't have your face."

"They say everyone has a twin out there somewhere," she laughs.

"God broke the mold when He made you. You're a one of a kind."

"You're probably right about that. I'm a mess."

"I like messes. I've been looking for a mess all my life."

"Good, then you came to the right place." She smiles and stares into his mesmerizing green eyes. "I like wimps…who cry over a sad story."

"Then you came to the right place too."

They nibble on their meals, but each of them is now smitten. Jake may be head over heels in love, but Pia is certainly in *'like'*. She does like him. She trusts him and she doesn't trust easily. And she has already had more fun with him than she ever had with Arty.

They are at her door. She does not invite him in as she knows what that means. She will not lead him on. He would have been content to continue the conversation for a few more hours, but it is late as they lingered at the table far longer than the elderly couple. Then they took a long, moonlight walk around the city before he drove her home. It is nearly midnight and he wants to kiss her goodnight. He would be happy kissing her hand and bowing, but she has given him no indication that she wants to be touched. So he bows anyway, but he does not reach for her hand.

"Thanks for a wonderful evening," she says as she waves with a tiny gesture. They are only two feet apart and the distance between them is killing him. He wants to pull her into his arms and kiss her passionately. He is envious of Arty since the bastard got to touch her so many times even if he never appreciated what he had. His loss is Jake's gain. If she could allow that creep to touch her flesh for all those months, the day will come when she will trust him to touch her. He will be patient.

She wants to invite him for the 4th, to join Portia and Ben, but she hesitates. She will sleep on it. He promises to call her at eleven in the morning, just to say hi. She is calling Portia at ten, and she will makes sure she is off the phone in time to take his call. Maybe she will ask him if he has plans for the 4th. Does she want to introduce him to Portia so soon? Are they in a relationship? He seems to want that, but she is uncertain.

Pia is still married. She is still frigid and afraid to be touched by this man whom she is enamored with. She still lives with her fears of fire and abandonment. But she does know one thing. She doesn't want him to go away, not yet, anyway. She needs him to stick around for a while…maybe for a century or so.

11

Pia slept soundly. There were no nightmares about the fire or about Nonna dying so suddenly. The air conditioner in the living room cooled the entire apartment and she did not wake in the dampness of sweat-soaked sheets. She wore her sexiest nightie to bed and thought about him while she drifted off, allowing her right hand to caress her own thighs. She moved her hand up a bit and touched herself as she thought about his magnetic smile and his trustworthy, honeydew melon eyes. She felt aroused, but she did not climax. Still, it was a delicious way to drift into dreamland with hope of avoiding the nightmares.

She woke refreshed. If she did have any bad dreams, she did not recall them. Sometimes she gets flashes at work of a nightmare where her brother is gagging to death in his crib. She doesn't recall the dream when she wakes, but then it comes to her while she is at her desk. She tenses up during those moments and coworkers often notice and ask her if she is OK. She always nods and mumbles that she just got a flashback from a bad dream. They all understand. They all know she is tormented by her past, but none of them ask many questions.

She is the odd duck at work, the girl who keeps to herself, who eats alone, and rarely makes a personal phone call. She doesn't socialize with any of her coworkers and most of them assume she will move on and seek employment elsewhere in due time. She doesn't seem to fit in and everyone wonders why she was hired in the first place. It's not that she is unlikable or incompetent, she is simply unknowable in the eyes of the people who work only a few feet away.

Pia is an enigma. She is the mysterious girl whose finger appears to have once worn a wedding band, who appears to have no family and few friends. They see her as a loner and they give her the space she requires. Even when a few of them donated used furniture and helped her move the scratched up table and antique bedroom set into her new apartment, she suspected it was an act of charity or even pity. She overheard two of them talking, expressing sympathy for her that was peppered with a touch of empathy. Everyone feels sorry for poor Pia, but none of them feel motivated to find a way into her heart or to learn about her demons. It was easier to be charitable and assume she wouldn't be sticking around very long.

One coworker, Laura, whispered something that caught her ear and weighed on her heavily. Pia is independent and she doesn't want people to pity her as if she is a mangy stray who is wandering the gutters in search of scraps.

"I do feel sorry for her. I think her mother died when she was young and she was sent to an orphanage. She reminds me of *Little Orphan Annie*. She's such a sad little girl. Pity."

Those words were burned in Pia's memory. Laura had uttered them during her first few months on the job and Pia never forgot the tone of voice that made her feel small and mocked. She hated to be ridiculed, it was the straw that broke her marriage. Had Arty treated her with more respect and dignity, despite the void in conversation and his inability to sexually arouse her, she would have stayed, she would have given him children. When Arty derided her, she tensed up inside and plotted her escape as if she was a prisoner who had been sentenced to life and she had little to lose. Like an inmate who steals a spoon and spends years digging a tunnel, Pia had found ways to save a few hundred dollars, her runaway money.

She had about $110 to her name when she married him, but he insisted they combine resources and open a joint bank account. Right after the honeymoon, he took control of the checkbook and insisted she live on an allowance. He gave her forty dollars each week, usually from his bartending tips, and it was often in the form of wrinkled singles and the occasional five-dollar bill. With the measly sum, she was charged with providing them with three meals a day. She also had to pay the paperboy, even though she cared little for the local tabloid, since Arty liked the comics on the fifth page. She had to keep Arty well supplied with his favorite, rather expensive, toilet paper. The forty dollars had to cover all paper products from towels to cups and napkins. And she had to buy soaps and shampoos with her allowance.

The worst part was the Laundromat. She did not drive and he rarely gave her a lift, so she used a small wagon to lug a basket of laundry to the facility each week. When she had a larger load of sheets and towels, she sometimes made two trips in a single week. This ate into her allowance since the coin-operated machines were a bit pricy and Arty liked his clothes to look immaculate.

He claimed a bartender made more in tips if he looked like he just stepped out of a high-class clothing catalogue. She ironed his long-sleeve white shirts and spray-starched the collars and the cuffs. She quickly realized he married her for the maid services. She was his laundress, his housecleaner, his cook, and his sexual release when he was in the mood. Of course, she worked just as many hours in the grocery store as he did hawking alcohol and flirting with the ladies.

He squandered his free time watching sports or lame TV shows when he wasn't tinkering with his car or hanging out with his buddies. She was fairly certain he had other women on the side, ladies who could be labeled as barflies or even cougars, but sadly, she didn't care. If he found sexual satisfaction in other places, he tended to leave her alone. At first, she assumed sex would get better over time. It did not.

Pia became resourceful when she went to the market with a fistful of coupons that she snipped from the local newspaper. At least the paper rag was good for something, she thought. She would buy day old bread and meat that was about to expire, just to save a few pennies. Arty liked Kellogg's Frosted Flakes, but they were expensive, so she bought a larger box of a generic brand and continued to fill the original name brand box with the so-called inferior cereal. Arty couldn't tell the difference, and if he did complain, she would simply shrug and pretend that Kellogg must have made a bad batch.

Since he took away her $110 when they married, she was determined to get it back, and when she finally hit her goal by Labor Day, she was ecstatic. But then she continued to save at an even more frenzied pace. When her secret savings approached the $200 mark, something wonderful happened, somebody dropped dead. The death of Arty's great-uncle provided her with hope and opportunity. She feared if she ran away on a normal day, he would hunt her down and drag her back. Even though he had never raised a hand to her, there were signs of sadism in his eyes.

They would occasionally watch a crime show on TV together and he sometimes seemed sympathetic towards the aggressive husbands who were locked up for spousal abuse. He would comment on how the feminists think they are equal to men, but they don't erect skyscrapers or build bridges. And when a TV judge would pronounce sentence on an aggressive husband, Arty would scoff and claim the judge was unfair.

She decided not to stick around long enough to wait for him to come home slightly inebriated after work and suddenly decide to slap her around. She had survived by obeying him and making sure she never created waves. She got along with him because she rarely disagreed with a word he said and if she did voice an opinion, she would quickly admit she had been wrong.

It is July 3rd now. She married Arty fourteen months ago after a two month courtship that began shortly after her 20th birthday. She first noticed him in the produce department, looking sheepishly helpless, about a month before her birthday. She was 19 and he seemed like a nice enough fellow. They talked several times over the subsequent weeks and he finally asked her out on a date. She hesitated at first, but it didn't take him long to convince her to trust him. Eight months after their first date, she hopped on a Greyhound and headed out of "Dodge", with no intentions of ever looking back.

It's time to call Portia. She decides to act as if the date with Jake was nice, but not go overboard with her praise. She knows Portia and if her mentor thinks she is falling for the guy she will be relentless and want to start planning a wedding. Pia is still married and a second wedding is the furthest thing from her mind.

"Morning," Pia says in a chirpy tone that reveals she has been up for hours. Portia has apparently just dragged herself out of bed.

"Hi, it's 10am, already?" she mutters as she sips on her black coffee.

"Yes, and Jake is calling me in an hour, so we can't talk too long."

"I see, so the date went well?"

"It was nice. I think I may invite him to come with us tomorrow. Is Ben definitely coming?"

"Yes, but I have bad news."

"What?"

"The Beach Boys were almost banned by some idiots in government, but then President Reagan said he liked them, so I thought they were back on."

"They're not playing?" Pia asks.

"Nope, they booked another gig somewhere else. So dumb."

"So who's playing?"

"I heard Wayne Newton," she complains.

"Well that's not the same," Pia agrees.

"But we'll still have fun. The fireworks are always great and we can bop around DC for the afternoon and grab food from some street vendors."

"OK, it will still be nice. Are you thinking about giving Ben another chance?"

"I am, but don't let him know that. I want to make the man grovel for at least another month or so. So tell me more about Jake."

"Well, he seems nice, for a car salesman," Pia replies, attempting to suppress the fact that she does like the guy.

"Oh, yeah, those car salesmen can talk a good game."

"But he says he's the poorest guy at work because he refuses to take advantage of people."

"OK, that's both good news and bad news."

"What's so bad? The guy has integrity."

"But he'll always be poor," she laughs. "You can't live on love alone."

"I know. But I don't care about money that much. Besides, he's smart and I'm sure he'll find a way to buy the house in the country with the farmer's porch. He wants to rock on a big porch in his old age and he thinks I might be the woman he wants sitting at his side."

"Oh, the guy either spins a good yarn or he is smitten, maybe both."

"He seems to like me, probably more than I like him. He does know I am still married."

"I told you I'll loan you money for the divorce."

"Not yet. Let me talk to Dr. Forte in September about the free lawyer. Anyway, I like him a little."

"More than you liked Arty at first?"

"More than I ever liked Arty," she laughs.

"What's the difference?"

"For one, Arty and I peaked on the first date. It was all downhill after that. Every time I see Jake, I seem to find more reasons to like the guy. But I'm not looking to fall in love and I want you to promise me you'll be cool around him. No match making crap."

"I promise to be good. And don't encourage Ben either. Make him suffer. He needs to woo me all over again if I'm ever going to trust him a second time."

"That's the thing about Jake. I feel like I could trust him with my life."

"Oh, I think you may be falling for this guy."

"I don't know. I have zero experience with the opposite sex, except for Arty, and that hardly counts. I've changed a lot in a year."

"Well, I have more than enough experience. I'll know if he's a keeper pretty quickly."

"Please don't embarrass me."

"I won't. I promise. So have Jake pick you up and meet up at my place around 1pm. Ben should be here by then."

"OK, what are you doing today?"

"I may go back to sleep. I'm so tired. But I need to clean the apartment and run to the supermarket." The word supermarket floods Pia's mind with thoughts of Jake and the day they first spoke about a melon. It seems when you least expect it, life can turn on a dime. Maybe she is smitten. She has so little to compare the feeling with and she refuses to be a wide-eyed schoolgirl who thinks all men are trustworthy. But Jake does seem quite honest and reliable. Time will tell.

She gives the apartment a quick dusting and then vacuums the carpet in the living room and bedroom. The bathroom needs cleaning, but she'll wait until after her shower. The phone is ringing. It's 11am and she knows it is him.

"Hello," she says cheerfully.

"Morning sunshine," he says.

"Nonna used to call me that," she laughs.

"How are you?"

"I'm great, how are you?" she asks.

"I'm over the moon. I had a date with an angel last night."

"Oh, you went out with another woman after you took me home?"

"Very funny. I only have eyes for you."

"And that definitely sounds like the kind of line men have been spitting out since the dawn of civilization."

"Probably since the first caveman bopped the first cavewoman on the head with a club and said ugh."

"Probably," she laughs.

"So what are you up to today? I don't have to work until Tuesday morning."

"I just did some cleaning and after I shower, I plan to scrub the bathroom."

"Yuk, that doesn't sound like much fun…except for the shower part. I wish I could be a fly on the wall while you shower. I wouldn't lay a wing on you, I would just drink in the scenery."

"You have a dirty mind, don't you?" she teases.

"Never met a man who doesn't, but at least I only have eyes for one girl in the shower."

"So you indicated. Sorry, I shower alone. I don't even allow flies to watch."

"Well, a guy can always dream…or daydream. I'll be daydreaming about you in the shower all day long while I figure out what I'm going to do today. I don't have a clue. I'll probably go have a late lunch with my mother and grandmother. They get home from church by noon and they usually eat around 1pm on Sundays."

"Would you like to come here for dinner?" she asks. She didn't plan to ask him to dinner, but the words just popped out of her mouth before she could stop them. "I'll cook. I owe you a meal."

"I would love to come. I'll bring a couple of bottles of wine."

"We're not getting drunk."

"No, but we can share one bottle. I'll bring a red and a white so you can decide what goes best with your culinary masterpiece."

"I warn you I'm no chef."

"I would be happy with a peanut butter sandwich so long as it was made with your hands."

"Are you sure you want to keep seeing me? You know about all my issues."

"Do I know about them all?" he asks.

"Well, most of them."

"No moths, no touching, no flames, anything else I should know?"

"I don't like to be ridiculed."

"I only want to adore you," Jake replies, sweetly.

"I may only be able to offer friendship."

"I definitely want us to be friends and having dinner with my new friend will make me very happy."

"OK, I need to shower. I'll see you around 6pm."

"I'll be there with bells on my toes, a single red rose, and a big, fat smile under my nose."

"You're quite the poet," she laughs.

"I have many talents that are soon to be revealed."

"I look forward to it. Bye Jacobus."

"Ciao Francesca."

It's nearly 6pm and the roast is in the oven. She wouldn't have dreamed of turning on the oven if the old, clunky air conditioner was still in the window. But the new one is keeping things perfectly comfortable, despite the heat emanating from the kitchen. She is wearing white shorts that barely cover her slim thighs. Instead of the typical zipper, there are four silver buttons in the front and she thinks they are kind of sexy.

This is not going to be a seduction as she is still keeping her distance from most human beings, but she did opt to wear the sexiest blouse in her closet which almost hides her lacy brassiere. She is even wearing one of her sexiest pairs of panties, not because Jake will ever see them, but because it makes her happy.

Suddenly she is nervous. Suppose he has too much to drink and forgets about the agreed upon boundaries? Would he force himself on her? Pia is 95% certain he is actually a virgin, a man who is waiting for the perfect first sexual experience, but men have needs. He may push her to allow him to kiss her or to fondle her breasts. If he crosses any lines, it will be over and she won't invite him to meet Portia tomorrow.

He did say he is free until Tuesday and she assumes he would love to spend the day with her and her best friend. And with Ben of course. She thinks the two guys would actually hit it off. Alcohol could be a game changer. She will definitely not open up a second bottle of wine. They each had two glasses of wine last night and he seemed completely sober. He was a perfect gentleman and she doesn't know why she is so apprehensive.

The bell rings. She freezes up and presses the button on the ancient intercom. She asks who it is. But she knows of course. She is filled with excitement, unlike anything she has ever experienced.

"May I help you?"

"Wine delivery for Francesca," he says. She can tell he is grinning.

"Come right up Jacobus." She buzzes him in and he bounces up the stairs two at a time. She has already opened her door and she watches him land on the top step as he nearly stumbles and drops the wine. She giggles. He is carrying four bottles. Is he insane?

"I couldn't make up my mind, so I bought all four," he mumbles, apologetically.

"Well, thank you. Feel free to take some home."

"I would rather drink them all here, just not all tonight."

"So you expect to be invited back?"

"I do."

"Well, it will depend on your behavior tonight."

"I'll be a very good boy, I promise."

"We shall see. Enter."

He steps in and places all four bottles on the kitchen counter before spinning around and complimenting her on her tidy apartment and the delicious aroma that is flowing from the oven.

"It may not taste as good as it smells," she laughs.

"It matters not, I am just happy to be here."

"I'm glad you're here too," she admits.

"Let's open one of those bottles. Can I help?"

"I can do it. Which one?"

"Ladies choice."

They are soon sitting on her sofa and chatting like old school chums who are catching up after a long absence. She feels like she has known him forever. It is an odd feeling for Pia. She knows so few people. She opens up to fewer.

"I want to play a game," he finally blurts out.

"So long as it doesn't involve taking our clothes off," she teases.

"Nope, it can be done with or without clothing. Clothing is purely optional."

"So what's this game?"

"Your husband's name is Arty, right?"

"Correct."

"When did you first lay eyes on him?"

"It was January last year. He was looking for a ripe melon just like you and I was working in the store. I got the job when I left the orphanage. When I first met you, and you asked about the melon, I was hesitant, it was all too familiar."

"I get it. So when you first saw his face and when he first spoke to you, if you had to rate the attraction level from one to ten, how attracted were you to him?"

"What kind of game is this?"

"Just trust me."

"I do trust you?"

"So, on a scale of one to ten… if there was absolutely no attraction whatsoever, you can say zero."

"I thought I had to pick a number between one and ten?" she teases.

"Or zero…"

"OK, I'll say a one. I didn't give him much thought."

"And then he obviously kept coming back, trying to get you to like him. So by February, what was his number?"

"Two…maybe…at best."

"And then when did you finally agree to go out with him?"

"March."

"Damn, it only took him two months. It took me six months."

"I'm a lot smarter now."

"So after that first date, what was the attraction number?"

"Three…a solid three."

"Then you kept seeing him and how did the number change?"

"By April it was still a three. It was exciting to have a boyfriend, my first one."

"And by May?"

"He proposed. I hesitated. I finally said yes. But he was slipping by then. Maybe closer to a two."

"And yet you said yes?"

"I was sent to a halfway house after I left the orphanage. It was creepy. There was one bathroom in the hall for eight of us. One girl was messy and would leave used feminine products on the floor right next to the toilet. She couldn't be bothered tossing them into the garbage. Another girl complained. That girl had a black eye and a split lip the next day. There was a lot of gossip, but no one complained after that."

"Sounds awful."

"Some of the girls *were* awful, leaving gobs of toothpaste all over the sink and there was hair everywhere. The shower was the most disgusting place of all. The walls were covered in hair and no one seemed to want to clean. So I started scrubbing the bathroom because I knew that's what Nonna would have told me to do."

"Nonna was very wise."

"When Arty proposed, all I could think about was having a bathroom that I didn't have to share with other girls. I would have more privacy and maybe we would have a baby. It all seemed a lot better than living in the halfway house."

"So you married the guy even though the attraction level was sliding from a three to a two. Did it ever rise again?"

"Nope, after the honeymoon, it was back to a one. By summer it was about a zero and by fall it was negative, can I assign a negative number to the attraction level?"

"Sure, the rules of this game are flexible."

"So by October, it was at a new low, about a negative three. I left in November. I saved up some of the grocery money. It wasn't easy since he controlled all the finances. He went out of town to a funeral and I got on a bus and came here."

"OK, now for the fun part of the game."

"Oh, there's going to be a fun part?" she teases.

"Definitely. So you met me in January as well, a year after you met Arty. What was the attraction level when we first spoke? Be honest now. Don't spare my feelings. Just tell me the truth."

"OK, well at first, it was creepy. I had become more and more uncomfortable with being touched and I was feeling a bit claustrophobic. Your comment about the melon reminded me of Arty. But the more you rattled on about being a virgin and about Sam and Marnie, I realized you were not Arty. When I walked away from you, I wanted to turn and smile, but I didn't. I guess I thought you were a solid two."

"OK, that's better than a zero or a one. What about over the weeks ahead, did you think about me at all, did my number change?"

"I thought about you. I figured we would never run into each other again. I did look for you the next time I went to that store, but I figured you were shooting hoops. Then in March, I moved here and I went to the supermarket. I was trying to face my fear of crowds. Tomorrow is going to me a little difficult for me."

"What's tomorrow?" he asks.

"July 4th. I'm meeting Portia and Ben to bop around DC and watch the fireworks after dark."

"I thought they broke up."

"They did. He is trying to make amends. But she'll make him sweat for a while."

"And the DC crowds will be hard for you?"

"Probably."

"Would it help if you had a body guard?"

"Know any?"

"I'm free."

"Portia told me to ask you to come if last night went well."

"And did last night go well?"

"You're here, aren't you?"

"So were you planning to ask me?"

"I figured I would see how tonight goes first."

"Makes sense."

"So you *would* go…if I ask?"

"I would."

"Good to know…takes all the pressure off."

"Kind of like kissing a first date when you pick her up to take the pressure off of the dreaded goodnight kiss," he laughs.

"I wouldn't know."

"So, was I still a two by March, before you ran into me a second time?"

"Maybe closer to a three."

"And then I asked you out and you shot me down and walked away. Was I a three by then?"

"Nope."

"Nope?" he complains like a schoolboy who was just told to stand in the corner.

"You weren't a three after our second conversation. You were a solid four by then."

"I was a four! I'm so excited. Arty was never a four!"

"True. He was only a three for about six weeks and then he went on a downward spiral," she laughs.

"So then we didn't run into each other until Friday."

"When you were on a date with gorgeous Claire," she jests.

"I wouldn't call her gorgeous, but yes, you nearly fell into my lap when you bumped into the table. I was hysterical inside, but I suppressed my laughter because Claire was glaring at you with daggers in her eyes."

"She did seem awfully possessive for a first date," Pia teases.

"And a last date," Jake laughs.

"Well she does have a boyfriend," Pia reminds him.

"So, I know we hardly spoke on Friday and it was awkward with Claire and all, but did my four change between March and Friday?" Jake prompts with a boyish smile.

"I think you slipped to a three after all that time. I figured we were two ships that passed in the supermarket. Then when I saw you with Claire, I admit I was a tiny bit jealous. It's just human nature, I suppose. You stayed a three though. Then when you practically chased me out the door, and offered me a ride home, and you left Claire at the table, I thought that was so weird. You slipped to a two."

"Oh, no…I'm on the dreaded downward Arty spiral," he mutters with a puffed out lower lip.

"No, you bounced back the next morning when I saw you on that bench, looking for me. As we walked to the bakery, you were a three again and by the time I agreed to go out with you, you were back to a four."

"Thank God, that was close," he shrieks, causing her to burst into laughter.

"I think we should eat."

"OK." He follows her to the kitchen and helps her serve the dinner. They sit at the only table and begin to cut their beef and nibble on peas and carrots.

"The mashed potatoes are out of this world. I figured you would make spaghetti and meatballs."

"Why, because I'm a first generation Italian girl?" she laughs.

"I guess."

"I do eat other food."

"Well, the roast is delicious. The gravy is perfect."

"It's from a jar."

"Well, you heated it up perfectly."

"Thanks. The potatoes are Nonna's recipe, it's one of the few things I can make well."

"I wish I had known her. I hope you meet my grandmother soon."

"We'll see."

"Back to the game. I was a four when you agreed to go out to dinner, my all-time high. What about when I took you home after our date last night?"

"You are really needy," she chides with a giggle.

"I am."

"You should buy a puppy…or adopt one from a shelter. You need to feel loved."

"I do."

"So, just to put you out of your misery, by the time we said goodnight after our big date, you had jumped to a six."

"What happened to five?"

"You sailed right past it. When you teased the waiter and the hostess, you nearly lost a point, but then you tipped really well."

"You noticed?"

"I noticed."

"So am I still a six? Have I slid off my pedestal?"

"Nope, still a solid six."

"Wow. Arty never made it to four."

"He did not."

"I'm overwhelmed and very grateful."

When they finally said goodnight, Jake stood in her doorway and grinned, feeling like that schoolboy who is about to kiss a girl goodnight for the very first time. It was an awkward moment, not because they have never kissed, but because he knows the rules. He is not allowed to touch her, not until she is ready.

"So, you still haven't asked me to join you guys tomorrow," he comments with a flirtatious grin.

"I almost forgot, yes, come, please join us," she replies.

"It would be my pleasure. What's the game plan?"

"Pick me up at 12:30. Eat lunch before you come. We'll leave your car at Portia's place and take the subway into the city. We probably won't get back until close to midnight. Is that OK?"

"Sounds perfect. Goodnight sweet lady and thank you for a perfect evening and a fantastic dinner. I'm stuffed."

"I'm glad you liked it. Thanks for all the wine. I'll see you tomorrow."

"Bye Francesca."

"Goodnight Jacobus."

As he slowly descends the staircase, he stops and turns to wave to her. She is still standing in the doorway, watching him leave, mesmerized by the back of his head. She likes the back of his head, it is one of her favorite things about him. He has a full head of reddish-brown hair, wavy and thick. The hair on the back of his head is fringed slightly over his shirt collar.

When he turns to wave, she smiles and calls out to him. "Oh, Jacobus?"

"Yes, Francesca?"

"I'm sorry, but you are no longer a six."

"I'm not?" he asks with a sad look of surprise.

"Nope. I would say you're a solid six and a half now."

"A new all-time high!" he calls out with glee as he bursts into song.

"I have often walked down this street before, but the pavement always stayed beneath my feet before. All at once am I several stories high, knowing I'm on the street where you live…"

The landlord opens his door, suddenly, and Jake goes silent. Pia peeks over the railing to watch their encounter, giggling to herself like a moonstruck teen.

"What's all the noise? It's after ten," the landlord barks.

"I am so sorry kind sir. I was merely celebrating the 4th of July a bit early. Happy Independence Day, sir," Jake declares with a broad smile.

"Same to you. Just keep it down. People go to sleep early around here."

"Roger," Jake replies as he looks up to see Pia watching the entire performance. She waves slightly and he does the same. He exits the building with a grin on his face and a bounce to his step.

She runs to the bedroom and opens the window, letting in the sticky night air, and pokes her head out as far as she can without risking certain death. She cannot see him as she cranks her neck and stands on her toes. But then she hears his voice.

"Are there lilac trees in the heart of town? Can you hear a lark in any other part of town? Does enchantment pour out of every door? No, it's just, on the street, where you live…"

He must be a *My Fair Lady* fan, she thinks. Or he adores Audrey Hepburn. He is singing the song that Freddy sings when he is smitten with Eliza Doolittle. Is Jake just as smitten? Is she? She told him he is now a six and a half. He probably sees her as a nine or a ten. But why? She is perplexed. She still feels he can do better. But he seems to be enthralled with her.

She continues to listen. He is far away now, likely getting close to the spot where he parked his car. But then his voice gets louder and she realizes he is still singing.

"People stop and stare, they don't bother me. For there's nowhere else on earth that I would rather be. Let the time go by, I won't care if I, can be here, on the street, where you live."

12

Washington, DC is crowded, as expected. The sun is blaring high in the sky and the foursome is skipping through the streets like Dorothy, Tin Man, Scarecrow, and the Cowardly Lion. Pia envisions herself as Dorothy, trying to find her way home, home to a place where she feels safe like the way she felt when she lived with Nonna in a humble home on Maple Street. Her imagination continues to run wild as she decides that Portia is the Lion, only far less cowardly. Portia is fierce and resilient, the rock who got her through some dark days in the orphanage. Ben is the happy-go-lucky Tin Man, trying to win Portia's heart back. That only leaves the goofy Scarecrow who can make Dorothy laugh as he shoves his ochre straw back up his sleeves. Jake is her Scarecrow, lanky and comical, and as the day evolves he is turning into a sold seven right before her eyes.

Ben and Jake are leading the way, carving a path for the ladies to follow, keeping Pia safe from the humans who are meandering about in every direction. There is enough of a distance between the men and the women to allow the fellows a chance to indulge in in a little guy talk.

"I think Pia really likes you. I've never seen her look so happy," Ben says.

"I hope so. I'm crazy about her. Head over heels," Jake declares. "What's going on with you and Portia?"

"I screwed up. I thought I wanted an open relationship and all I did was mess up the best thing that ever happened to me. I went out with a few girls, but I didn't sleep with any of them. I was so distracted thinking about Portia the entire time. I have apologized and begged for her forgiveness, but she hasn't decided if she'll be able to ever trust me again."

"But you're here. She invited you to be with us today. That's a good sign."

"True. But I know Portia. She won't make it easy for me. I'll have to earn back her trust."

"You can do it, man. Just romance her. It will be worth it."

"Are you a romantic, Jake?"

"Absolutely, and I fully intend to woo Pia, if she'll allow me to."

"I guess you know she doesn't like to be touched," Ben whispers as if it's a state secret.

"I know. She said she even stopped hugging Portia."

"But she hugged her today," Ben comments. "So she is getting better. Like I said, I can tell she really likes you."

"And I know she is still married and the guy wasn't very good to her," Jake says.

"He's probably the reason she doesn't like to be touched."

"That and her difficult childhood."

"Yeah, she's had more than her share of heartaches," Ben sighs. "I really like her. I like you too. I hope it works out."

"And I hope Portia takes you back. The four of us could have some great times together."

"You want kids?"

"Definitely. I want it all, the picket fence, the farmer's porch, the swing set in the backyard. I want grandkids someday so that I can spoil them rotten. I want to find that special forever love, the kind you find in literature or romantic movies."

"Yup, you're definitely a romantic. I want all that too. I want to teach my kids to throw a football, even if I have all girls."

"I want to teach my kids how to make a proper layup. Although lately, my game is off."

"Why?" Ben probes.

"I've been distracted. I think I'm in love, *madly* in love."

"Hey, you two, wait up," Portia calls out.

"And what have you two been gossiping about?" Pia asks, impishly.

"We'll never tell," Ben teases.

"Just guy talk…you know football, basketball, that kinda stuff," Jake adds, innocently.

"Well, we've been talking about you, Jake," Portia declares as Pia shoots her a look of concern. She promised Pia she would not embarrass her.

"We think you're not really a virgin, Jake. We think you're just making that up."

"I never said that," Pia utters as she holds her hand to her heart.

"I'm just messing with you, Jake," Portia laughs.

"Are you a virgin, man?" Ben asks.

"Yup, and proud of it. I've dated a bunch of girls. We kissed a lot and fooled around a bit, but I want my first time to be with the woman I love."

"She may be right in front of you," Portia adds.

"I think that may be true," Jake agrees as he looks into Pia's eyes.

"Let's go find something to eat," Pia suggests as she changes both the subject and the trajectory of their route. "Let's cross the street."

Everyone knows Pia is embarrassed, but surprisingly, Jake seems proud to tell the world he is saving himself like a young Victorian bride, he is saving himself for marriage, or at least for the girl he hopes to marry.

They find a food truck and grab some wraps, turkey for the women and roast beef for the guys. Then they sit on a patch of grass and sip on lemonade as they nibble on their lunch. Pia is laughing at Ben's humor and giggling like a toddler who is being relentlessly tickled each time Jake makes a witty comment.

The four of them are basking in the sunlight, happy and carefree, celebrating the nation's birthday when it happens. None of them realize what is occurring at first. Only Pia.

"Hello, Pia," he says, calmly. He is standing and the four of them are sprawled out on the lawn. Pia cups her hands over her eyes and stares up towards the blinding sun, unable to quite make out his face, but she knows. She knows that voice. She stands in shock, but then takes a step backwards as he attempts to embrace her. Jake stands to protect her, to quickly assess the situation, but it is too late for that.

"No, Jake, please sit," Pia commands. "Excuse me everyone. I need to talk to someone." Pia and Arty wander towards the Washington Monument in silence until he finally begins the conversation.

"I thought the Beach Boys were playing today."

"We all did. Some kind of screw-up by the government. I'm surprised to see you here."

"I have an old buddy who just moved to DC. He still doesn't know a soul and he asked me to come visit for the weekend. He's around here somewhere. I lost him in the crowd."

"Oh," she says. "Are you still living in the apartment?"

"No, I bought a house, I paid cash. It's really nice, there's even a swing in the backyard, one of those gliders for two."

"How did you pay cash?"

"I wanted to surprise you. I've been saving up for a down payment."

"But you said you paid cash. How much was the house?"

"Forty-nine grand."

"But how?"

"My great-uncle left me some money."

"But you said you hardly knew him."

"I know, but I also knew he was loaded. And he hated most of the family. He didn't love me, but at least he didn't hate me. Anyway, he left me sixty grand. Can you believe it?"

"That's great. I'm happy for you."

"Are you living down here?"

"In Maryland," she admits, unable to lie, but unwilling to give him her exact address. She is purposely unlisted in the phonebook.

"Why'd you leave me, Pia?"

"Why do you think?"

"I get it. I was a lousy husband. I should have been kinder to you."

"Are you seeing anyone?" she mumbles.

"No, I swear, Pia, I have only had sex with three girls in my whole life and the other two were before I met you. I have never cheated. I just flirt sometimes, it's part of being a bartender. It goes with the territory."

"You swear you never cheated on me?" she probes.

"I swear. Listen, one of the waitresses gave me an article from a women's magazine about being a better lover. I know I was selfish. To be honest, I had no idea how to please you. I've learned a few things about sex, about women, and about myself. I want to be a better lover, a better husband, a better man. I want you back Pia. I just had no idea where you were until now."

"I can't go back."

"Are you seeing that guy?" He tenses up and clenches his fists. She can tell he is jealous, getting angrier as they speak.

"I went out with him a couple of times. We're really just friends. I have never even kissed another guy. You are the only man I've ever been with."

"But you hated the sex, didn't you?"

"It hurt at first and I never climaxed. I just never got it. What's the big deal?"

"You can learn to reach an orgasm, and then you may like it."

"You *have* been reading," she comments.

"Listen, I won't try to make you come back, but I forgive you for running away. I'm not mad. I was a jerk. I should have paid more attention to you. Our wedding vows were for better or worse. We *are* still married. If you come back, it will be different. The house is great. You won't have to work. I got a promotion. I'm a manager at the restaurant and I only work two nights a week and three day shifts. I can support us. We don't have to pay rent. I'll still give you forty bucks a week for groceries, but you won't have to work. We can have a baby."

"Forty bucks is nothing. The laundry alone costs five or six bucks a week."

"A hundred dollars then. And you are done with the Laundromat. There's a brand new washer and dryer in the house. I just don't know how to work them very well and my whites are all pink now," he laughs. "I'm an *idiot*."

"You used to call me an idiot if I burned the bacon or the toast. I hated the way you made fun of me. I would never do that to you."

"I'm sorry. I was completely wrong. I should have put you on a pedestal and treated you like a queen."

"I don't want that. I just want respect and kindness."

"I promise I am a changed person. I have missed you so much. I cry myself to sleep some nights. I looked for you. I even put up posters all over the county. I had no idea where you went."

"Did you buy new furniture?"

"Only a little. I want you to pick out a new bedroom set with a king size bed. You can buy all the curtains and rugs you want. You can even take over the checkbook and control all the finances. You could put me on allowance."

"Thirty bucks a week, that's all I would give you for cigarettes, beer and car parts."

"I gave you forty."

"I had to pay for the laundry, the food, and your expensive toilet paper," she says, sarcastically.

"True. I was such an asshole. It took me a few months to figure that out. At first I was worried sick. Then I got angry at you for leaving. Then I got angry at myself for driving you away. I really have changed, Pia." He attempts to put his arm around her and she steps back.

"Don't touch me." He looks shocked and bewildered.

"What's wrong?" he asks.

"It's not just you. I don't like to be touched by anyone anymore. I'm seeing a psychologist. She's trying to help me. I'm still afraid of fire too. And I don't like being in a crowd like this."

"No problem. There are other shrinks back home. You keep facing your fears. I'm OK with that. I'll even sleep on the couch. I won't touch you until you're ready. In a few weeks, you'll feel differently. But when you invite me back into the bed, I will go slowly this time and focus on pleasing you. I promise."

"I don't love you, Arty. I never did."

"But you married me."

"It was a mistake. I hated living in the halfway house. I shouldn't have said yes. I'm sorry."

"Would you have left me if I had treated you better?" he asks.

"I don't know. Maybe not. But I was so unhappy. I don't think we make each other happy. I don't think you love me either."

"I do love you. At first, it might have been more about sex and I shouldn't have treated you like a maid. I was a moron. But I know I love you now. Just seeing you makes my heart beat faster. I love you Pia. Just give me a chance to prove it. And if you allow me to love you, maybe you will start to love me back. We'll have a baby, maybe a few. Whatever you want. I never hit you, you know that. I never would. I'm not that bad."

"You're right. You didn't hit me, but emotional abuse can be just as bad. How do I know you won't stop appreciating me as soon as I come back?"

"If I revert to old habits, you can cut my allowance. Punish me. Force me to wake up. I'll give you complete control of everything.

The house is in my name, but I'll have the deed changed. You'll be a joint owner of it all."

"I can't promise anything. I have a good job now. It pays well. I have health insurance. It's paying for my psychologist. I have a few friends. I have a life here, Arty."

"And you have a life back home too. We took vows, Pia. For richer or for poorer, but now we are richer. As soon as you come home, we'll go buy some furniture and you can pick it all out. Please give me a second chance, Pia. That's all I ask. Give me a year and if you want out, I won't argue. We'll get divorced and split up everything. You'll leave the marriage with some real money in your pocket. Just give me a year."

"Suppose I make you sleep on the couch for that entire year?"

"I'll understand. Then we can get an amicable divorce. But at least we will have tried. Just give us one more chance to make it all work."

"I would want to work. I don't want to just stay home. And I would find a better job now that I have some skills."

"Whatever you want. You'll wear the pants in the family. I was a complete failure as a husband, but I've been talking to some of the waitresses and my eyes are open now. They made me realize I pushed you away. When I found out about my inheritance, I was so excited for us. I wanted to share the good news. But you were gone and I kept praying you would come back. I can't tell you how happy I was to see you sitting on the grass eating lunch with those people."

"Those people care about me."

"I care about you, Pia. I really do. I do love you. I just need to show it more. My father was a complete ass. I modeled myself after him and that was a huge mistake. It's not your job to starch my shirts or wait on me like you are my servant. The waitresses at the restaurant really gave me a tongue lashing. They made me realize it was all my fault. You were very brave to just take off with very little money. I don't know how you pulled it off."

"I saved up a few bucks. I had a friend down here, from the orphanage. I never told you about her. She was my life preserver in case things continued to erode. And they did. You practically raped me some nights when I told you I was exhausted. You climbed on me like I was a carnival ride so you could satisfy your needs. You never cared about what I wanted, what I needed. You knew I was a virgin, just a kid out of the orphanage, a kid without a mother or a grandmother to confide in. I didn't even have any girlfriends. I felt so alone and living with you only made it worse. You were a terrible partner. Even roommates are kinder to one another. You were awful to me, Arty. Just awful."

"I'm glad you got that off your chest. And you are right. But I swear things will be completely different. Six months. Give me six months to prove it. After that, I'll pay for the divorce and sell the house. You'll walk away with at least twenty-five grand. Take a leave of absence from your job. You can come back here in six months and I won't fight you. Just give me six months to prove my love, to prove I've changed, that I've grown up. I'll sleep on the couch. I won't touch you without permission. I won't do anything against your wishes."

"I still don't love you," she declares, averting eye contact.

"But could you, over time?" he pleads.

"I don't know."

"Will you at least think about it?" She nods.

"I will think it over," she mumbles, partly to appease him, partly because she is more confused than ever.

"Can I at least get your phone number, and maybe your address? I want to write to you. I'll send you love letters. I'll show you I have changed. We got married too quickly. I'll court you like I should have done last year."

"OK, let me think about it. Has your phone number changed?"

"No, same number."

"I'll call you, I promise."

"When?"

"When will you be back home?"

"I leave tomorrow. I'll be back Tuesday night."

"I'll call you Wednesday, are you working that night?"

"No, I'll be home by six."

"I'll call you at seven on Wednesday and we can talk further. I need a day or two to think. This is a lot to process. I have a lease, a job, friends, and a good life here."

"I'll buy out the lease. I've been saving. I still have some of the inheritance. I have fifteen thousand dollars in the bank. I'll mail you a check for five-thousand to cover any expenses you have to make the move back. I'll come get you if you like. Or you could just go back with me tomorrow and skip town on your landlord."

"I wouldn't do that."

"I know."

"I have to get back to my friends. I'll call you Wednesday night at seven."

"Promise?"

"I promise. I never break a promise."

"I know. Thank you, Pia. I wish I could at least hug you." She just stares and he nods. He watches her walk away. He does not pursue her.

She finds them all in the same exact spot. Portia has wrapped up the lunch and she is holding it for her. They all look worried and concerned. Jake looks terrible, like his world just came crashing down on his head.

"Was that him?" Portia ask, but she knows. Pia nods as tears stream down her cheeks. Portia opens her arms and Pia allows her only friend to hold her. Portia rocks her while the men helplessly watch. Then they all sit back down on the thick grass to talk.

"What did he say?" Portia asks as Pia attempts to compose herself.

"He's visiting a friend. He just happened to bump into us. He wants me back. He says he changed."

"Do you believe him?" Portia asks as Jake stares like a frightened animal in the wild, wondering if he is about to lose her. How can he compete? She is married to the guy.

"I think he is being honest. He talked to waitresses at work and read some articles. He knows he was a terrible husband. He swears he has never cheated on me. He got a big promotion at work and he inherited money from his great-uncle. He bought us a house, he paid cash. He wants to go furniture shopping and he wants me to pick out everything. He offered me complete control of the finances. I would be giving *him* a weekly allowance. He promised to sleep on the couch for now. He is asking for six months. If he's still on the couch in six months, he'll pay for the divorce and sell the house. I'll walk away with about twenty-five thousand dollars. That's what he said."

"And he knows you don't want him to touch you?" Portia asks and Pia nods.

"He knows I'm seeing a psychologist. He blames himself for being a selfish lover. He's been reading articles from women's magazines about pleasing a woman. But he promised he will not touch me or do anything without my approval."

"What did you say?" Jake finally asks with a look of hopeless despair.

"I told him I don't love him. I said I've never loved him. I just wanted to get away from the halfway house. I said the marriage was a mistake from the beginning and I was never happy."

"How did he respond?" Portia asks.

"He said he loves me and he wants a chance to prove it, to help me to love him back."

"So now what?" Jake asks, knowing he has no right to advise her.

"I promised to call him Wednesday night at seven. He's heading home tomorrow. He wanted my phone number and my address, but I refused. He wants to mail me five-thousand dollars to buy out my lease and settle my affairs down here. He offered to come get me when I'm ready. He wants to mail me love letters and woo me."

"So, you didn't give him your address or phone number?" Portia asks.

"No, I told him I need time to think. I mean I did take marriage vows for better or for worse. He said things will be completely different. When I am ready to let him into my bed, he wants to have a baby, maybe a few. He wants to prove he has grown up. He says he appreciates me now. He admitted he was a total jerk."

"So, will you call him from home?" Portia asks.

"I'll probably use a payphone so he can't possibly know where I am. I won't even call from Wheaton. I would like to call him from Baltimore so he doesn't have a clue where I am. I need time to think."

"I'll drive us to Baltimore as soon as you get out of work on Wednesday," Jake offers. "We can grab dinner and you can make your call."

"Tell me what you're thinking Jake," Pia finally says as she unwraps her food and takes a small bite. She is suddenly famished.

"OK, here's what I think. You called me a six and a half last night and you said he was never more than a three. You said he was a negative number when you left. Let's say he has grown up a lot. People can evolve. But will he ever be a four or a five in your opinion? You said you don't love him, that you never loved him. Then why uproot the life you have been building here just to honor a marriage vow you made to a justice of the peace? I know I have a vested interest in keeping you here. We all want you to stay here. We all care about you. But we want you to decide what's best for you. I will respect your wishes. If Wednesday night becomes our last dinner together, I will honor your wishes and treasure the time we spent together. I'll probably spend the rest of my life searching for someone that rocks my boat like you do. I know what I'm looking for now. You said I was a one or a two at first and now I'm a six and a half. You were a ten for me, a ten out of ten. And now, well, let's just say your number is off the charts." He smiles and she nods as more tears threaten her dark eyes. She hugs Portia again and whispers something in her ear.

There is an awkward silence while Pia continues to munch on her wrap. Ben has said nothing. He wants to interject his thoughts, but he is not sure it will be appreciated. Finally, he speaks without reservation.

"Pia, I don't know you that well, but I do like you and I certainly respect you. I hardly know this character, but I can tell he adores you. It's in his eyes. We all deserve to be adored. I don't know if your husband adores you or if he ever did, or if he ever could. But if you think your husband feels the kind of passion for you that I think Jake feels for you, then go to him if you think you must. But you may be throwing away the best thing that ever happened to you. I blew it with Portia because of a ridiculous moment of pure insanity. I wanted to keep seeing her, but also find out what I was giving up out there. It didn't take me long to realize I wasn't missing a thing. I love Portia with all my heart, and I screwed it all up." Ben begins to cry and Portia throws her arms around him.

Pia stares at Jake, and for the first time, she is tempted to touch his hand, just for a moment, or even fall into his waiting arms. But she cannot move her muscles. She feels paralyzed and yet she yearns for Jake, for his touch.

"You didn't screw it up, I still love you, I still adore you," Portia sobs. Jake is the only one of the foursome with dry eyes and he is close to losing control of his own emotions. The day had started off so brilliantly with so much hope, so much potential, and now a dark cloud has descended upon them all as the crowd thickens with festive patriots.

"Will you take me back?" Ben pleads. Portia nods.

"I adore you, you big jerk," she mumbles as she kisses him.

Suddenly, Ben moves to his knees and looks into Portia's eyes. "Will you marry me, Portia? I vow to never even look at another woman."

"Are you being serious?" she sobs, wiping away her tears.

"I am."

"Where's the ring?" Portia laughs.

"We'll pick it out together. It will be a joint effort. You point and I'll pay. Marry me Portia. Make me the happiest man on the planet."

"What do you think, Pia?" she asks. "Should I marry this jackass?"

"I think you should follow your heart," Pia whispers.

"OK, Jake? Your opinion?"

"I'm a total romantic. I can see the two of you are crazy about each other. I say go for it!"

"OK, I'll marry you, you big lug. But it will be a closed marriage, completely monogamous and if you even mention the words open relationship again, I'll cut off your pecker."

"Deal, I love you, Portia," Ben exclaims.

They fall back into one another's arms and Jake makes a joke. Pia laughs and smiles at him. "Never in the history of mankind has a woman accepted a marriage proposal, while gazing up towards the Washington Monument on the nation's birthday, and promising if the man screws up again, she will humbly cut off his penis."

They all begin to laugh hysterically and at that moment, Jake moves up to a solid seven and a half. Pia does care for him, but she is extremely conflicted about Arty. She needs time. Time to think.

13

Restful sleep avoided Pia after the holiday fireworks as she tossed and turned, dreaming she was drowning in a puddle of moonlight. There had been no flirtatious banter when she said goodnight to Jake before heading to bed to ponder Arty's words and face her fears. The nightmares were suffocating as she saw herself scrubbing floors like Cinderella, while a bunch of unwashed urchins demolished the house and Arty guzzled down a fifth of bourbon and ordered her to put more starch in his shirts.

Her dreams were also permeated with images of the fire that destroyed her childhood home and during those moments of restless sleep she saw Gaetano being strangled by smoke, trapped in his crib, while her parents crawled courageously to save their baby boy. She awoke at 4am, drenched from anxiety and perspiration, and she climbed from her bed and turned the air conditioner up high. But the temperature in the apartment was 70 degrees and her sweat-soaked sheets were not the victim of Maryland's brutal heat wave or the stifling humidity, but rather the aftermath of agonizing dreams that were plagued by her usual fears and visions of Arty stealing both her oxygen and her self-respect.

She took a cold shower to wake herself up and wash away the misery as she had no plans to return to her damp, disheveled bed sheets. After a cool shower, she felt refreshed and she stripped the mattress and replaced the sheets with a brand new set that she had been saving for a special occasion. Pia ate breakfast at five and pondered Arty's proposal of granting him a second chance and abandoning the life she had recently carved out in Maryland. She had made Jake promise not to contact her until Wednesday. She gave him her work number and asked him to call her after lunch. She promised Arty she would call, but she was uncertain about involving Jake. A voice in her head told her to cut Jake loose and provide him with the opportunity to find a better girl, a girl without so many issues, a girl without a husband.

She picked up a notebook and drew a vertical line down the center of the first page, labeling the two columns. Pros and cons of returning to Arty. She began with the pros as they were the more challenging ideas to internalize.

Money, a house, honoring the marriage vows, Arty paying for the divorce in six-months if it didn't work out, easing her guilty conscience, a baby, a second chance… It was difficult for her to write the words and even more difficult to believe any of it was worth walking away from her new life, walking away from Portia, away from Jake. The apartment was OK, but she could leave without hesitation. She grabbed it because Portia had asked her to move out when she was depressed over Ben. The job paid well, but she cared little for her coworkers and the daily routine could be monotonous and mind-numbing.

She would always be a part of Portia's life, but her best friend was now engaged to marry and she would be rearing children and moving to the suburbs in a few years. She couldn't stay in Maryland just for Portia. Her dear friend was moving on with her life and Pia had to do the same.

And then there was Jake. Had Arty not appeared out of nowhere, she might have fallen in love with Jake. But it was more of a crush at the moment, a fantasy, a wish-upon-a-star kind of dream. Jake is handsome and charming. She had fantasized about meeting his family, his mother, his grandmother. Pia had even thought about that farmer's porch and those two rocking chairs where they might both plop down their aging bodies in a half century or so and reminisce about the good old days.

But Jake and Pia had only really gotten together for a single weekend, despite a convergence of coincidences that brought them both to the produce aisle on two occasions and the chance meeting while Jake was on a dinner date with captivating Claire.

Despite the chocolate croissants in the park where their pinkies had briefly intermingled and Sunday's evening serenade on the street where she lives, it was all simply a lark. They hardly knew one another and Arty is her husband. He deserves a second chance. We all do.

She leaves for work on the early side since she rose from her nightmares before 5am and she heads to the office with a heavy heart and a life changing decision to ponder. She will be the first to arrive and she will ask to leave a half hour early on Wednesday. Maybe Ben or Portia could drive her to Baltimore should she decide to abandon her newfound friendship with Jake. She fears Arty. She knows if she calls from Wheaton, he may attempt to track her down. She told him she is living in Maryland and she would rather not take any chances that he could somehow trace the call. She is still uncertain if she is going to give him that second chance and should she deny him, she fears his reaction will be fierce.

He must not know where she lives or how to contact her. She was careful not to introduce her husband to her friends as she stumbled off towards the Washington Monument to allow Arty to say his peace. But she does not trust him. Despite her misgivings, she is seriously considering taking that leave of absence and negotiating a settlement with her landlord. She is considering moving into Arty's new house and putting his words to the test.

In a worst case scenario, he will rape her, beat her, threaten her, and disappoint her beyond repair. Then she will take what is hers and drain his bank account to pay for a divorce. She will return to Portia and crash with her once again while she picks up the pieces of her shattered life. If a worst-case scenario should unfold, she may even give Jake a second chance since everyone deserves a second chance, even Jake, even Pia. But will Jake have moved on?

Jake is wonderful. He will make some lucky girl a fine husband someday. Pia is relieved that she was unable to allow him to touch her, for had they made love, it would be that much harder for her to walk away, and if Jake lost his virginity to her and then she left him, he would have been absolutely devastated.

Tuesday was long and dull. Her coworkers bantered about their long weekend, but Pia did not engage as she was lost in her thoughts. They were used to her keeping to herself, but finally, Marie asked her a question.

"So, Pia, what did you do for the long weekend?"

"Oh, I went to the fireworks at the mall."

"Did you have fun?"

"I guess."

"You seem glum, even more so than usual. Would you like to talk about it?"

"I may need to take a leave of absence. There is a family crisis back in New York."

"I thought you didn't have any family," Marie challenges. Marie is her supervisor and she has been kind to Pia at times, but she has also regretted hiring such a gloomy girl. Still, she knows Pia's life has not been easy, and while Pia may find it difficult to mingle with her coworkers, Marie also knows her apprentice is very young. She believes there is still hope for Pia Petrocelli.

"I have a confession, Marie, can we talk in private?"

"Of course, let's go into my office." Pia follows the stout, older woman and before she takes a seat in front of the imposing work desk, she shuts the door, instinctively, to allow them some privacy. Marie does not object since she can tell by Pia's body language that the girl is in some kind of trouble.

"I have a secret. I should have told you earlier."

"Take your time," Marie says with a maternal gaze. She has a small fridge in her office and she offers her a soda, but Pia declines.

"You know I was in an orphanage?"

"Yes."

"When I left there, I was in a halfway house, barely making ends meet with a minimum wage job in a grocery store. I had never really known any boys and I had never been on a date. Then a guy started talking to me and after two months, I went out with him. He seemed nice and he talked me into marrying him two months later. I think I just wanted to get away from the place I was living where I had to share a bathroom with a bunch of other girls. A few of them were pretty disgusting."

"So, you're married?"

"I left him after six months and came down here. I have one close friend…from the days at the orphanage. She came here first. She's two years older than me. I stayed with her and she helped me find this job. Now I have an apartment and I actually went on a date this weekend…I guess I had several dates with the guy."

"Is this new guy a good man?" Marie asks. Pia's tale intrigues her. Marie is a fan of two daytime soap operas, and she videotapes them every afternoon in order to indulge her passion for drama, so Pia's story fascinates her.

"Jake is a good man. I met him six months ago while shopping and we ran into each other a few times. I finally went out with him Saturday night and then he came over to dinner Sunday. We had a lot of fun. Then he joined me and my friends to bop around DC on the 4th. That's when it happened…"

"What?" Marie asks with wide-eyed curiosity as she leans in and begins to salivate with an almost sadistic nosiness.

"I ran into Arty," Pia mumbles as she blinks back her tears.

"Arty is your husband?"

"Yes. I've been saving for a divorce. He didn't know where I disappeared to. I just left while he was out of town at a funeral. He told me his deceased uncle left him some money and he bought a house for cash. He wants me back and he promised he is a changed man."

"Did he beat you?" Marie asks in a demanding voice as if she is prepared to hunt down her husband and make him pay.

"No, but I was a little afraid of him. He drank more than he should since he is a bartender. I guess it's an occupational hazard. I had zero experience with sex and I was a virgin on our honeymoon. He wasn't violent, but he was what Portia calls a selfish lover."

"Who's Portia?"

"My friend from the orphanage. She's my only real friend in the whole world."

"Except for Jake now that you went out with him," Marie adds.

"I do see Jake as a friend, but we really just started to get to know each other."

"What did Jake say about Arty?"

"He knows I never loved Arty. He thinks I should stay here."

"But Jake has his own agenda?" Marie comments.

"He thinks he is crazy about me, but it's too soon for him to know that."

"So, are you considering going back to your husband?"

"Yes. I made a list of pros and cons. He has money now and a house. He promised he will be more attentive and less selfish. One of our issues was money. He controlled it all. He says I will be in control now.”

“A man will say anything to get what he wants.”

“He swears he never cheated on me, but I have my doubts.”

“Did you like any of the sex? Sorry to be so bold.”

“No. It hurt a lot at first. Then it was just something I wanted to get over with. That worked for Arty since he could satisfy himself rather quickly and then just go to sleep.”

“I see. You know I was married twice. The first one died and I divorced the second. To be honest, I didn’t love either one of them. I had a nice little figure in those days. I married too young, like you, and when he died, I was lost. But I wasn’t in deep mourning. Then I married on the rebound and your Arty sounds like my ex. I never reached an orgasm with either of them, but over the years, I learned how to get there. I dated a few guys and I learned to pleasure myself. I became more relaxed in bed by the time I hit 35. They say a woman’s sexual peak is in her thirties, while it’s more like 17 or 18 for men.”

“I think I’m frigid. I don’t even like to be hugged by anyone. I’m seeing a psychologist, but she is away for the summer. I’m supposed to see her right after Labor Day.”

“What does she say about your being frigid?”

“We are taking it in small steps. She convinced me to shake her hand on the first visit.”

“So, you and Jake didn’t sleep together this weekend?”

“Oh, no. We didn’t even kiss. The closest we came to human contact was when our fingers touched accidently. He understands and he is extremely patient.”

“He sounds like a keeper.”

“He deserves better than me. I’m frigid and married.”

“So this leave of absence would allow you to move in with your husband for a few weeks to see how it goes?”

“Yes, he asked for six months. If I still want a divorce after that, he promised to pay for it and sell the house. He said I would walk away with about $25,000 so I could make a fresh start.”

“And you would sleep in the same bed?”

“No, he wants me to pick out a new bedroom set. He said he would sleep on the couch until I am ready to invite him to sleep in the bedroom.”

“Again, men will say anything to get what they want.”

"That's why I want to sublet my apartment, so I can still come back."

"Well, I could give you a leave of absence, without pay of course. You would lose your health insurance after 30 days. But I am willing to keep your job open for up to six months if you need me to. To be honest, I've been having my doubts about whether you are a good fit here. You don't socialize with the others, but I still like you, Pia. Your work is more than adequate and I feel a bit sorry for you."

"I don't want pity."

"I know. I was the one who got a few of the others to scrounge up some used furniture for you. I asked Greg to deliver it to you in his van. I mean they were all glad to help, but they may not have done it had I not pushed them."

"I appreciate that."

"I never had any kids, Pia. My first husband died when I was pregnant. People thought I miscarried because I was so devastated by his death, but that wasn't it. He was a quiet man, a pretty boring guy. I think I married him to get away from my domineering mother. I miscarried because I have one of those bodies that has trouble getting to the second trimester. I got checked out and the doctor said it would be hard for me to have children. My second husband had two kids. His first wife kicked him out for cheating, so I should have known better. He didn't want any more kids."

"So, are you close to his kids?"

"No, I never see them. They always lived with their mother. I tell you this because in some ways you are like a daughter to me. Despite your standoffish ways, I have a soft spot in my heart for you."

"Thanks, I appreciate that. You have always been kind to me. One of the reasons I am so introverted is because I didn't want anyone to know much about me. I have been living in fear of Arty. I was afraid he would find me. So I've been secretive."

"Then why would you consider going back to that?"

"I don't know. I'm so confused. I haven't made up my mind. I'll call him tomorrow night at seven. I promised. I'm going to have a friend take me to Baltimore and call from a payphone."

"Why Baltimore?" Marie asks.

"I guess I'm paranoid. I have this terrible feeling that Arty is going to find a way to trace the call. He doesn't know where I live. I wouldn't give him my number and I'm not listed in the phonebook.

So I just figured if I call from Baltimore and he figures out where I made the call from, he'll think I'm living there."

"It all sounds like a James Bond novel to me," Marie laughs.

"I must seem like such a loser," Pia mumbles as she stares at her shoes and struggles to make eye contact with her supervisor.

"The opposite, Pia. You are a winner, a survivor. How old were you when you ended up in an orphanage?"

"Twelve, after my grandmother died."

"What about your parents?"

"They died in a house fire when I was four. My baby brother died too. It was just me and Nonna after that. She had a heart attack when I was twelve and a half. She died before I found her."

"You are definitely a survivor. I think you are a very brave, young woman. Leaving your husband had to be difficult."

"I scrimped and saved almost $200 before I escaped on a bus."

"It breaks my heart to think about your baby brother, and your parents of course."

"I was staying over with Nonna. It was a Saturday night. If I had been home, I might have smelled the smoke. Maybe I could have saved them all."

"You were four, sweetheart. You can't blame yourself."

"I live with a lot of guilt."

"You shouldn't." Pia almost tells Marie about sticking the knife in the toaster. She still thinks she caused the fire, but she decides to suppress the thought. She has already told her too much.

"I'll tell you what I decide on Thursday," Pia finally mutters as she looks up.

"Do me a favor. Stay until the end of the month either way. That's, let me see, Friday, the 29th. Stay until then. I'll get your health insurance to stay in place until September 1st. I can fudge the paperwork a bit. If you let me know you want to come back before September, you won't lose your insurance."

"OK, but I may not leave at all. I'm still on the fence."

"I can see the pros…the house, money, honoring your marriage vows, getting him to pay for a divorce. What about the cons?"

"He could be lying. He might force himself on me. If that happens, I'd leave him right away. He also might still try to control the money so he can control me."

"You never loved him, not even on your wedding day?"

"The only thing I know about love is the feeling of trust and warmth I had with Nonna. I love Portia too. She got me through some dark days at the orphanage. I never felt those kinds of feelings for a man. I even thought I might be a lesbian."

"Do you still think you could be a lesbian? I ask because I entertained the same thoughts for a time. I even dated a woman for a few months."

"That surprises me. It didn't work out?"

"She helped me figure out how to have an orgasm, but in the end I realized we were just friends. Men…I can't live with them, but I don't really want to live without them. I just joined a gym. I plan to drop fifty pounds and put myself back out there. At my age, I at least know what I'm looking for."

"Well, I realized I am attracted to men. I'm very attracted to Jake…and I trust him."

"Then I would let that play out and put Arty on hold for the rest of the year. Rethink things next year. If Arty is true to his word, he'll still be waiting if it doesn't work out with Jake."

"I'm still afraid to have Jake touch me. I'm such a mess."

"But you like him and he is being patient and kind?"

"Definitely. He's amazing. He claims to be a virgin. He has dated lots of girls, but he is saving himself for the right girl."

"And you believe him?"

"Not at first, but yes, now I do."

"And he thinks you might be her, the right girl?"

"Seems that way, but I have no way of knowing if he's said those words to other girls before."

"That's why you need to play this out. Jake could be your future. Arty is the past. Take it from me, sweetie, if you never loved Arty, you never will."

"I shouldn't be in a relationship until I get my head screwed on right. I was making progress with the psychologist. It's just my luck she had a two month trip to Europe planned. She did leave me a colleague's card, but it's a man. I don't want to start over, talking about my issues, especially with a man. I chose a woman doctor on purpose."

"The problem with orgasms is as old as time. I know lots of women who have never had one. Some men are lousy in bed and some women are afraid to masturbate. Have you tried it?"

"Yes, but no luck so far. I feel funny about doing it."

"You shouldn't. If you can get there alone, then it will be that much easier to get there with Jake. You already know what sex was like with Arty. Why go back to that?"

"He claims to have been reading articles about pleasing a woman. He says he has changed. I think he appreciates me more now."

"Does he really love you?"

"I doubt it."

"I think he just wants what he feels is his. Men think they *own* us. Well, they're living in the wrong century. No one owns you Pia."

"I know."

"So talk to me on Thursday and if you do plan to take a leave, will you stay until the end of the month?"

"I will. I would have stayed at least two weeks. I'll definitely stay until then."

"I hope you decide to stay permanently, or at least for a few years. I think this talk has brought us closer. We should go out for drinks on Friday, just the two of us. Think about it."

"I will. Thanks for being so understanding."

"And everything we discussed is just between us girls. It's your business and I will not gossip about it around the office. I promise." Even as Marie utters the words, she is thinking about telling a few people. It is a juicy story, right out of one of her soaps. But she also respects Pia, so she'll try to keep her big mouth shut.

Later Tuesday evening, Pia calls Portia and asks her to drive her to Baltimore. She'll treat Portia to dinner and they can celebrate her engagement. She doesn't want Jake to take her. That would just make things too hard.

"Are you sure you don't want Jake to take you?" Portia asks.

"I'm sure. I plan to tell him tomorrow. I think we should stop seeing each other for now. I need to figure some stuff out."

"Are you really considering going back to him?"

"I'm on the fence. My supervisor said she'll keep me insured until September 1st if I stay until July 29th."

"You told her?"

"I did. I told her a lot of stuff, more than I ever dreamed I would reveal to anyone at work. But it all just came out. I didn't want to lie about any of it."

"Does she think you should go?"

"No, she thinks I should see where this thing with Jake is heading."

"I agree with her. I like her."

"I mentioned you to her too. She knows you're my only real friend."

"Ben's your friend too. We both want you in the wedding. Will you be my maid of honor?"

"I would be happy to do that. I guess I would be a matron of honor."

"Not if you get divorced first," Portia laughs.

"When will you tie the knot?"

"We're thinking about next summer, maybe August or even September. It's so hot down here in August. September would be my preference."

"So, it's a year away?"

"Yes, and Ben wants to buy a house in Alexandria."

"Virginia?"

"Yeah, it'll probably be even hotter. They have some beautiful neighborhoods and great schools. Ben wants at least two kids."

"What do you want?"

"Maybe three or four. I always dreamed of having a big family of my own. I guess lots of orphans feel that way."

"I can't think about having kids. I don't even want to be touched by a man."

"That'll change. You started hugging me again."

"I know."

"Maybe you can hug Ben down the road. He can be your test man. At least you know he is safe. If he grabbed your ass, I would beat him to death."

"He wouldn't do that," Pia laughs.

"He better not. I trust him. You can trust him too."

"So, you'll take me to Baltimore? I'll buy you dinner."

"Save your money. I'll pay."

"But, I want to toast your engagement."

"OK, you can buy me a drink. I'll take care of dinner. It will be fun. While you make your call, I'll finish a novel I'm reading. I could just get drunk, but then who would drive us back? You really need to learn to drive, girl."

"I know. I need to become a real grownup."

"Well, you are 21 now."

"So, I'm leaving work early tomorrow. Can you pick me up at 4:30?"

"Sure, that'll work. We will hit some traffic, but we may as well get on the road."

"I'm nervous."

"You don't have to make a decision tomorrow. Just hear him out. Then tell him you'll give it some more thought. Or tell him you've decided to stay right here. Just don't agree to anything until you've thought it through."

"I have a lot of thinking to do. I'll probably have a hard time sleeping tonight."

"You never seem to get a good night's rest."

"I know. I think the last time I really slept well was the day before Nonna died."

"Better days are coming, my friend. And for what it's worth, Ben and I really liked Jake."

"I know. He is a good guy. I like him too."

"I hope you don't break his heart."

"Me too. Me too. Goodnight Portia."

"Don't let the bedbugs bite."

14

Pia's night was restless, but that was nothing new for her as she scrutinized the ceiling in her semi-darkened bedroom and thought about Jake, wondering why she was considering abandoning him. Maybe she should tell Arty she needs a few months to wind things down at work. That would buy her time, time to think. The problem is that Jake would want to keep seeing her if she sticks around and that might confuse her even more. Or it could help her realize that she is falling in love for the first time in her life. She knows she never loved Arty, but the question that haunts her is…can she ever love any man?

She thinks of herself as broken emotionally, incapable of true love. Pia may have caused the wiring in the kitchen to overheat with her imprudent behavior, but she was only four. She may have murdered her entire family, maybe that's why God took Nonna from her. Perhaps she doesn't deserve to be happy, but would God seek vengeance on a four-year-old child? Pia is not religious, but she does sees God as a fatherly figure, not a vengeful entity who is consumed with fiery wrath.

Pia knows she cannot be responsible for something she did at age four, but her conscience still weighs on her. Nonna left a lot of papers in her desk and after she died so suddenly, social services helped Pia sort through them.

One of the papers was a police report that indicated the fire started in the kitchen. They also found her mother in the hallway right outside Gaetano's room and her father was found a few feet from the crib. Both of them had been desperately trying to reach their baby boy while he cried hysterically in his bed. The image is burned in Pia's mind and it haunts her when she closes her eyes.

She dreams about sticking the knife inside the toaster along with her fuzzy recollections of seeing fiery sparks. The lights flickered, she is certain of that. Did she cause the wiring to become damaged, frayed and threatening, lurking behind the pretty, yellow daisy wallpaper? She tried to research such a question many years later, but the results of her reading were inconclusive at best.

She is back at work. Marie has been overly attentive like a mother hen who is concerned for her chick. Her coworkers seem to find Marie's behavior odd and curious, but none of them says anything to Pia. They are gossiping amongst one another, Pia is certain of that, and she cannot help but wonder if Marie kept her confidence.

Pia munches on a tuna sandwich at her desk while she awaits Jake's call. The others have all retreated to the lunch room or braved the afternoon heat to grab some food at one of the local eateries that cater to the DC crowd of busy office workers. She is grateful for the privacy when the phone rings.

"Hello," she says as she gulps down a bite of her sandwich.

"Hi gorgeous," Jake says cheerfully.

"Hi Jake. I'm glad you called. Portia has agreed to drive me to Baltimore tonight. We're having a girls' night out to celebrate her engagement."

"I see. So I won't be seeing you after all?"

"No, I'm sorry. But I do appreciate the offer."

"And have you decided what to tell him?"

"I'm still thinking. I did speak to my supervisor about taking a leave of absence, depending on what I decide. She was very nice about the whole thing."

"Can I ask you something?"

"Sure."

"Do you have any feelings for me at all?"

"I do. I really like you. So do Portia and Ben."

"Am I still a six and a half?"

"Maybe a seven," she replies.

"And Arty never hit four?"

"You know the answer to that."

"So what does that tell you?"

"It tells me you and I could have a future together, but first I need to confront my past and my demons. I still don't know why you would want to waste time on a frigid girl who is still married."

"Because this particular girl is worth it."

"I really appreciate how much you seem to like me."

"You were my ten from the moment you first spoke to me and you have remained a strong ten ever since. When you bumped into the table at the restaurant, Claire no longer existed. You could have said dump the chick and come home with me and I would have followed you like a puppy in heat."

"Do puppies get horny?" she laughs.

"This one does. But you don't seem to get it. I would rather be with you, sitting several feet apart, than be wrapped in the arms of another woman. Just being in the room with you, listening to your voice, makes me happier than I've ever been."

"It must be those pheromones."

"That's probably part of it. I felt like I found my soulmate when I met you. And after spending all that time together last weekend, I am certain of it. I'd do anything for you. Anything."

"I must say, if you ditched Claire to follow me home, I would have thought that wasn't very gentlemanly of you," she teases.

"I agree, it would have been a terrible thing to do to someone, but that just shows you how much power you have over my heart."

"You said you would do anything, is that true?"

"Definitely."

"Then stay away from me. Don't call. Don't come around. Wait for me to figure this all out. Trust me. I will call you as soon as I am ready to move forward. And if I never call, you must move on. Give me a few months. If after say, Halloween, you haven't heard from me, then assume I'm dead or making my marriage work. Either way, you have to move on with your life. You'll find someone. But I don't want you to stop dating. If you sell a car to a pretty lady tomorrow and you want to ask her out, go for it. Don't wait for me, don't rely on me. That's what I want from you."

Jake is silent. He has no words. The thought of never seeing Pia again has paralyzed his voice…his heart. She knows he is upset and she waits. Finally, he speaks.

"OK, I'll wait until Halloween. I hope you call me sooner. If I haven't heard from you by then, I'll figure you have made a new life for yourself. But I promise you this. I will never forget you. Not even if I live to be 100. I'll never forget you, Francesca Pia Petrocelli."

"Thanks for being so understanding. I need to figure all this out without any distractions. I have your number and I know where you work. I'll be in touch as soon as I can. I do like you Jake. You are a seven and I know that number could easily go higher. Let me work on all my issues, let me deal with Arty. Give me time Jake, that's all I ask. But if I vanish, promise me you will live your life to the fullest and find yourself the right girl to sit on that farmer's porch with you in your old age. Promise me."

"I promise. I still hope that girl is you."

"I know. A part of me hopes it's me too. I have to get back to work now."

"I think I'm in love with you Pia," he finally blurts out as tears fill his eyes.

"I'm sorry, Jake. I'm sorry if I've hurt you. You're a great guy, certainly someone most girls could fall for. I just might be all wrong for you. I am so sorry. Goodbye Jake."

"Don't say goodbye, not yet. Just say see you later."

"OK, see you later alligator."

"See you in a while crocodile," he responds with a choked up voice. She can tell he is on the verge of tears and she hangs up the phone and covers her face with the flat of her palms. She feels awful inside, as if she just ran over a kitten in the street. She knows she crushed his hope.

He wanted to drive her to Baltimore, to listen to her conflicted arguments after her phone call to Arty. He wanted another chance to win her heart and she denied him that. She begins to sob for a moment, but then she hears a few of her coworkers coming down the hall and she quickly composes herself and wipes her swollen eyes. Then she buries her nose in her work and doesn't even look up as three of them enter the room with laughter and camaraderie. They are a tightknit group and she still feels like an outsider.

15

Pia and Portia laugh as they nibble on appetizers and down their whiskey sours. The traffic had been backed up for miles and it is time to call Arty. Portia tells the waiter to hold their dinners until her friend returns to the table. With Portia's nose buried in her romance novel, Pia finds the nearest payphone and makes her call. It is one minute past seven.

"I was so afraid you wouldn't call," Arty mumbles.

"I always keep my promises," she says.

"How are you?" he asks.

"Confused, but OK."

"I don't know what else I can say or do to prove to you I have changed," he continues.

"Can you tell where I am calling from?" she probes boldly.

"I assume you are home, why?"

"I'm at a payphone. I'm having dinner with a friend and I can only talk for a minute."

"Are you on a date…with a *guy*?" he persists. He seems annoyed.

"Does it matter?"

"I'm still your husband…it matters."

"Well, I'm with my girlfriend. We're celebrating her recent engagement."

"Oh, tell her I said congratulations."

"I had this eerie feeling that you would be trying to trace this call somehow to find out what city I'm living in."

"I wouldn't to that, Pia. I wouldn't even know how."

"I guess I'm being paranoid."

"I've never given you a reason to fear me. I've never raised a hand to you."

"You did force me to have sex sometimes when I told you I was too tired."

"I didn't physically force you. I just begged and persuaded you at times. You never seemed to like sex, but now I know that was my fault. You were a virgin. All you knew about sex was what you experienced with me and I was a lousy lover. I didn't try to find out how to help you enjoy it or how to help you relax. I've grown up since then. Just give me a chance to prove it."

"OK, here's what I am willing to do. I'll call you again this weekend. We'll keep talking two or three days a week for the month of July. If things between us continue to evolve, I'll come back in August. I need to have many more conversations with you in order to figure out what to do, what I want."

"Can I come visit you this weekend?"

"Don't you have to work?"

"Actually, my days off are Mondays and Tuesdays. The restaurant is closed then. Can I come visit you on Sunday and stay with you until Tuesday? I could get someone to cover for me on Sunday."

"I'm not ready for anything like that. But I'll call you on Sunday night. What time is good?"

"I should be home by nine Sunday night."

"I'll call you Sunday. Then we can talk on Tuesday too since it's your day off."

"What about Monday?"

"I'll need time to process our Sunday conversation. You can't rush this, Arty. If we have any chance of starting over, you are going to have to be patient with me. It's the best I can offer."

"You *have* changed. You're much more confident now," he mutters.

"Is that a good thing?" she asks.

"The old Arty would have said no," he admits. "But like I said, I've changed too. It's a good thing. We will rebuild our marriage, but as equals. I swear I will never bully you again. If you are too tired for sex, I won't push it."

"I may not *ever* be ready for sex again. Are you willing to risk that? I'm seeing a psychologist as I told you. I can't deal with anyone even touching me right now. I can barely hug Portia sometimes and I've known her forever."

"I understand. You have your childhood trauma. I know you are still struggling over that. And the marriage started off badly when I didn't exactly think about your needs very much. I was an asshole. I appreciate you now, more than ever. I do love you, even if you don't believe me. You're the only girl I have ever loved, the only girl I ever want to love."

"Then stop thinking of me as a girl."

"What?"

"Think of me as a woman. I'm 21 years old and I live in my own apartment and support myself. I'm a woman now. Call me a woman. Think of me as a woman."

"I get it. You've grown, but so have I. I swear."

"So, I'll call you at nine on Sunday night."

"OK, and don't worry about me tracking your phone. That's not something that would have ever crossed my mind. Even if you give me your address, I'll never just show up unannounced. I know that would only push you away. I want to win your heart. You may have married me for all the wrong reasons. We hardly knew each other. I want you to come back, but only for the right reasons."

"I do think you have changed, Arty. This is a good beginning if we are going to rebuild our marriage."

"Great. That's all I ask. I'll give you as much time as you need. And I decided to get two bedroom sets since the house has three bedrooms. We'll make the third bedroom into a den and later it can become a nursery if we have a baby. I'll sleep in the guest room and you sleep in the master. There is a master bathroom and it will be all yours. I'll use the hall bathroom. You'll have all the privacy you need. We can eat together and watch TV. We'll watch what you want to watch. I'm going to get cable and we'll have a bunch of new channels. I know I was selfish, always watching sports and stuff you didn't care about. I know what I did wrong. Let me make it right."

"I'll talk to you on Sunday."

"One thing, I'm sleeping on a crappy mattress. Is it OK with you if I pick out the guestroom bedroom set? I'll leave the master empty until you return. I want you to pick that stuff out. I have the old sofa, but when you come, you can pick out the dining room and the living room furniture too."

"We'll have a dining room?"

"Yup. It's a really nice house, Pia. And it's all paid for thanks to my great-uncle. I just pay the taxes and the utilities. It's great. You'll love it."

"It sounds great."

"And I'll teach you to drive and buy you a brand new car of your own. You can pick it out of course."

"How much money do you have?"

"Over fifteen grand. I'm able to save a lot every week. Life is going to be so different this time, Pia. Trust me."

"I'll talk to you soon."

"I love you, Pia, I really do love you."

"Bye Arty."

"Bye Pia."

Pia returns to the table and Portia waves to the waiter. He dashes off to the kitchen to alert the chef that they are ready to eat as soon as possible. Portia puts down her book and waits for Pia to speak.

"He sounded so sweet. He is so hopeful. He told me he loves me. He wants to teach me to drive and buy me a brand new car. He wants me to pick out most of the furniture. He actually asked my permission to go buy a bedroom set for the guestroom so he can sleep there. Our old mattress was pretty awful. He wants me to pick out dining room and living room furniture. I would have a real dining room…"

"Hold on, are you seriously buying all this?"

"Sort of. But I didn't make any promises. I told him I need time to think and we will need to have many conversations before I make up my mind. I'm calling him on Sunday night at nine."

"So that's the plan, let him slowly wear you down with promises while he begs you to come back? Any guy can say the words, say they love you. Actions speak a whole lot louder than words."

"Yes, but so far his actions are pretty good. He promised he won't just try to find me and show up unannounced. He says he sees me as a woman. Before I was a scared little girl. He does seem to have changed."

"What about Jake?"

"I told him to back off. I promised to call by Halloween after I figure this all out. I told him if he doesn't hear from me by then, he should just move on with his life. He'll probably forget me by Labor Day."

"Do you have feelings for Jake?"

"I don't know. He's a great guy. He's handsome, and funny, and with his personality he can obviously sell a car easily. The guys is charming. He could sell sand in the desert."

"Do you trust Jake?"

"I do."

"Do you trust Arty?"

"I'm not sure."

"Do you have feelings for Arty?"

"A little. We do have a history together."

"So, the plan is to just keep calling him and let him slowly convince you to give the marriage a second try?"

"I think so. But that doesn't mean he won't screw up. If he loses patience and hands me an ultimatum, I'll probably tell him I want a divorce."

"So you may be wearing him down, testing his patience?"

"Exactly, one of us will eventually cave. Either I'll give him a second chance or he'll push me away."

"But you could lose Jake by then."

"It's a risk I have to take. If Jake is as smitten as he claims to be, I suspect he'll give me time while I figure myself out. I still have my issues with intimacy."

"And with fire," Portia reminds her.

"It's true, I live in fear of being trapped in a fire, like my poor parents. I dream about it. It's my greatest fear."

"I suggest you buy one of those ladders for escaping a fire if the master bedroom is on the second floor. At least you have a fire escape at the apartment."

"I always liked your place since it's on the first floor, but I couldn't find an apartment I could afford on the bottom floor."

"Will you continue seeing Dr. Forte in September?"

"Definitely…if I'm still living in Maryland. Otherwise I'll get a referral for back in New York."

"I still can't believe you may be going back after all you've been through."

"I'm still confused. I have to admit Arty sounds very sincere. He is treating me like a queen. He never treated me this well, not even when we were first dating or when we got engaged. I think he has changed."

The waiter brings their dinners and the conversation comes to a temporary halt. But Portia is not happy. She can see how Arty is manipulating Pia and she needs to help her friend keep a proper perspective. She is hopeful that Arty will eventually screw up and reveal his true nature. He's probably simply putting on an act and Portia is determined to help Pia expose the truth.

Portia is selfishly trying to keep Pia in Maryland. She loves her and she hates the idea of her going back to New York. She doesn't know Arty, but the glimpse she got on July 4th told her all she needs to know. Jake is far handsomer, far more athletic looking, and apparently far more confident. But the most important thing about Jake is his utter devotion to Pia, despite all her demons. Portia suspects Arty will have very little patience with Pia once he gets her back. He will expect her to invite him back into her bed within weeks. He will try to control her and dominate her life again. A zebra doesn't change his stripes overnight. Arty is who he is and Portia wants Pia to open her eyes. But she knows this is a decision that only Pia can make.

16

Pia told Marie about her conversation with Arty. She promised to give Marie at least two weeks' notice before leaving. They can work out the health insurance at the time should Pia decide to take the leave of absence. Marie is worried about Pia, but she knows she is not actually the girl's mother. Only Pia can decide what is best for her.

July evaporates as the Maryland heat index continues to cook the sidewalks and drain the ambition out of pedestrians who roam the streets and fantasize about mushroom-colored, blissful beaches and shimmering, turquoise water. Arty and Pia talk every other day during the month and she finds herself remembering some of the things that first attracted her to him. His ability to make her laugh was at the center of their relationship, especially when they were first courting. Arty had offered Pia privacy from sharing a bathroom with strangers and the security of shared expenses. She hated eating alone and Arty could be good company when he wasn't preoccupied with fixing his car or the money he had bet on the outcome of a football game.

Arty continues to court Pia. Their conversations grow deeper and more meaningful than their entire time together before she boarded a Greyhound bus and fled from him. She learns he hopes to have two children, a boy and a girl. He likes boy names like Richard or Jonathan, and girl names like Rebecca or Jennifer. But he is completely open to naming their daughter Francesca or Pia. He never liked his own name, Arthur, and he definitely prefers to give their son a different first name.

But in the end he wants Pia to name their children. She would be the one carrying them in her womb for nine long months. She would be the one to go through the agony of child labor and the months of nursing and nurturing the helpless creatures her body had created. Arty seems to have changed, he has learned how to open up and reveal his own inadequacies and fears. He always hated his father and he felt sorry for his mother. His father died long ago, but he has no fond memories of the man who was a drunkard and a poor role model.

Arty swears he will never raise a hand to his own child or to his wife. He endured his father's belt as a child and he watched his mother suffer the back of her husband's hand. Arty's mother is now living in Florida, dating a life insurance salesman. She calls Arty a few times a year, Christmas, his birthday, and sometimes on Thanksgiving. They are not close, but Arty is glad she is still part of his life.

He has a sister who moved to the west coast long ago and she stays in touch with their mother, but she and Arty seldom speak. She is older and she ran away from their abusive father long ago and never looked back. Arty thinks she is working in show business as some kind of assistant to a Hollywood producer. Maybe he will reach out to her once Pia comes back. His sister has never met her own sister-in-law. Arty's mom wasn't at the wedding either, but she did meet Pia once when she was visiting friends in Ulster County. She was cordial, but she saw Pia as a mere child and she wondered if Arty knew what he was doing.

As Pia gets to know her husband better during their phone conversations, she finds herself wishing they had been able to confide in each other when they were first married. Maybe life would have been better if Arty had bared his soul earlier. But Arty had suppressed his feelings and his silence weighed on their short marriage.

Pia is beginning to like Arty more and more. But she still isn't in love with him. How does one define love? How does one know if they are truly in love with someone else? How could Jake have been so certain of his feelings for Pia? It is a mystery to her.

She finally came to the conclusion that if Arty and she continue to forge an actual friendship, then maybe she can learn to love him. Nonna once told her it was common in the old country for families to arrange marriages. Couples were not in love when they exchanged marriage vows as they were practically strangers. But when a friendship began to grow, it often turned to love. Life was harder in the old days where survival was at the forefront of most marriages. There simply wasn't time for romance and fanciful dreams. Life was about keeping a roof over their heads and food on the table, much like the squirrels who focus on hoarding nuts and building nests in trees as winter descends upon them. Survival.

And then children come along and survival becomes more challenging, especially if the youngsters are sickly. Marriages were contractual arrangements where the husband and wife were a team who battled life's challenges like loss of income, disease, fire, famine, and injuries. Were these folks from yesteryear in love? They probably didn't have a lot of time to ponder such poetic notions. They were bound by marital law and God's law. They were a legal unit who shouldered great responsibilities in order to keep their children alive.

Pia has not talked to Jake since July 6th. He has kept his promise to give her time, to give her space. But that doesn't mean she isn't thinking about him. She wakes each morning wondering what he is up to. Is he dating? Is he miserable? She falls asleep each night focused on Jake, hoping to dream about chocolate croissants in the park and moonlight serenades about the street where she lives.

Jake is always in the back of Pia's mind, despite the talks she continues to have with Arty. She can't forget Jake, she knows she never will. She has been pondering the lessons that Nonna taught her and asking Nonna's spirit to guide her in her decision.

One day she was walking home from the grocery store, pulling her little cart, when Nonna seemed to send her a sign. She watched a family playing in the park across the street from her building. Her eyes were fixated on the bench, the one where Jake perched his body on that Saturday morning before July 4th, hoping to catch a glimpse of her on the street. The mother sat on the bench, holding a baby on her lap, while the father played with two older children. They were tossing a ball around and laughing. Nonna's words echoed in Pia's mind...*family...that is the essence of life.*

Arty and Pia had agreed to marry and start their own family. Had she selfishly baled on their marriage vows far too early after a mere six months? Didn't all young marriages go through growing pains? Maybe after children came along, Pia would begin to see the goodness inside her husband as he tossed a ball to their son or daughter.

On July 29th, she gives Marie her notice. Her last day of work will be August 12th. Arty agrees to drive down to Maryland and pick her up on Sunday, August 14th. He will get the day off. He won't need to return to work until Wednesday. On Monday, they will go furniture shopping. Pia will sleep in the guestroom until her new bedroom set is delivered and he will happily sleep on the lumpy sofa while they await the new living room furniture.

They hope to find furniture that is readily available so that they can build their little nest quickly. Arty promises he will never touch Pia until she tells him she is ready to resume their marital relations. Then they will discuss having children. Pia is beginning to yearn for a family of her own, for a house filled with the joyous laughter of little ones running about. Someday, she hopes she and Portia will be able to rent a house on the beach for a week in the summer where their children can all build sandcastles and dodge saltwater waves.

Portia is beginning to accept Pia's decision and she is also dreaming of a future where they will both be mothers. Orphans often grow up without siblings and that leaves a hole inside their hearts. Children can fill that void and bring love back into their lives. Pia's maternal instincts are kicking in and she plans to seek out a new psychologist to help her find her way back, to help Arty find his way back into her bed, back into her heart.

She arranges for someone to sublet her apartment and leaves the secondhand furniture behind. She departs Maryland with a few suitcases, much like when she first arrived. She does take a few kitchen items with her, but she leaves the rest for the person who will sublet the place. She tells her landlord she will be in touch.

Marie hopes Pia will return within six months. She and Pia grew closer in July and she wants the girl to be happy. She doubts Arty could ever make Pia happy, but of course, Marie has never known true love herself.

The ride back to New York is filled with lively conversation. Arty memorized some new jokes and he continually makes her laugh during the seven hour drive. They stop for food and bathroom breaks, but they are at the house by dark. When Pia first sees the house from the outside, her jaw drops. Arty had sent photographs, but the place is huge and it is all theirs.

During the remainder of the month, Arty continues to sleep on the lumpy sofa, but by Labor Day, he is sleeping on a new couch that is far more comfortable. The master bedroom set is still on backorder and Pia is quite comfortable in the guestroom. Arty picked out a beautiful bedroom set for the guestroom and he finally admits that one of the waitresses from work helped him with his selection. She is an older, married woman and she tried to find something she thought his wife would approve of.

The dining room set arrives by mid-September and the master bedroom set is promised by Halloween. Pia thinks about Halloween often since that's the deadline she gave Jake. There has been no communication between them and she did make him promise to move on with his life after trick-or-treating passes by. She is tempted to send him a letter and mail it to his workplace, but she continues to suppress such urges. It may be better to help him forget her by vanishing and creating the illusion that she had been merely a figment of his romantic, vivid imagination.

She speaks to Portia at least twice a week, telling her that Arty has kept all his promises. He never attempts to hug her or even hold her hand. They are platonic roommates for now, but they continue to laugh a lot and play cards or board games on Monday or Tuesday nights when Arty is off. Pia found a new job after Labor Day, working in an office. Her skillset made her eligible for positions she would have never applied for in the past. The salary isn't much, but she can use her paychecks to splurge on anything she wants.

Arty began giving her driving lessons after she passed her written test. He has been so patient, never yelling or criticizing. It is like he is a different person and she is enthralled with this new Arty. But there have been signs of infidelity like a bit of lipstick on his white shirt collar or the occasional whispering into the phone when he thinks she is in the shower.

Oddly, this does not bother her as much as one might think since she is not attempting to satisfy any of his carnal needs. She wonders why she is not angry about this.

Ironically, she finds herself possessed with envy for the girls who might be dating Jake. She wonders if he is still a virgin. But she is committed to making her marriage work and she is confident that Arty will stop fooling around with other women once she became a dutiful wife again.

A part of her is curious. Is he really a selfless lover now? Could he please her? Could he help her reach her first orgasm? The longer they wait, the stronger the sexual tension between them continues to simmer like spaghetti water that never quite comes to a boil. There are moments while they are splitting a bottle of wine over a game of cards, when their fingers touch accidently, or one of her feet inadvertently rubs against his foot. These small flirtations do not trouble her and she finds herself more relaxed around him. But she is certain that he is struggling to keep his distance and yet he continues to be a perfect gentleman.

She made her first appointment to see a New York psychologist, someone Dr. Forte recommended. But the sessions will not begin until early November, well after the Halloween deadline she gave Jake. She thinks about Jake far too often and she wonders if he is daydreaming about her. But she has been back with Arty for a month now and things are going smoothly for the most part.

Jake is walking up and down her street, pacing, wondering, waiting. He has been doing this on the evenings when he feels he may go mad if he does not return to the bench where he sat on the morning after his date with Claire. Sitting on that bench or walking by her window makes him feel closer to her, even if she is no longer near.

Absence has indeed made the heart grow fonder. Jake is madly in love with Pia and he wants the world to know it. He has already confessed his feelings to his dear mother and beloved grandmother. They were overjoyed for him until he told them the bad news, that the girl in question is married, that she has likely returned to New York to give her husband a second chance. Then their hearts slipped into sadness for they knew Jake was setting himself up for heartbreak and sorrow.

He begins to hum the words he had once declared through song when he disturbed her landlord and serenaded the neighborhood. He is on the street, on the street where she once lived. Suddenly, a light appears in the window and his heart begins to race with anticipation as he runs to her outside door and rings the bell with trembling fingers. Is she back? Has she returned?

It seems like an eternity before he hears the voice. It is not her, it is a male voice and his heart sinks as he glares at the door in quiet desperation.

"Who are you?" he exclaims.

"Jake, is that you?" the voice asks.

"Yes," he utters in confusion.

"It's Ben. I'm subletting from Pia. You want to come up?"

"OK," Jake agrees as the door buzzes and he pushes hard. Maybe Ben can tell him something about Pia. He has missed her so much that he can no longer focus on his job or on shooting hoops with the guys.

Jake bounds up the stairs with a secret prayer that he will find Pia standing in her doorway with a sweet smile and welcoming arms. But he knows this is mere fantasy and he takes a deep breath as he approaches the landing. Ben is standing in the open doorway, waving as if Jake might have forgotten, forgotten where Pia's door is located in the dimly lit hallway. But that is of course absurd, he could never forget where Pia once cooked him dinner and climbed deeply into his fragile heart. Never.

"Come in brother," Ben proclaims with a smile. "Want a beer?" Jake nods and the two men plop into the soft sofa and crack open cans of Budweiser.

"Why are you living here?" Jake asks.

"I'm staying until Pia's lease runs out on March 1st unless she comes back earlier. My lease was up and I moved here to be closer to Portia. Portia and I are hoping to rent a house together by February   and   start   making   wedding   plans."

"When are you getting married?" Jake asks as he looks around, recognizing so many things she left behind like the cracked lamp and the yellow gingham kitchen curtains.

"August something, I forget the date. Portia knows. It's about a year away."

"And Pia?"

"She's well. Portia talks to her a couple of times a week. She just found a job back in New York and her husband is teaching her to drive."

"I see." Jake's heart is crushed. The guy is living with Pia, teaching her to drive, something he had hoped to do for her. He was looking forward to finding her a great deal on a used car and surprising her with it as a gift as soon as she got her license. He had had so many plans for them, but he is quickly beginning to realize it has all been a fantasy.

"I guess the husband is still sleeping on the couch. Apparently, the guy has been a perfect gentleman."

"So Pia is really happy?"

"I guess so, she just found a new shrink, but Portia says she won't be able to start seeing her until after Halloween."

"Halloween. She told me if she doesn't contact me by then that I should forget I ever knew her."

"How are you Jake?" Ben probes with an empathetic frown.

"Still hopelessly in love with her, Ben." Jake's eyes are watery and Ben goes to fetch two more beers. He doesn't know Jake well, but the two of them did bond a bit on July 4th and Ben feels sorry for Jake. But there is little he can say to alleviate the guy's pain.

"I'm sorry you are so hung up on her. I guess you should try to put it all behind you," Ben mutters as he hands him a second beer.

"I can't. I love her."

"Have you dated at all?"

"I can't."

"I get it. When Portia and I split up, I was miserable. I thought I had lost her forever and I was the one who wanted the open relationship. Right after my first date with another girl, I knew I had made the worst mistake of my life. I imagined Portia on a date with another guy, and it made me crazy. I guess I am monogamous after all. It was so stupid of me."

"Imagine me lying in bed every night, unable to sleep, thinking of her with him."

"But he hasn't touched her. At least that's something."

"He gets to share meals and laugh with her, and snuggle up in front of the TV with her," Jake complains, almost choking on his own words.

"I doubt there's any snuggling. You know Pia."

"That's about the only thing that keeps me from going insane. But I haven't seen her in over two months. I miss her man, I'm mad about her."

"For what it's worth, Portia says Pia really likes you a lot. She just needs to give her marriage one last try. I suspect the guy will blow it. Pia already found lipstick on his shirt collar."

"The bastard."

"Pia's not that upset according to Portia. She knows he has needs and she's not ready to invite him into her bed."

"I could never cheat on her like that. If we were together, even if I couldn't touch her, I still wouldn't touch another woman."

"Well, you're a saint, Jake, cuz lots of other guys would."

"I know she's a lot. She has her demons. But I love her with all my heart and I would never cheat on her, even if we continued to be celibate. As long as we were together, I would be happy. I adore her."

"I guess you shouldn't give up then, not even after Halloween. I'll tell you what, I'll talk to Portia. Maybe we can all put our heads together and come up with a way to get you and Pia back together. This husband of hers will screw it all up eventually. He had to be a real jerk to drive her away the first time. I doubt he's really changed much."

"Would you do that? I promised Pia I would give her time. Part of me wants to drive to New York and try to find her. But I did promise I wouldn't do that."

"Let me see what Portia can do. She's on your side. I mean she is completely loyal to Pia, but she is not on the husband's side at all. Portia still thinks Pia should come back to Maryland. That's why she convinced me to sublet the place. Pia can come back anytime she wants and from what I know, her old boss feels the same way."

"Have Portia tell her I would drive up there and bring her back anytime she likes. Tell her I can't stop thinking about her."

"I'll relay your message."

"Thanks man. You're a pal."

Jakes leaves half of the second beer behind when he exits the building. He doesn't want to drive with two beers in him. He's distracted enough as it is and traffic in Wheaton is crazy. He decides to completely sober up by taking a walk in the park. He will retrace their steps on the day they headed to the bakery and bought the warm croissants. That memory is etched in his mind and carved into his heart.

He remembers when her finger touched his. She didn't wince or pull back, despite her insistence that she doesn't like being touched.

It was one of the most erotic moments of his life. She is the one. She's the one he wants sitting beside him on that farmer's porch in his old age. He is certain of this and he just cannot give up on her. He will not give up.

17

Pia got her driver's license in early October. Arty says she is a natural behind the wheel. Today they are going car shopping. As Arty pulls into the car dealership, a salesman instantly greets them. For a brief moment, Pia sees Jake. The salesman even resembles Jake from afar. The entire time they are perusing the vehicles, all she can think about is Jake. She is certain that her Jake is a far better salesman than this guy who appears to be willing to say anything to close the deal.

She finally decides on a burgundy-red Mustang. It is her dream car and Arty smiles as she sits behind the wheel for a test drive. He is likely envious since he drives a boxy sedan with a rusty fender. But he wants Pia to be happy. They come to a price and Arty agrees to pay cash. They'll pick up the car in two days.

Pia is over the moon about her own brand new set of wheels. And she loves Mustangs. She never thought she would actually own one and she doubted she would ever get a driver's license. She has to give credit where credit is due. Arty has kept all his promises except one. She is certain he is having an affair.

When they get back to the house, she thanks him. A part of her wants to hug him with gratitude, but she dares not. They sit down to eat lunch and she finally confronts him on his extramarital affair.

"Arty, don't get upset, but I've noticed the lipstick on your collar. I've overheard you on the phone with her. Is it serious?"

He looks like a deer in headlights as he formulates his first response. All his instincts tell him to lie, but he know she is too smart for that. She is very composed which helps him to stay calm.

"It's not one girl. I've been having sex once in a while to ease the tension. There are three waitresses. One is married, but her husband has lost all interest in sex. She's a little chubby since she popped out three kids for the guy. She had her tubes tied since she's done with having babies and the husband never touches her. She has needs. So we fool around now and then. She knows you are going through your own issues with intimacy. Her husband actually knows about it and he accepts the fact that she needs sex. He prefers she does it with me since he knows I'm not trying to steal her from him."

"The husband knows?"

"Yes, he likes me. It's not a relationship. It's just sex."

"He must be a very understanding man."

"The other two are single, young. They just like sex. One of them started hitting on me because she wanted more hours. I gave her what she wanted, even though she has no seniority. She paid me back with casual sex, mostly in the car, you know, oral sex."

"I see," Pia says. "And the third girl?"

"She's just horny. Her boyfriend dumped her and she flirted with me a few times. We've done it twice. None of these girls are relationships. I'm not in love with anyone but you. They are just using me for sex and I guess vice versa. I know it sounds bad, but it's the truth. I just couldn't go on being celibate. I mean I waited a long time for you to come back. After you did, I thought you would come around in a few weeks. But you still don't want me to even hug you."

"You're right. I wanted to hug you to thank you for the car, but I was afraid you would want more."

"Could I still get that hug? Even hugs might help me to stop looking for sex. A hug, a kiss, a slight shoulder rub. It doesn't have to be sex, but I need some kind of intimacy in this marriage. I'm begging you to at least try."

She stands and he follows her lead. She takes him into her arms and holds him for a full minute. Her body feels so good to him after all this time. He cannot help himself and he reaches for her right breast. She pulls away in shock.

"You just told me you've been having random sex with three women. You promised to respect my wishes. The minute I hug you, you cop a feel!"

"We *are* married. We have had sex before."

"Bad sex, selfish sex to get you off," she responds in anger.

"What do you want from me?"

"I want respect. I want you to stop screwing around and give me time. I'll be seeing the psychologist in a few weeks. Don't blow this now. You can't rush me."

"How long will I have to wait to touch my own wife's body?"

"We agreed on six months if I need it. After that, we will talk about it or talk about divorce. A divorce lawyer would crucify you over all these women."

"And what would a judge say about you withholding sex from me?" he whines.

"My psychologist would defend my actions. It's not my fault."

"I'm sorry. I don't want to fight. Let's just eat lunch."

"Will you stop having sex until the six months is up?"

"That would be around your birthday," he comments. "Is there any chance you'll want me before then?"

"I don't know."

"OK, I'll break it off with all three of them. I promise."

"I hope you didn't expose us to any diseases," she mutters as she nibbles on her salad. He doesn't respond. He simply sulks without saying another word and she is immediately transported to the early days of their marriage when they often ate in silence. Pia is starting to believe he has not really changed. Not when it comes to some things.

But he did buy her a new car and if she leaves him, she intends to keep it. It is being registered in her name. It will be all hers. She has never owned anything of real value before. The new furniture for the master bedroom should be delivered within weeks. The store keeps changing the date, but they have assured them it will not be much longer.

Arty leaves for work the next day around 10am. Pia is off. The office where she is working has shut down for a few days for remodeling. The staff are still being paid. It's like a vacation for her and she is excited about picking up the Mustang tomorrow. She decides to call Portia at work.

"Hello, Portia speaking," she says in her professional work voice.

"Hello, Pia calling from New York," she exclaims in her nonprofessional voice.

"Hey stranger, it's been nearly a week. Sorry, I've been so busy."

"Making wedding plans already?"

"No, not really. We did check out a few venues. You have to book them a year in advance, but we're still contemplating what we want. What's new with you?"

"Three things, I got my driver's license!"

"Wow, I'm so proud of you. Congratulations. Is he going to buy you a car?"

"That's the second thing. I pick it up tomorrow. It's brand new and paid in full. It's all mine."

"What did he buy you, a VW bug?"

"Nope, something cooler. He bought me a burgundy-red Mustang!"

"Oh, my God, that's my dream car," Portia screams, causing a coworker to flinch.

"Mine too. We used to fantasize about them together in the old days."

"I remember. Of course I am still partial to the first generation, the ones they made in the sixties and early seventies."

"True, but this one has eight miles on it. I want to keep it forever."

"What's the third big news?"

"That one isn't a good thing," Pia grumbles.

"What did the bastard do?"

"Well, yesterday I hugged him for the first time to thank him for the car and he promised to behave himself."

"Did he hurt you?"

"No, nothing like that. He just copped a feel. But I made him back off. I told him to give me my six months, til around my birthday. Then we will either talk divorce or we will start fooling around. I want him to prove he is serious about his promise. And I need to start seeing my new shrink in a few weeks. I still have lots to figure out."

"So the third thing was the hug you gave him?"

"Actually, no, the third thing is he has been having sex with three different waitresses. One of them is married. He says it's just sex, not anything more. He claims my keeping my distance is driving him mad."

"What did you say?" Portia whispers as she suppresses her anger.

"I asked him to stop and he said he will. But he is struggling with celibacy now that I am so close. He really wants to prove to me that he can be a better lover. But I still can't think about intimacy. It was difficult enough to hug him for the first time."

"How did you get yourself to do it?"

"I pretended I was hugging you at first. And then I started fantasizing," Pia admits.

"About what?"

"Guess," Pia teases.

"About Jake?"

Pia is silent for a moment. Finally, she admits the truth. "I still think about him constantly. The car salesman reminded me of him, but he wasn't nearly as nice or as handsome."

"So you *are* conflicted between Arty and Jake?"

"I am, but maybe I'm just kidding myself. He has probably moved on," Pia sighs.

"He hasn't."

"How do you know?"

"He stopped by your apartment. I think he walks by it a lot like a lovesick calf. When he saw the light on, he must have thought you were back. He rang the bell and Ben let him in."

"Oh my, what did he say?" Pia asks as her heart begins to race.

"He is madly in love with you, girl."

"Oh gosh."

"And I think you have feelings for him too."

"And now he knows Ben is subletting?"

"Yes, and he is clinging to the hope that you will come back."

"I am so confused. I assume the first time I actually let Arty into my bed, I'll know what I want. When he bought me the car, for a moment, I thought I could fall in love with him. He is different in lots of ways."

"Maybe he appreciates you more now. You had to leave him to wake him up. But he has been cheating on you, even if it's just sex. If Ben did that, I'd strangle him in his sleep."

"I think I was relieved that there were three different women. He isn't having a real affair. He isn't plotting to run away with one of them."

"Maybe it would be better if he ran away with someone else. You could sell the house and the furniture and drive your new Mustang back to Maryland with a bank account full of money."

"He would never leave this house. He loves it."

"Well, I'm glad you're OK. He hasn't hit you or forced himself on you?"

"No, but I can see it's eating him up inside. I try to keep well covered so I don't get him excited. I walk around in a robe that nearly touches the floor when I'm not fully dressed. I always double check the lock on the bedroom door when I'm undressing and I never leave the bathroom door unlocked, not even if I'm just brushing my teeth."

"Why, does that turn him on?" Portia laughs.

"It's just a habit. I don't want to step out of the shower and find him standing there."

"It must be weird being back. Are you starting to have some feelings for him?"

"Sometimes, when he is especially sweet like when he took me for driving lessons. He was so patient with me. He never yelled once, not even when I ran over a garbage can. I felt awful. Suppose it had been a child. He paid the neighbor for the can and he apologized for me, but I couldn't even look the guy in the eye. I know it was just an old dented trash can, but the fact that I lost control of the car freaked me out. I'm better now. I'm ready to drive alone for the very first time."

"Well, call me in a few days. I need to get back to work."

"I'll call you soon. Thanks for listening. Next time, we'll talk more about the wedding plans."

"Stay safe, Pia."

"Bye, Portia, I love you."

"Right back at you."

18

Arty drives Pia to the Ford dealership at 11am on his way to work. He tells her she should come to the restaurant for a free lunch and show him the new car. She thanks him again and even pats him on the shoulder before he drives off. The salesman sits with her for well over an hour, going over some paperwork and then showing her all the bells and whistles on the car. Most of it is pretty self-explanatory, but the guy definitely likes to talk. He seems to be flirting with her and prolonging the exchange.

He is sitting in the passenger seat, showing her the radio knobs and the controls for heat and air conditioning when their hands touch and she flinches. He seems surprised and he laughs.

"Are you OK?" the salesman asks.

"I'm fine. I don't like to be touched."

"I'm sorry. It was an accident, I assure you," he says as he opens up the manual for the third time to show her how to change a flat tire.

"It's OK, I have to go. I'll read the manual myself."

"Please don't make a fuss about this. I could lose my job."

"Don't worry. It was nothing. Thank you for everything."

"Be careful backing out," he says as he exits the vehicle.

She finds him condescending and patronizing, but she smiles and waves as she wrenches her neck to look behind her. She adjusts her mirrors one last time and slowly backs out. When she puts it in drive, she takes a deep breath. The windows are open and she enjoys the cool air rushing through her hair as she enters traffic.

It is the first time she has ever driven alone and she continually looks around to make sure there are no garbage cans near or reckless drivers sneaking up on her. Pia feels so grown up now at 21, now that she has a license and her own set of wheels. It means freedom. She could simply head south or west and never look back. But she isn't ready to cut the cord with Arty, not yet.

The vehicle has a lot of pep and she is having a ball. She carefully keeps a safe distance from the cars in front of her and she applies the brakes slowly as she approaches a traffic light. The hardest thing about it is not operating the pedals or steering the car. The most difficult part of this new adventure is finding the actual restaurant where her husband works.

She has been there many times, but she has never been the one behind the wheel. She makes a wrong turn and realizes she is heading in the opposite direction. Finally, she pulls into a gas station and asks for directions, which makes her feel a bit foolish. The man asks her if she needs gas and she tells him the dealership just filled the tank. Pia explains it is her first time behind the wheel by herself. She is a new driver and the car has 13 miles on it. She has been driving in circles.

The elderly gentleman admires the car and happily explains the simplest way to get to the restaurant. She is grateful and she makes his day with a sweet smile. She is a pretty girl, but she actually doesn't know it. Men notice her more than she realizes.

The directions are simple and there are only four turns. She makes a left at a supermarket and thinks of Jake and his hunt for a ripe cantaloupe. She makes a right after passing a park and she recalls chocolate croissants with Jake smiling from ear to ear. As she makes the next right, she passes a used car lot and she thinks about women like Claire who are likely flirting with Jake at that very moment. Finally, Pia makes another left and she can see the neon sign ahead. She is nearly there.

It is after one now and the lunch hour will be winding down. Maybe her husband will take a break and dine with her. He sees her pull in and dashes to the front door to greet her.

"Nice car, beautiful," he calls out with a grin.

"That's what the man at the gas station said," she laughs.

"He called you beautiful?" Arty probes with a wrinkled expression.

"No, but he did call the car beautiful."

"The dealership gave you an empty gas tank?" he asks as he admires the car once again, walking around it. "Close all the windows before you get out."

"They gave me a full tank, I stopped for directions. I got lost."

"And the man at the gas station flirted with you?" Arty queries with a jealous scowl.

"A little, but he was about 75 years old," she laughs.

He makes sure the car is locked and holds the front door for her. She enters the restaurant feeling like such a grownup, the wife of the boss.

"Sit here. I'll get a menu," Arty offers.

She takes a seat and looks around. Nothing has changed much since the last time she visited him. She wonders if any of the three waitresses are working. The ones her husband has been having sex with.

"Today's special is meatloaf. It's really good. I made sure they saved some for you if you're in the mood for it."

"Can you eat with me?"

"Sorry, I grabbed a bite of a burger earlier. I'm too busy right now. But I'll stop and visit in a bit."

She studies the menu, sitting up straight. Nonna continually emphasized posture as they danced around the kitchen. Finally, a waitress approaches her table.

"Hello, I'm Marsha, are you ready to order?" the waitress asks. She is young and pretty and Pia wants to ask her if she has ever performed oral sex on her husband. But instead she orders the meatloaf. Marsha brings her a soda and tells her it won't be long.

She studies the other waitresses. Two of them are chubby and both are wearing wedding bands. She wonders which of them was satisfying her carnal needs with her husband. Arty stops by the table and says hello, distracting her from her curiosity.

"Are they here?" Pia probes casually, but with conviction.

"Who?" Arty asks.

"The waitresses you had sex with."

"Babe, please keep your voice down."

"Is it a secret?"

"Of course. We don't broadcast that kind of information."

"Have you told them all you aren't going to have you know what with them anymore?"

"I will. Two of them were off for a few days. They just got back today. I haven't had a chance to talk to any of them yet."

She is served her meal and she eats slowly, methodically, as she ponders her next move. The old Pia would have been too timid to speak up for herself, but she refuses to be the laughing stock of the restaurant. She can feel the eyes of some of the staff on her. She believes many people know about Arty's sex life. It disturbs her.

When she has eaten half of her meal, she tells Marsha to clear it away and stands. She digs into her purse and finds a five-dollar bill and drops it on the table. The meal is free, but waitresses work for tips.

"Arty," she calls out as she approaches him. He is giving a busboy some tips on cleaning the tables with seltzer.

"All done, babe?" he asks. "I already took care of the check."

"I want to use your office."

"Sure, you need to call someone?"

"No, I want you to send them to me, one at a time."

"Who?"

"You know who."

"Oh, please don't do this."

"I want to have a word with each of them."

"They're busy, babe, they're working."

"It's almost two, they're not that busy. I'll only need about a minute or two with each of them. This is nonnegotiable, Arty."

She heads to his office and makes herself comfortable. Arty takes a long breath of air and stares at the closed office door. He is panicking, but he knows it will be far worse if he makes a scene. Finally, he approaches the chubby, married waitress and explains the situation. She nods, fighting back her tears, and then she slowly walks towards the office.

She taps and Pia tells her to enter. She walks in and Pia commands her to close the door behind her and to take a seat. The waitress obeys without saying a single word.

"What's your name?" Pia asks.

"Terry."

"Do you know who I am?"

"Yes, you're Arty's wife."

"Good. I can see you are married." She nods. "Arty tells me your husband has lost interest in sex."

"I'm so embarrassed," Terry sobs as she can no longer suppress her emotions.

"It's OK. You're not getting fired. I just want it to stop now. Are we clear?"

"It will never happen again. I am so sorry. It was just sex."

"You can go now. Don't make me come back. I won't be nearly as gracious next time." Terry nods and leaves in a hurry, shutting the door behind her.

Pia is pleased with herself. She took control of the situation and asserted her authority. She is not the boss, but she is married to the boss and Terry obviously doesn't want any trouble. The second waitress doesn't even knock, she just opens the door and walks right in.

"Hi, I'm Joyce, I guess you're Arty's wife?"

"Yes, close the door and take a seat. This won't take long."

"Good, I just got a table."

"Why are you having sex with my husband?" Pia asks.

"I'm sorry. He gave me more hours and he made me feel like he expected me to show my appreciation. It was just a few times, just oral sex. I'm sorry you had to find out about it. I have no interest in stealing your husband, I swear."

"It stops now, do you understand?"

"I do. It will never happen again. I promise. I apologize."

"Good, now go earn a living and don't make me come back here." She nods and leaves, closing the door behind her. She is young, about Pia's age, and she looked scared. Pia laughs to herself. This has been easier than she expected. One more to go.

She doesn't knock, she barges in and plops herself down without a word. She looks hostile. Pia stands and shuts the door herself. Then she confronts the gum-chewing woman with teased hair and far too much eye makeup.

"And you are?" Pia asks.

"Marla."

"You know who I am?" Pia asks and the waitress nods as she chews on her gum like a cow munching on grass.

"What's this about?" the waitress demands.

"I want you to stop having sex with my husband."

"That's up to him. He's the boss."

"Well, he'll tell you the same thing, but I wanted you to hear it from me."

"You don't scare me. I could kick your ass."

"I see. So I assume you have no intention of apologizing," Pia says as she attempts to remain calm. She loathes this woman.

"For what? Arty told me you don't put out. The guy has needs. I have nothing to apologize for."

"You can go now," Pia says.

"Good. This was a waste of my time."

Pia sits and ponders what just occurred. She waits for Arty to come find her. For some reason, she is not angry or even jealous. But she did not appreciate the lack of respect displayed by the gum-chewing waitress who just slammed the door in her face.

"Hey, how's it going?" Arty asks, sheepishly.

"Sit down, please," Pia says. He closes the door and complies.

"I wish you hadn't done that," he mutters.

"I wish you hadn't put me in the position where I felt I needed to confront these women."

"You're right."

"I want you to fire Marla. The others apologized and promised it will never happen again. Marla was rude. She told me it was up to you and she felt no remorse."

"She is a tough character," he admits.

"And I really resent that you told them about our personal situation."

"I'm sorry."

"I am about to start seeing a new psychologist. Would you tell them about my visits to doctors? Would you like me to talk about your personal health issues at my new job?"

"No."

"I want her fired."

"I can't, she could sue the restaurant for sexual harassment."

"Fine, then cut her hours back a little each week. Keep cutting her back until she quits."

"OK."

"And don't you dare have sex with any more women. I won't stick around if I suspect you are doing it again."

"I know. I was wrong."

"And when I am ready to have sex again, I plan to screw the new bartender."

"What?" Arty groans with horror.

"I'm joking, but even the thought of it freaks you out, doesn't it?" He nods and tears swell in his eyes.

"I'm such an ass. I didn't even enjoy it all that much. It wasn't as if I was in love with any of them. I don't even like Marla as a person. She kind of scares me. None of the waitresses like her."

"Well, then cutting her hours will be the right thing to do. None of the other waitresses will feel any sympathy for her."

"Probably not."

"I felt very awkward eating my lunch. It felt like everyone was watching me, like they all know our personal business."

"I should never have said anything to any of them. They are all a bunch of gossips. I mean they knew you disappeared and most of them blamed me for mistreating you. A few of them really did help me educate myself with magazine articles and books. Marla only started working here right around the time you came back to me. She assumed we weren't having sex and I didn't contradict her. I guess I got caught up in the moment. I do get very frustrated sometimes."

"Look Arty, for the most part you have grown up a lot. You certainly treat me more like an adult now. I love the car. I like my new job. I really do love the house and I can't wait to see the new bedroom set. But you have to show me the respect I deserve. The thought of me screwing someone at my new job would upset you, I'm sure."

"Well, of course. Especially since you won't let me touch you."

"Even if we were having sex, you would still be mortified if I had sex with someone else."

"You really never cheated when you were in Maryland?"

"Cheated? I never even hugged anyone except for Portia."

"I swear it won't happen again. No one here is judging you, I promise."

"You know, I actually don't care what any of them think of me. I know who I am. I have been faithful to you. I have never even kissed anyone else, not ever. But I still have some issues to work through and all I'm asking for is a little patience and a little respect. If I find lipstick on your collar or I hear you whispering to someone, I'll pack my suitcases and drive into the sunset. And nothing will ever convince me to come back again. I will expect you to pay for a divorce and I will sign the papers. I don't even care about splitting the house money. Your great-uncle gave you the money. The house is yours. But I feel like I've earned something and I'll just take the car and leave you forever."

"It won't happen. No matter what, I will not stray again. I swear on the graves of my dead grandparents."

"OK, we'll make a fresh start. I'll try to hug you goodnight when I can. It will be a beginning for us. And cut down Marla's hours for next week."

"I will, I promise. I'm sure she'll move on within a few weeks."

"Good, because I'm never setting foot in the restaurant again, not while she's working here. Got it?"

"Got it."

"I'm going home now."

He stands and is about to open the door when she tells him to wait. He turns and she slips into his arms. He holds her and closes his eyes, enjoying the warmth of her body. Then she releases him and he lets go.

"Thanks for that," he whispers.

"I'm getting better. I told you I was starting to feel better. Just be patient."

He nods as she walks out the back door so she doesn't run into any of the waitresses again. He follows her out and escorts her to her new car, unlocking the driver's side and opening the door.

"You look great behind the wheel," he comments with a warm smile.

"Thanks, my husband bought it for me, he's a sweetheart," she teases.

"I'm trying, babe, I'm trying to be a better man."

"I know you are. We are both trying. See you later, alligator."

"Drive carefully, don't get lost again," he laughs as she backs out. And then she waves as she hits the gas. A year ago she would have never had the nerve to confront those three women. A year ago, she was scrimping and saving her pennies so that she could run away like a scared rabbit. She is no longer afraid. She feels stronger than she ever has.

As she retraces her path back towards the house, she takes note of landmarks. She needs to learn how to get to places. She has the license and the wheels, but her sense of direction is pathetic in her mind. She wonders how she ever navigated the Metro and she laughs at her own shortfalls. Maybe she can buy a map of the area and start studying all the roads. She'll learn.

Her thoughts run to Jake. He wanted to teach her to drive. He spoke of finding her a car. She does like him so much, he is a very special guy. She wonders what it would feel like to be in his arms. Hugging Arty no longer disturbs her, but she still doesn't want to encourage him to get too frisky. She has never thought of Arty as more than a four. He was almost a five for about an hour as they picked out the new car together. Then he admitted to his infidelity and he slid back to a one. He is a solid three again, but it is difficult to see him ever making a new high. And Jake continues to be a seven and a half in her mind...maybe even higher.

But Pia feels we must play the cards that life deals us. She agreed to be Arty's wife when she was a timid kid, barely 20 years old, still living in that halfway house and sharing that filthy bathroom with a bunch of strangers. She'll be 22 in a few months and she is so much stronger, so much more confident. She realizes she can touch Arty, let him hug her, but she will be stingy with her hugs. He needs to earn them. He must pay a price for humiliating her.

Pia has no plans of returning to the restaurant for the foreseeable future as she was uncomfortable and somewhat embarrassed that the staff appears to know so much of her personal business. That is the most unforgiveable thing that Arty did to her. He made her look like a crazy person because of her phobias and some of the staff probably feel sorry for Arty. They must be wondering what he sees in her. A part of her wishes he would change jobs and make a fresh start. Maybe she can help him look around for a new job.

She hopes Jake is well. He continues to live in the recesses of her mind and in at least one chamber of her heart. He was so sweet to her, so persistent, and yet completely respectful. Pia knows she will keep him in her heart for the rest of her days. She'll always remember eating chocolate croissants with him on a park bench. She will never look at a croissant again without thinking about Jacobus Sean McGuire.

19

Jake is having dinner with his mother and grandmother. His basketball game has improved since he has found a way to concentrate on his moves by blocking Pia out. It is not easy, but he simply focuses on the net and the man he is guarding. It's a kind of meditation where he blocks out the real world and pretends he is an NBA rookie showing off his talents. But when darkness takes away the sun, and he lies in bed alone, he thinks of her. He worries about her and he finds himself dreaming of the girl in the grocery store who helped him pick out a melon.

"So, Jake," his mother says as they sit down to eat, "what's new?"

"My layups have finally improved," he jokes.

"We aren't talking about basketball," Nana teases.

"You mean am I dating anyone?" he asks. He knows where this is going. It's always the same conversation. His mother wants a grandchild and his grandmother just wants him to settle down and stop living the life of a carefree bachelor.

"Of course," his mother says as she hands him a platter of roast beef and tells him to serve himself.

"The last girl I kissed was named Claire. She actually kissed me and asked me to dinner. I sold her a car. I think she actually has a boyfriend. Anyway, I took her to dinner and this other woman who I met in a grocery store a couple of times bumped into our table. It turns out the other woman was living around the corner from the restaurant. I asked her out once, but she shot me down and then I thought I'd never find her again."

"So what about Claire? She has a boyfriend?" Nana asks.

"She just wanted to use me for sex, Nana," Jake declares, knowing he may be embarrassing his sweet grandmother.

"Jake, behave yourself," his mother laughs.

"Anyway, I like the girl from the grocery store, not Claire," Jake announces. "I think I'm in love with her."

"Oh my God," his mother exclaims. She has been waiting for him to fall in love for years.

"But she is married, Mom," Jake admits.

"What?" Nana gasps. "Jake, you know better than that."

"When we met, she was separated, but now she moved back to New York to give her husband a second chance. He mistreated her."

"Poor girl," Nana whispers to herself.

"I'm hoping she'll come back once she realizes a leopard doesn't change its spots."

"Does she love you too?" his mother asks as she puts down her fork and looks into her son's troubled eyes.

"I don't know. She has some problems with intimacy. She grew up in an orphanage. Her grandmother took care of her until she was twelve because her parents and baby brother died in a fire when she was four. Then her grandmother died and she was placed in the orphanage. She had no experience with men or boys and when her husband asked her to marry him, she hardly knew him. But she was alone and she agreed. She left after six months. She had a friend from the orphanage who lives in Wheaton. Then she got her own apartment."

"Around the corner from the restaurant?" Nana asks to see if she is following all of this.

"Right. I watched for her and ran into her the morning after I had the date with Claire."

"The girl with the boyfriend who kissed you when you sold her a car?" Nana probes as his mother giggles. His grandmother is trying very hard to keep up.

"Yes, Nana. And we had a lovely conversation and a walk in the park. She bought me a chocolate croissant."

"Claire?" his grandmother asks with a confused expression on her wrinkled face.

"No, Nana, the grocery store girl. I had more fun with her eating that croissant than I have had with all the girls I have ever dated combined."

"Oh, you have it bad," his mother teases.

"I do, Mom, I love her. I am sure of it."

"You said you *think* you love her a few minutes ago," Nana reminds him with a twinkle in her eyes.

"I know what I said. But I do love her. I do."

"What do you mean by intimacy problems?" his mother asks.

"It's terrible about her family dying in a fire and then her grandmother dying when she was twelve," Nana adds.

"Horrible, poor girl," his mother agrees.

"She has been through a lot. But she's amazing. She started seeing a psychologist to help her sort it all out. She started feeling uncomfortable in crowds. She doesn't like to be touched right now."

"So you have never touched her?" Nana asks.

"Our fingers touched a bit when we both reached into the bag of croissants. She didn't seem upset by that. But I have not hugged her or kissed her or even tried to hold her hand."

"Did you see her again after the croissants?" Nana asks.

"Yes, we had a wonderful dinner date that night and then she cooked supper for me the next day. Then we joined friends of hers in DC for fireworks on the 4th. But that's when everything got crazy."

"What happened?" his mother asks.

"We ran into her husband in DC. He's from New York and he was visiting a friend. He had no idea where she was. She just got on a bus and vanished last November."

"This is like one of my soap operas," Nana comments.

"So have you heard from her?" his mother asks.

"I'm in touch with the friends from July 4th. She is sleeping separately from her husband and she's about to start seeing a new psychologist. She still doesn't want him to touch her and I guess he is complying with her wishes for now."

"I think you must forget this girl," Nana mutters with a frown.

"Your grandmother is right, Jake. She's a married woman who is trying to mend a broken marriage. She's back in New York. You have to let her go."

"I know Mom, I'm trying to forget her, but it's not easy."

"Love never is, son, it never is."

They continue to eat in silence, but both women fully realize Jake is tormented over this young woman. Jake's mother has never seen her son so distraught over a girl before. She wishes she had words of wisdom for him, but nothing comes to mind. Finally, his grandmother speaks.

"She may come back Jake, but you can't wait forever. If you love her with all your heart, give her a little longer. When did she leave?"

"In August. I haven't seen her since July 4th, but we spoke on the phone two days later. She was confused, but I guess she decided to give the guy a second chance. He's all wrong for her from what she told me. She doesn't love him."

"It is complicated," his mother admits.

"Give her six months, Jake," Nana declares. "By Valentine's Day, close this chapter of your life."

"Her 22nd birthday is February 12th," Jake says.

"Then give her until then," Nana repeats. "Give her time."

"I am concerned about her intimacy issues," his mother adds. "If she can't make it work with her husband, what makes you think she can make it work with you?"

"She likes me a lot more, Mom. She trusts me."

"Of course she does," Nana agrees. "You're a good boy."

"He's a man now, Mom," his mother responds to his grandmother's comment.

"Yes, you're right. Jake is 23, the same age as his grandfather was when I married him. We only want the best for you, Jake," Nana says with a sweet grin and a pat on the shoulder.

Suddenly, Jake smothers his face with the flat of his hands and begins to sob. Both women rise to comfort him. Each of them wraps her arms around his broad shoulders and holds him like he is still the toddler they both adored two decades ago. They hate watching him suffer like this. They will pray for him…and for the girl who bought him the chocolate croissant in the park.

20

P ortia calls Pia on Sunday night, but there is no answer. She leaves her a message, telling her friend she is just checking in. She had expected Pia to call her and when it started to get late she reached out. Now she is worried. So she calls Ben.

"I can't reach Pia. She was supposed to call me an hour ago."

"I'm sure she is fine," Ben says. "It sounds like things are working out for her. She likes the new job. She has her own wheels now."

"I know. But I have a weird feeling in my gut. I left her a message."

"That's all you can do. I bumped into Jake today."

"Where?"

"He was sitting on a bench near the apartment. I think he assumes Pia will wander by one day. I suspect he hangs out there a lot."

"He's really got it bad for her. He has my vote, but Pia is calling the shots here."

"Why do you think she stays with her husband?" Ben asks.

"Hard to say," Portia admits.

"You know her better than anyone."

"I think she feels she owes him a second chance."

"But she never really loved him?" Ben asks.

"I don't think she knows what love is, not the romantic kind. She's had so little experience. She married the guy to get away from the halfway house. It was a pretty horrible place. In some ways, she preferred the orphanage. She was so lonely and broke. I can't say Arty swept her off her feet, but he did give her a place to hide from the world."

"What do you think spurred the fear of touching thing? When she first got here, I remember her hugging you."

"I don't know. She is filled with demons and regrets. She blames the fire on herself."

"But she was four years old."

"She stuck a knife in the toaster on the morning of the fire. She thinks she caused some damage in the wall when sparks started flying. She thinks she caused the fire and she regrets not being there when it happened. She assumes she might have been able to wake up her parents, to save her baby brother."

"That's a heavy burden to be carrying around," Ben comments, sadly.

"I know. And when her grandmother died, she felt so lost. When I first met her at the orphanage, she was so introverted, so scared. I helped her climb out of her shell, but when I aged out, I think the walls started closing in on her. Then she aged out and she ended up in that awful halfway house. I was lucky I had a cousin down here to take me in, even if she was a crazy old bat."

"So she married a guy she hardly knew to get away from the halfway house and now she thinks she owes him something?"

"I guess. If he had treated her right, she never would have run away. I just can't believe he has changed that much in such a short time."

"Me neither. Call me when you finally reach her."

"She may call back, but it could be late."

"Call me anyway. I don't mind if you wake me up."

"If I wake you, we could have phone sex," she laughs.

"Well then call me in the middle of the night even if she doesn't call."

"You got it, champ."

"I miss you during the week."

"You can stay over all weekend. We'll have lots of sex."

"I can't wait until we are living together."

"Me too. You are the man of my dreams."

"So you have forgiven me for thinking I wanted an open relationship?"

"I forgave you a long time ago. But don't let it happen again."

"Never. I only have eyes for you, Portia."

"I'll call back around 3am."

"I look forward to it. Wear something sexy."

"How will you know?"

"I'll know," he laughs.

21

Pia takes a long drive on Sunday evening while Arty is at work and stops by the restaurant to watch the parking lot for a while to see if he is having oral sex in his car. She still doesn't trust him. Portia is expecting a call from her, but it slips her mind. She is heading home around 9pm when she makes a wrong turn and gets completely lost and drives around for over an hour before she finds her house. She really needs to buy a map of the area.

Arty gets home right after her and finds his wife in the kitchen, brewing some herbal tea. She hugs him briefly and offers him some tea, but he refuses. She can smell the bourbon on his breath and she knows he had at least one drink, but he seems pretty sober. He appreciates the hug as it encourages him to be patient.

While she sips the tea on the sofa, he joins her, carrying a glass of bourbon in his right hand. She looks at him and asks how much he had to drink at work.

"Just one. A customer wanted to buy me a drink. The boss can't say no to that. But it was just the one."

"And this one looks like a double," she comments.

"I guess. I just felt like another. But I won't be going back out tonight. I'm fine. Is the bedroom set coming on Tuesday?"

"Yes, I'll be at work. It's supposed to be delivered between 10am and 2pm. At least you're off. Make sure you keep an eye out for the truck," she reminds him.

"Will do. I was wondering if we could christen the new bed and sleep together Tuesday night. No touching, just sleeping together. Maybe a hug or two? A little cuddling?"

"I'll think about it," she says, softly.

"That's all I ask. The machine is blinking by the way."

"Oh, it's probably a message from Portia. I was supposed to call her and I forgot."

"Didn't you hear the phone ring?"

"I took a drive. It's such a magical night with the moon so full and so many stars shining. But I got lost again. I just got home a little while ago."

"You weren't out with another guy, were you?" he teases.

"Well, Robert Redford asked me out, but I told him he wasn't my type," she laughs. He nods and sips on his bourbon, wondering if she would ever give him a taste of his own medicine. But he knows she is frigid, so he doesn't worry about movie stars.

"You know Pia, all marriages go through growing pains, especially during the first few years. After children come along, everything seems to fall into place. All you have to do is talk to me about anything that is bothering you. I'll listen and I'll try to help you if you just give me a chance."

"I'm trying," she says. She wonders why his touch continues to repulse her. She can handle a brief hug, but the thought of making love to him nauseates her. Is it Arty? Or is it her? Perhaps she can't make love to any man, not to Arty, not even to Jake.

"You should let me show you how much better I've become in the sack after reading all those articles. I swear I'll be gentle and I'll stop whenever you say."

"Not tonight, Arty."

"When the new bedroom set gets here, please," he pleads.

"We'll see. I want to give you a second chance. But maybe I'm just broken inside. Maybe you would be better off without me."

He sips on his drink and seems to ponder her words. She may be right, but he isn't ready to give up on her yet. He still finds her sexy and he is determined to take what is his, what he feels he has bought and paid for with both patience and hard work.

After a break in the conversation, Pia finally yawns and says goodnight. He reaches for her and she waves. She is afraid to hug him again. He has been drinking and she knows he might grab on and refuse to let go. She ascends the stairs slowly, praying he will not pursue her, but he is too tired and tipsy to move. She blows him a kiss from the top step.

"Goodnight, Arty."

"Don't let the bedbugs bite," he laughs as he chugs the remainder of his drink and pours another.

Just after 2am, as she sleeps soundly in the guestroom, dreaming about moving into the master bedroom in two days, Arty spends another night on the couch. He is restless after three double bourbons, but he finally falls asleep with a lit cigarette in his mouth.

The fire spreads quickly, first igniting his large pile of car magazines, then moving rapidly to the drapes, the lampshades and the pillows that are strewn about the living room. Arty is out cold and the smoke doesn't wake him at first.

Finally, he gasps for a breath as the old stuffed chair, his favorite chair, begins to burn with ginger-red flames shooting out from the sides of the cushion. He leaps to his feet and screams for her, but the bedroom door is shut tight, locked, protecting her from the heat and from roaming drunks.

"Pia, Pia, wake up, there's a fire," he screams as he stumbles and trips into the kitchen doorway.

He grabs the largest towel he can find, quickly soaks it and beats back the flames. But there is no use. He never did buy that fire extinguisher even though Pia had reminded him several times. He runs towards the stairs, but the banister is on fire and he cannot safely climb more than three steps. The smoke is black and thick and he continues to scream for her. He cannot see the guestroom door as the noxious smoke burns his eyes, but he listens for her. He shouts to her to wet some towels and run for her life.

"Pia, Pia, fire, fire," he shrieks in a drunken panic. He is still inebriated and his legs feel rubbery as a part of him believes he is merely having a nightmare. The flames are spreading rapidly and the heat is too much for him as smoke fills his lungs. He gasps for air and runs through the kitchen, out the backdoor in a drunken panic. He races towards a neighbor's house to beg for a miracle.

The neighbor's wife calls for help while her husband turns on their hose. He attempts to extinguish the fire that has engulfed the front porch of Arty's house. But there is no use as windows shatter from the heat and the porch burns like a bonfire on the beach.

"Where's your wife?" the neighbor screams out in the post-midnight madness.

"She was upstairs. I couldn't get to her. I was asleep on the couch." Arty falls to his knees in despair.

"Did you try to wake her?"

"I screamed for her over and over," he sobs.

"Hold the hose, keep trying to slow it down. I'll go check on the fire department," the disoriented man yells as he runs back into his house. He and his wife were sound asleep only minutes ago and now they are suddenly engulfed in someone else's nightmare.

Arty is back on his feet. The heat from the fire forces him to step back as he watches fingerlike, dancing flames shoot from the roof. The entire house is on fire and there is no sign of Pia. He thinks about the bedroom set that has not yet been delivered, silently grateful that something will be spared. He glances down the side street and sees the new Mustang, wondering why she didn't park it in the garage. His car is in the garage. It is likely too late to save it, but least one of their cars is safe.

Then his thoughts return to Pia. How can he be thinking about new furniture and cars while his wife is trapped in the blaze, in the thick, black smoke? He remembers how distraught she had been when she first mentioned her family dying from smoke inhalation. She has lived her life in fear of fire and now she is the victim of his carelessness. He knows he was drunk, smoking on the couch. He knows it is all his fault. He wonders if the firemen will point the finger at him. Will he be blamed?

The neighbor returns. The fire department has been alerted. It won't be long. Arty drops the hose and collapses from shock and exhaustion and the neighbor gets a whiff of his breath that reeks of bourbon and cigarettes. He wonders what caused this unthinkable tragedy. He grabs the hose and continues to spray water on the porch, fearing the fire will claim his own home as its next victim while several bushes burst into flames.

Arty is whimpering like a child, calling out her name. "Pia, Pia, I'm sorry, Pia." The neighbor pats him on the shoulder with his left hand while he holds the hose steady in his right. His wife comes running with a blanket and a large tumbler of cool water. She covers

Arty's shoulders with the wool cloth and helps him sip some water as she attempts to comfort him.

"Pia is inside?" she shrieks. She knows Pia. They wave to each other often. Her heart aches for the girl. The neighbors are retired, so Pia is a mere child to them. Arty looks much older with his newly grown beard and his small pot belly. The neighbors never thought much of him, but they like Pia. The girl seemed so sweet, yet so vulnerable.

"Pia, Pia, Pia," Arty continues to scream as he remains frozen on his knees while water drips down his chin. The neighbor's wife squints and cups her hands to her eyes as she stares into the fire, praying for a miracle, but she sees nothing, only flames and smoke.

Finally, they arrive. The sirens alert them all that the trucks are near. Two trucks screech to a halt as a dozen men begin the onerous task of battling the hellish monster that is determined to ignite the entire street and turn all the homes to ash. Ladders and hoses are dragged and carried, men with helmets and face shields carry axes as they confront the demon flames.

More neighbors wake and glare at the fire from their bedroom and living room windows. Some throw on jackets and brave the cold night air as they inch closer to the chaos. Two neighbors drag Arty by his arms, towards their own home, away from the heroes who are trying to salvage the house.

The windows that have survived the fire are destroyed by their axes as the fire travels across the shingles and engulfs the brick chimney. The firemen cannot get near the roof as it has turned into a hellish blaze and all they can do is contain the disaster from the front and sides. Finally, a few men go towards the back of the house. The attached garage is burning and the stench of burning rubber fills the air.

While the firemen continue to fight the flames and avoid being consumed by the black smoke, several neighbors bring coffee and muffins to Arty and the elderly neighbor who had held the hose until his hands burned from the encroaching heat. One of the neighbors convinces Arty to move further back, but he resists at first as he is mesmerized by the inferno that has paralyzed his thoughts.

Arty is overcome with grief. The house meant so much to him, to both of them, it was giving them a chance to carve out a real future together. His mind is incapable of realizing Pia is likely gone, having finally confronted her worst nightmare. He regrets never buying that fire extinguisher and just when his despair feels like it could not get any worse, he remembers. He never called him back.

He never called the insurance man back. Because he bought the house for cash, he had no obligation to purchase fire insurance. But he intended to do it, he knew it was the smart thing to do. When Frank gave him the quote, he balked and said he wanted to do a little comparison shopping. He promised to call Frank back. Then he went to DC for the 4th and found Pia again. He forgot all about Frank and the fire insurance.

Arty begins to weep hysterically and the neighbors attempt to console him, but how does one reconcile with such loss. Pia was so young, just starting her adult years. Most of the neighbors are senior citizens and they shoot glances at one another as if to say the girl is with God now. Arty is crying for his loss now, the loss of his home, for his utter stupidity for not calling Frank back. He refuses to accept the fact that Pia is gone.

"Pia will be so mad, she'll be so angry with me..." he keeps mumbling. "Pia told me to buy a fire extinguisher. She reminded me to call Frank last week. Pia will be so disappointed. What will I say to her? Pia, Pia, Pia, I'm sorry, Pia. Forgive me, Pia."

22

Portia calls Ben at 3am. He is hoping for phone sex as she had promised, but she is in no mood. Something is wrong. She knows it. Pia never called her back. It's just not like her.

"Hey sexy, I've been waiting for you," a sleepy Ben mutters as he touches himself with anticipation.

"Ben, something is very wrong. Pia never called me, I know in my gut she is in trouble."

"OK, calm down, I'm still half asleep. Maybe their phone is out of order. Call the operator. They can check on it. Then call me back."

"OK, I'll call you back."

Portia taps her foot on the linoleum as she sits in a kitchen chair and waits for an operator. She tells her she is very worried about her friend. The operator is very sweet and accommodating. She waits, it feels like minutes drag on and finally the operator returns to the line.

"I'm sorry, the number you are calling is out of service. I don't know anymore. But I would try again in the morning."

Portia thanks her. She is relieved, assuming a branch fell on the telephone line. Phones do that sometimes, they just stop working for a while. She calls Ben back.

"Everything OK?" he asks. He had dozed off for a few seconds, but now he is sitting up in bed, propped against several pillows.

"I'm not sure. The operator said the phone line is down. She said to try again in the morning. It's too late to call Arty's restaurant. I guess I'll try to get some sleep and wait til morning."

"How about the phone sex, since we're both up?" he prompts with a bit of boyish charm.

"I'm beat, babe. I'll jump your bones next weekend. I promise. Sorry we couldn't get together today. I had that work baby shower and a bunch of errands to run. I'll make it up to you next weekend."

"OK, I guess I'll try to get back to sleep. Let me know when you finally reach Pia."

"I will. Nighty-night sweetheart."

"You too, precious Portia. I love you."

"Ditto baby."

Portia tosses and turns for hours. She and Pia share a bond that was forged in the loneliness and desperation of spending their teen years in a county orphanage. Neither of them was very adoptable since most folks prefer the little ones and except for the love they shared with one another, they felt abandoned by the world. But now Portia has Ben and the two women still have one another. Whenever Pia is in trouble, Portia gets a knot in her stomach. It is as if they are somehow linked by their experiences, wired together in some kind of psychic phenomenon.

Portia's dreams are generally pleasant compared with Pia's nightmares of fire and discovering Nonna on the kitchen floor with an oversized wooden spoon still clutched between her still fingers. Pia has been tormented by her dreams since she was four years old, but now it is Portia who is consumed with such troubled angst as she attempts to catch a few winks.

Jake is having a bad night as well. He woke at four and could not get back to sleep. He has not spoken to Pia in months and it is killing him. He needs to hear her voice. He feels connected to her as well and he knows something is wrong. But he promised her he would back off and allow her some space to figure out her future.

Around half past five, Jake finally calls Ben in a panic. He was having strange premonitions as if Pia was calling out to him from a tunnel of darkness and her voice sounded like the wind in winter as it howls through bare branches and wanders down lonesome alleyways.

"Hello," Ben croaks as he wipes away some sleep sand.

"Ben, did I wake you?"

"Who is this?"

"It's Jake. I'm worried about Pia. I had a dream about her and it was so real. I feel like she's calling out for help. Maybe I'm crazy. Maybe I'm just going mad, I don't know."

"Actually, Portia is worried too. She woke me up at 3am to tell me she can't reach Pia. I told her to call the operator. Apparently, the line is down. I'm sure everything is fine."

"Do you know her address?" Jake demands.

"I do. She's sent me a few letters to tell me stuff about the apartment."

"Please give it to me."

"What will you do?"

"I'm not sure."

"OK, but if anyone asks, you didn't get it from me." Ben gets out of bed and stumbles into the kitchen. He looks through a pile of papers in the junk drawer and finally finds one of Pia's letters. He reads the return address to Jake.

"Sorry to have disturbed you, Ben."

"Don't do anything crazy, Jake." But Jake has already disconnected the call. He calls the operator and asks for information. Pia lives at number 8 Elm Street. He asks for a phone number for some of the other houses. He asks for numbers 6, 7, 9, and 10. The operator insists he needs a name and he explains it is a matter of life and death. He uses his charm, his salesman's gift for gab, and he promises the operator that she will be saving a life. Finally, the woman relents and gives him two phone numbers, one for number 6 and the other for number 10. The first number is for Sydney Anderson. The second house belongs to Bonnie Edwards.

It's not quite 6am and Jake knows he should wait, but he makes the first call. His heart is thumping so loudly he can hear it beating. His breathing is labored in panic as the phone rings.

"Hello," a woman says with a frantic air in her voice.

"Mrs. Anderson?" Jake asks.

"Speaking."

"I'm so sorry to disturb you."

"I've been up most of the night. Who is this?"

"I'm a friend of Pia's and I'm worried about her. She lives in number 8."

"Where are you calling from?"

"Silver Spring, Maryland. My name is Jake McGuire."

"I am so sorry to tell you that number 8 burned down during the night. The firemen are still there putting out the fire."

"What about the people who live there?" Jake gasps, frantically. "Is Pia all right?"

"I'm so sorry to tell you this. It appears only her husband got out in time. We are all devastated for them both."

"Are you sure?" Jake shrieks into the phone in disbelief.

"I'm afraid so, Mr. McGuire. I am so very sorry to be the bearer of such tragic news."

"No, no," he mutters as he disconnects, refusing to accept her words. He sits for a few moments, tears streaming down his face. And then he slams his right hand on the kitchen counter and screams *"No! Pia!"*

Jake dials the second number and a woman answers. He takes a deep breath as he hears her voice.

"This is Bonnie," she says calmly.

"Excuse me, I'm calling to check on Pia in number 8. I'm a friend from Maryland."

"Did you hear about the fire, sir?"

"I did."

"The husband was taken away in an ambulance. The firemen are inside the house now, probably looking for the wife's body. The house is pretty bad. No one could have survived such a fire. I am so sorry."

"Pia might have survived. It's still possible, isn't it?"

"I suppose. Would you like to leave your number? I can call you when I know more."

"Yes, please. I'll be right here waiting. My name is Jake McGuire."

"Let me get a pen and paper to write down the information, Jake. Such a tragedy. At least the firemen kept it from burning down the entire neighborhood. I'll be right back."

Jake's tears continue to drip on the counter. When she gets back on the phone, he gives her the number twice. Then he makes her read it back to him. He thanks her and slumps into a chair as he hangs up the kitchen phone.

"She was so afraid of fire, she wouldn't let the busboy light the candle in the restaurant. It's like she knew, she knew the fire was coming for her…" he hysterically mutters to himself. Finally, he calls Ben back and tells him what he just learned.

"No, no, this can't be happening," Ben proclaims. He has been woken up for the third time since 3am. He is wide awake now and he tells Jake he will call Portia. Jake hangs up quickly so he can wait for Bonnie's call.

Ben dials Portia and lets the phone ring a dozen times. Even her machine isn't picking up. He puts on some coffee and tries again. This time a sleepy Portia answers.

"Hello," she mumbles.

"Portia, Jake just talked to Pia's neighbors. There's been a fire, it's bad. Pia's house burned down. Arty was taken away in an ambulance."

"What about Pia?" she screams into the phone, scarcely awake, thinking this has to be a bad dream.

"The neighbors say she was unable to get out. The firemen are still there. One of the neighbors is going to call Jake back when she knows more, but two neighbors claim she couldn't have survived. I am so sorry, so sorry." Ben knows Portia is crying, he is too. This news is unthinkable, especially for Portia. No one knew how much Pia feared fire more than her best friend, the girl who comforted her so many times at the county orphanage.

Portia is too overcome with grief to speak. Ben tells her he is on his way over to her house. He told Jake to call Portia when he knows more. Ben dresses quickly, skipping his morning shower. He shuts off the coffee and grabs a cup to go. It's going to be a long day, an awful day.

23

Portia is sitting on her bed when Ben walks in. He has his own key. He finds her sitting cross-legged, looking through a photo album, wiping away her tears as fast as they fall before they hit the paper. A lone tear drips onto a photograph of Pia and Portia screams as she wipes it dry with a tissue, blotting it carefully to keep the picture from smearing.

"Hey, babe, I'm here. Has Jake called?"

"No," she cries out as he sits and she falls into his waiting arms. He holds her like she is a child. Portia has suffered her own demons. She was orphaned young as well and she knows loss. Finally, she releases Ben and picks up the album again.

"This is Pia when she was thirteen. A lady at the orphanage took the picture and gave it to her. When I left, she gave it to me, telling me to never forget her, as if I could ever forget her." She continues to sob.

Ben takes her into his arms again and rocks her, smothering her with affection, trying so hard to find the right words. Finally, he speaks from the heart.

"Pia knew love. She still remembered her grandmother and she still felt loved by you. She loved you so much," Ben says.

"Stop talking about her in the past tense. She could still be alive. It's still possible." Ben nods and offers to put on some coffee. She tells him she can't eat anything, but coffee will help her focus. What do they do? If Pia is gone, will there be a funeral? Will she be able to show her respect and comfort Arty, the man she despises?

Ben is in the kitchen when the phone rings. He grabs it at once, accidently spilling coffee grounds into the sink.

"Hello, this is Ben," he mutters, fearing what his ears are about to acknowledge.

"Ben, it's Jake. She's alive. *She's alive!*"

"Portia, Portia, she's alive," Ben screams. Portia comes running and they both put their ear to the phone as Jake continues.

"The firemen found her in the bushes behind the house. She made a rope out of the bed sheets. They think she hung from it and then dropped into the bushes and crawled away from the fire until she passed out from smoke inhalation. She's in the hospital. The neighbor said she's not in great shape, but she is alive. She's alive!"

"We're going to New York," Portia declares.

"OK," Ben agrees without protest. His boss won't be happy, but screw it.

"I'm going with you. I have a big car, a four-door sedan. I'll drive," Jake insists.

"How soon can you get here?" Portia demands.

"I'll be there in less than an hour. Pack a bag." Jake hangs up.

"You have some clothes here, Ben," she proclaims. "I'll pack up stuff for both of us." Ben nods. He keeps a toothbrush and a razor at Portia's as well. They are going on a road trip.

"Mr. Thompson, how are you feeling?" a nurse asks as he opens his eyes.

"Awful," Arty mumbles.

"Well, I have some wonderful news for you. The firemen found your wife. She's alive, sir. She's alive."

"Is this a joke? She was trapped. She never got out of the house," he shrieks.

"She climbed out a window and fell into some bushes. She took in a great deal of smoke, but she's going to make it. She's in ICU."

"Are you sure?"

"Her name is Francesca Pia Petrocelli Thompson according to the police."

"Yes, that's her, that's her. I want to see her."

"I'll get someone to take you to her, just stay put for a bit. You've been through a horrific experience."

"What about my house?" he demands.

"I'm sorry, I don't have that information. But be thankful. Houses can be rebuilt."

"Not without insurance money," Arty grumbles. He is overjoyed that Pia survived, but now he knows he will have to face her and explain how his irresponsible behavior nearly killed them both and destroyed their home. He is filled with remorse, wracked with guilt. He has destroyed any chance for them to have a future together.

He dozes off for a while and dreams she is dead. He is at the cemetery, weeping, begging for her forgiveness. He is sweating and tossing when the nurse wakes him. He jumps when she touches him and swings both arms. His right hand slaps the nurse across the face and she flinches with slight pain.

"Mr. Thompson, Mr. Thompson, calm down. You were having a nightmare. You're in the hospital. You're going to be fine."

"Was it a dream? Is my wife really alive?" he pleads.

"Yes, and we're taking you to her. Sip some water first." He obeys and tries to compose himself. Finally, the nurse helps him out of bed and an aid assists him into a wheelchair. The man helps Arty settle his toes on the footrests and once he is secure, they are off.

"My wife and I were in a fire. I thought she died. They said she got out a bedroom window. She's in ICU…"

"That's where I'm taking you, sir. Hold on now. I'm so glad your wife made it out. Such a terrible ordeal for you both."

They travel down a corridor to the elevators. The aid pushes the button and they wait. Arty is very impatient and he complains about the slow elevator.

"Is it ever coming?" he groans.

"It's getting close. Both elevators are on the floor below us."

"Why aren't they moving?" Arty complains.

"Probably helping some sick folks on or off. Just be patient."

"Patience is not my strong suit. People are always asking me to be patient. I am so sick of being patient."

"Well, for now you are a patient in the hospital," the aid jokes.

"Very funny," Arty scoffs.

The right elevator opens and the aid pushes the wheelchair inside. They are alone and the aid hits the ICU floor. As the door closes, Arty hopes it will be an express and not stop at every floor.

When the door opens again, the aid pushes him down another corridor and then turns left. A policeman is sitting outside of one of the doors. It is Pia's room.

"What's the cop doing here?" Arty frantically asks. He is paranoid now, fearing he is going to be blamed for the fire.

"I really couldn't say, sir."

"Excuse me," a nurse asks, "are you Mr. Thompson?" Arty nods. "How's my wife?"

"She is asleep. Don't wake her. Just sit with her until she comes to. We medicated her. Her lungs were injured from all the smoke. The doctors are still unsure about the extent of the damage. Be patient."

"Everyone wants me to be patient lately," Arty whines. "Why is there a cop by the door?"

"The police are investigating the fire for potential arson. The policeman is supposed to speak to your wife as soon as she opens her eyes. I'm sorry, it's out of our hands."

The aid pushes Arty close to the door and the policeman introduces himself. Arty scowls rudely and tells the aid to bring him to his wife now.

He sits quietly as he was told to do. He is relieved to see her face. She is scratched up and her face is slightly burned. Her hands and forearms are wrapped in gauze and her neck has a bandage on the right side. Her hair is disheveled and singed, but it is Pia. He is certain. Arty is not a man of faith, but he looks up towards the ceiling and utters a simple prayer. "Thank you God. Thank you for saving her."

The aid leaves him. The ICU nurse will call when it is time to bring him back to his room. The policeman is within earshot and Arty begins to whisper to Pia.

"It was an accident, babe. I tried so hard to save you. I couldn't get up the stairs. I screamed for you to get wet towels. I'm so proud of you for climbing out the window. It was so brave of you. We're going to make it, babe. We'll find a way to rebuild the house, to rebuild our lives." He doesn't mention his mistakes. He never called Frank, he never took out the insurance policy. He never bought the fire extinguisher. His mind is racing. Maybe the owners of the restaurant will help, perhaps the community will have a fundraiser to rebuild. People have big hearts. All is not lost. The bedroom set is paid for. They will have to hold onto it for now. They could sell the Mustang and buy a used car. He still has some money in the bank. He'll find a way to start over.

Finally, she opens her eyes and stares. Her face is frozen and expressionless. He is anxious. A nurse checks on her and alerts the officer that she is awake. The policeman insists that Arty is wheeled into the waiting room while he speaks to Mrs. Thompson. Arty is angry and nearly curses at the police officer, but he bites his tongue and yells out to Pia.

"I love you, babe, with all my heart. I love you."

As Arty is wheeled out by one nurse, a second nurse helps Pia take a sip of water. She is on a morphine drip and she checks it and asks Pia if she is in pain. Pia shakes her head, her eyes tell the nurse differently. She is simply being strong.

"Mrs. Thompson, I'm Officer Riley. I won't take up much of your time. You live at number 8 Elm Street? Just nod if that's true." Pia nods.

"Are you sure you don't want more pain medication?" the nurse asks. Pia shakes her head. She has still not found her voice.

"I'm sorry to tell you the house burned, but you escaped. Your husband is in the waiting room. His injuries are less severe. You took in a lot of smoke and you have trouble speaking. The doctors will explain it all, but if you can speak, I need you to tell me what happened to you for the police report."

She is silent for a long moment. Then she attempts to talk. Her voice is faint, almost a whisper, but she tells him she doesn't know how the fire started. She was asleep.

"I...trapped...upstairs.   Smoke...under...door. Made...rope...sheets. Window...falling..."

"Can you remember how the fire started, Mrs. Thompson?" Pia shakes her head and mumbles that she was sleeping. The officer nods. He has written down her words, but he seems unsatisfied. For some reason, he suspects there is more to the story. He already thinks very little of the husband. The man was rude and defensive. Cops can read people. Arty told a detective that the fire was an accident. He blamed it on a candle that Pia left burning. A lie.

As Arty is wheeled back in, he looks white. He is fearful that he is about to be arrested, accused of a crime. Is smoking in bed a crime? Is he going to be held accountable for her injuries?

"Hi babe, don't you worry. I'll take care of everything. You just rest and heal. I know it is hard for you to talk. You must have inhaled a lot of smoke. The fire was an accident. I don't know what happened. I woke up on the couch and saw the flames everywhere. I tried to get to you, but the stairs were on fire. I screamed for you to run, to wet some towels. I'm so sorry. I thought I lost you. I am so grateful you are alive. Screw the house. We can go back to the old place. I'll bet it's still empty. I'll call your boss for you and explain. You just get better."

While Arty continues to ramble, Pia says nothing, she doesn't even attempt to speak. She is in shock and his number has hit a new low. She suspects he was smoking and fell asleep. There is no other explanation…other than deliberate arson. But Arty loved the house, he wouldn't have burned it down. If he wanted Pia gone, he just had to say the word.

She wonders if he took out a life insurance policy on her. She ponders if he tried to kill her. Her health insurance just kicked in. Arty has health insurance at his job. She is grateful for that.

Pia thinks about Arty running for his life and leaving her behind. Maybe there was nothing he could do but call for help. She doesn't know what to think and she is in pain. The nurse checks on her and can see the agony in her face. She ups the morphine and tells Arty she needs to sleep. She has already summoned the aid to wheel him back to his room. While they await the aid, the nurse asks Arty to stop talking and allow his wife to rest.

Arty thinks the nurse is abrupt and rude, but he says nothing. He sits quietly, staring at Pia's face. She looks weathered, as if she has aged a decade or more, but she will heal. She is young, she is a strong person. She feared fire and smoke all her life and it seems her fate finally caught up with her. Arty is filled with regret, wishing he had called Frank back, wishing he had bought the fire extinguisher, wishing he had listened to his wife.

Arty is back in his room, nibbling on lunch, when the doctor comes in and tells him he should be discharged in the morning. He is there for observation, but his injuries are minimal. Arty asks about Pia. The doctor is one of many physicians who are on Pia's case.

"Your wife has burns on her hands, arms, feet, and neck. Most of them are first degree, which are considered mild. But some of the burns on her feet and hands are second degree which is causing her pain due to swelling and blistering. She will have scars, but the plastic surgeon doesn't believe surgery is warranted. Thankfully, she escaped without third degree burns. Her lungs are my biggest concern at the moment."

"How bad is it, Doc?"

"The X-ray wasn't as bad as we feared, but we need to take a second chest X-ray later today. Sometimes the first one can be inconclusive. There is definite swelling in her nasal passages and throat, but we have that under control. The swelling in her airways is causing respiratory distress and that's part of the reason she is on morphine and oxygen. A fire can produce compounds that damage the body's oxygen use at the cellular level."

"I don't follow, Doc," Arty complains.

"Fires can produce hydrogen sulfide and cyanide, which can be deadly. If there is a reduction in her red blood cells, there will be a depletion of oxygen in her blood. That could cause the white blood cells to die. She needs them to fight off infection or clots. We are giving her platelets to rebuild her blood cells. Other organs can be burdened by the blood supply issues, including her kidneys. We need to keep a close eye on her carboxyhemoglobin level."

"You're losing me, Doc," Arty mumbles.

"We are inserting a small scope into her airways today to assess the damage. We will also be able to suck out some of the debris in her airways. She will be sedated for this procedure. It will take time for the lungs to fully heal. There may be lung scarring which could lead to chronic shortness of breath as if she has severe asthma."

"Can she talk?" Arty asks.

"Not much, nor do we want to encourage her to strain her voice. She is hoarse and in pain. She needs rest, medication, blood work, another X-ray, and lots of tender loving care. When you get her home, you will need home nurses for a week or so and you will be expected to step up and take care of her."

"We lost our home in the fire. I'll probably sleep in my office and shower at the gym. I'm not sure what to do about Pia."

"She may need to be transferred to a rehabilitation facility when she is discharged. But she'll be with us for at least a week. Hopefully, she'll be out of ICU in a few days when she is completely out of danger. The burns will hurt for a while, but it's her blood oxygen levels and her ability to breathe properly that are our primary concerns."

"I appreciate everything you have done for both of us."

"That's what we're here for. I'll have a social worker stop by to discuss your wife's situation. She will need a good amount of care for the next month or two."

"When can she get back to work, Doc?"

"Let's not get ahead of ourselves, Mr. Thompson. It may be a long time before she is ready for that. There is another concern, she is in shock. This is normal for a victim of such an ordeal, but her level of shock is severe. Does she have a history of having survived a similar tragic event?"

"Yeah, when she was four, her whole family died in a fire. She wasn't there. She was at her grandmother's house. But she has been afraid of fire ever since I've known her."

"I thought you said she left a candle burning?" Arty ignores the question. "Does she have a psychologist?"

"We were separated and she was living in Maryland. She had a shrink down there. She has an appointment to see a local psychologist in November."

"See if you can find out the names of both psychologists, the one in Maryland will be more helpful, but we should alert the doctor she is supposed to start seeing. I'm afraid that appointment will likely be postponed under the circumstances."

"Thanks again, Doc. I'll see what I can find out."

"I better run."

"Thanks for giving me so much of your time, Doc. My wife is a fighter. She'll be just fine."

"She's young, she has that on her side." He smiles and walks out of the room and Arty begins to sulk. He wishes he never brought her back to live with him.

He now thinks he would be better off without her. She may turn into an asthmatic invalid and he doesn't have the skills or temperament to play nursemaid. And they have no house. She can't stay in a rehab forever. The insurance won't pay for that.

He begins to plot and plan. Maybe she can go back to Maryland and stay with her friend, Portia. Portia can take care of her. When she gets better she can come back. He is planning to ask the staff at the restaurant to start a local fundraiser so he can rebuild the house. It will be better than ever if they can just raise a bunch of cash. The neighbors will all feel sorry for them.

He'll play the part of the doting husband for now. He needs Pia so he can gain sympathy from strangers who have deep pockets. As he continues to scheme his way out of his mess, he wonders if he would be happier with one of the waitresses, one of the girls who loves sex. He has been told that he is a good lover by one or two girls over the past year. He doubts Pia will ever appreciate his skills in the bedroom. She has barely allowed him to hug her over the past two months.

It's time to cut her loose. A part of him wishes she had not survived the blaze, but since he doesn't have any life insurance on either of them, he would have had a real problem paying for a burial. He needs to sell the Mustang and salvage some cash. Maybe his car survived the blaze. Maybe it can be fixed. He could forge his wife's signature and sell the Mustang privately. Hopefully, all the documents are in the glove compartment because if the title is in the house, he will be up a creek.

He is determined to be nice to Pia while he raises some cash, but he has decided to move on as soon as possible. He is fed up with her phobia over touching and her recent demands. She criticizes him for drinking and smoking so much and she constantly wants new stuff for the house. Now they have to start over and being a bachelor again suddenly appeals to him.

Arty has not changed much. He is still the selfish fellow he always was and it only took one turn of events to bring out the worst in him. At first, he was afraid he would be charged with arson or attempted murder, but so far it looks like he is in the clear. Now he just wants to rebuild his life and send Pia back to Maryland. He needs sex and she has just taken a huge step backwards. He has run out of patience.

24

Portia, Ben, and Jake arrive at the hospital while Arty is speaking to the doctor. They are in a waiting room while a hospital volunteer tries to get them some information. Portia is sick with worry, but she is grateful, thankful that Pia is alive. When the nice woman told her Pia is in ICU, she trembled at the thought of third degree burns and disfiguration.

"She'll pull through," Ben says to comfort his fiancée.

"She may be severely disfigured," Portia sobs as she fights back her tears. She is a strong woman, but she has a weak spot when it comes to Pia. Hasn't the girl suffered enough in her life?

"I don't care if she needs plastic surgery," Jake declares. "I love her. I'll take care of her no matter what."

"Calm down, dude," Ben says. "She still has a husband."

"I wish he died in the fire. How the hell did it happen? Pia doesn't smoke, but I'll bet that bastard does."

"It could have been electrical or some kind of freak accident," Ben says.

"Why are you defending him?" Jake demands.

"Calm down both of you," Portia insists as she wipes away her tears with the tips of her fingers. "Let's just focus on helping our friend get through this. This is not just about her physical injuries. She has lived in fear of fire her entire life and she has to be emotionally paralyzed right now. I have Dr. Forte's number. I'm going to call her after we speak to Pia first. She hasn't started seeing a new psychologist yet."

"Excuse me, the ICU nurse said one of you may visit the patient. She said to keep your visit to no more than ten minutes. The patient may not be able to speak, so please don't encourage her to do anything that could cause her further pain."

"I'll go," Portia insists, much to Jake's dismay.

"Can we take turns?" Jake asks.

"The nurse really wants to limit visitation," the volunteer insists.

"I don't need to go up," Ben says.

"I'm her sister and Jake is her brother. Can we each see her for a few minutes?"

"You'll have to discuss that with the nurse when you get up there." The woman is polite and professional. She takes her job very seriously. She gives Portia a paper badge to wear and smiles. "I hope your sister gets better soon."

"Thank you," Portia says as she begins to head for the elevator. She turns after a few steps and waves to Ben. He waves back and mouths the words, *I love you.* She forces a half-smile and hurries towards an open elevator before the door shuts on her.

"That was smart of Portia to say you are Pia's brother," Ben mutters. "We couldn't say you're her boyfriend with her husband around."

"I wonder if they're in the same room," Jake mumbles with concern. He hopes not.

Portia is on the elevator with two men, one is likely the father. It appears the younger one's mother is ill. She is in ICU as well. She wanted to buy some flowers in the lobby gift shop, but the sign downstairs said flowers and balloons are not allowed in ICU. She understands, but it feels wrong to be walking in empty handed. Maybe when Pia is up to it, she can bring her one of her favorite treats, a chocolate croissant.

The three of them get off the elevator together and Portia follows the two men. The younger one looks to be no more than twenty. They speak to the nurse at the desk and the younger one breaks into tears. His father comforts him. The news is not good. Finally, they walk towards one of the private rooms and Portia steps forward.

"Bad news?" she whispers.

"The man's wife is gravely ill. May I help you?"

"I'm here to visit Pia Petrocelli."

"Who?"

"I mean Pia Thompson. Petrocelli is her maiden name."

"And you are?"

"Her sister, Portia. Portia Petrocelli," she lies.

"Please keep your visit short and don't encourage her to try to speak. She is hoarse and she should rest her vocal chords."

"I understand. Our brother, Jake, is downstairs. Can he come up for a few minutes after I leave?"

"I suppose, but only him. We need to allow the patient to rest. She'll be going downstairs for more tests in a few hours and the doctor wants her to sleep until then. She really needs lots of rest in order for her body to heal."

"Thank you. May I go in?"

"Yes," she says as she points. Portia nods.

As Portia passes one of the other rooms, she sees the man holding his wife's hand. The son is crying and Portia's stomach tenses. She doesn't know what to expect. Pia could be completely unrecognizable.

She peeks in and squints in the dim lighting. Pia is alone in the room and she is connected to monitors and unfamiliar contraptions. The first thing Portia notices is the bandages around her arms and hands. Her feet are bandaged as well, but they are covered with a blanket and Portia doesn't see the full extent of her burns.

Pia appears to be asleep and Portia quietly pulls up a chair. She wants to take her hand, but she knows better when she sees the bandages. She sits and waits for Pia to open her eyes for a few minutes. Portia is relieved that her face looks far better than she imagined. Her skin is red and blotchy and there is a small bandage on her neck, but she would recognize her in a crowd. Pia's hair looks like it went through a cyclone and the ends look split and scorched. Portia takes a deep breath and waits.

About four or five minutes elapse and the nurse sticks her head in. She can see her patient is still asleep. She checks the monitors, adjusting the morphine drip again, stumbling around enough to stir the patient. Perhaps she is less than quiet intentionally so that Portia can see her sister open her eyes. It works.

"Hi," Portia whispers. "Don't try to talk. Nod if you can. Are you in a lot of pain?" Pia shakes her head and Portia forces a smile.

"Your sister can only stay for another five minutes. Then we'll send up your brother for a few minutes. After that, I want you to try to sleep for a few hours before we wheel you back downstairs for another chest X-ray." The nurse leaves and Pia looks at Portia in confusion.

"My…brother?" she mutters.

"Try not to talk, sweetie. I told them I'm your sister so they would let me up. They're only allowing immediate family and we can't stay long. But we're staying for a few days. We'll be back tomorrow. Maybe we can visit longer then."

Pia shoots her a quizzical look and she knows. Gaetano is her brother, the only sibling she ever had. He was a toddler when he died. She tells Pia that Ben and Jake are downstairs. She will be sending Jake up in a few minutes.

"I was so scared. At first, the neighbors told Jake you died in the fire. Then we found out you were alive. You jumped out a window. You're my hero. I'm sorry you are suffering, but your body will heal. You're still young. I'll take care of you. You should come back to Maryland and let me nurse you back to health."

"Brother…Jake?" Pia whispers.

"Yes, we told the staff Jake is your brother. Do you want to see him?" She shakes her head no. But she appears to be conflicted.

"Are you sure? He came such a long way to see you. He cares for you so much. He drove. He has a big car. Please let him just stick his head in."

Pia looks sad and Portia assumes she doesn't want Jake to see her looking so awful. She removes a small brush from her purse and gently brushes Pia's hair. Tears fill Portia's eyes, but she blinks them back and continues brushing and whispering to her friend, telling her how much she loves her.

"There, now you look quite presentable. Believe me, Jake will see only the beautiful girl he fell head over heels for. Let him come up for a minute, Pia."

She doesn't nod, but she doesn't shake her head either. Portia takes that as a yes. Pia continues to stare at Portia and the older girl gently kisses her on the top of her head.

"I love you so much, Pia. You do recognize me?" Pia nods. "So I'll send Jake up?" Pia hesitates, but she finally relents with a slight nod.

"Love…you…too."

Portia breaks into tears, but she quickly wipes them away with the heel of her palms. She apologizes for losing control. She tells Pia she looks good, despite her injuries. She is not lying as she had feared Pia's face would be burned badly. She is relieved.

"I'll be back tomorrow. I'll leave the phone number of our hotel at the nurses' station. If you need us to bring anything tomorrow, anything at all, try to let the nurses know if you can. They can call the hotel later. Anything at all. I'd bring you the moon if I had it in my power. I love you more than anything. Just rest. You look really good, despite what you've been through. You are still beautiful on the inside and on the outside. I love you so much, Pia. I'll see you tomorrow."

Pia attempts to smile, but it comes off as a crooked smirk as she nods to her friend. Portia backs out of the room slowly, never taking her eyes off Pia. She finally waves with an abbreviated shake of her wrist and turns away.

"Excuse me, can I leave the phone number of my hotel. If my sister needs anything, please call me anytime. I'll be back tomorrow. I'm going to send our brother up now, his name is Jake."

The nurse hands her a small pad and a pen. Portia writes down her name and the number at the hotel. As she writes, the nurse explains Pia's injuries. The worst burns are second degree, mostly on her feet and hands. Her lungs are a concern and Pia is struggling to breathe. The second X-ray will tell them more.

She thanks the nurse and walks away with tears filling her eyes. When she gets to the elevator, the man and his son are once again waiting. They are apparently going out to buy something for the man's wife. She appears to be craving a vanilla shake. Portia wishes she could bring Pia something to brighten up her day just a little, but the nurse made it clear to her that Pia cannot eat or drink much at the moment. She can only take very small sips of water from a straw. The nurse did place an ice ship against Pia's lips for a few moments, moistening the dry, chapped skin. Pia looks like she has a bad sunburn, but Portia knows the bandages cover something that is far worse.

Portia rides down one floor with the men. The doors open and more visitors enter the elevator along with people in white coats who are discussing their dinner plans later. Hospital employees often seem so jovial, despite the sadness all around them. It is part of their routine to encounter grieving families along with ecstatic new fathers and grandparents.

When they reach the lobby, Portia heads towards Ben and Jake and the two men go in a different direction. She cannot help herself and she calls out to them.

"Your wife will be in my prayers, sir," she declares with a comforting look. The older man turns and nods. The younger man stares at his shoes as he plods along as if each of his feet weighs fifty pounds. Worry can weigh on a person's limbs and heart like an albatross of agonizing anguish.

As Portia approaches the guys, she breaks into convulsive sobs and Ben's eyes portray deep concern while Jake's eyes exhibit fear and panic. "She has bad burns on her feet and hands. Her arms are bandaged as well, along with her neck." Portia can barely get the words out of her mouth and she collapses in Ben's arms.

"Can I see her?" Jake gasps with an anxious look.

"You can…" she sobs, "but not for long. Don't make her talk. Her face just looks like she has a bad sunburn. She is scratched up and her hair is a mess, but I brushed it…I brushed it for her."

"Is her husband up there?" Jake asks with a tense look of dismay.

"I didn't see him."

"OK, you go up, Jake," Ben says as he carefully removes the badge from Portia's lapel and hands it to Jake. Jake nods and tells them he'll be back in a few minutes.

"I told the nurses to call the hotel if she needs anything, anything at all," Portia sobs as Jake hurries towards the elevators.

"That's good. I guess we'll come back in the morning," Ben says. It's more like a question and Portia nods in agreement. They sit and wait for Jake.

Jake rides the elevator alone and he is soon on the ICU floor. He stops at the nurses' station and announces himself. He asks about Pia's husband, calling him his *brother-in-law*. Just muttering those words turns his stomach. Arty is no brother to him. He blames the man for nearly killing Pia.

"Her husband visited her this morning. He is upstairs in his own room."

"Is he injured as well?" Jake asks.

"His injuries are superficial, but the doctors decided to keep him overnight for observation."

"Thank you. I'll go see my sister now."

"Be very quiet. Don't let her talk much. Ask her questions where she can nod. I can only let you stay for a few minutes." Jake thanks her, but a smile evades him.

He tiptoes into the room and sits in the chair Portia had occupied. Her eyes are shut. He studies the bandages on her hands and arms. Her neck is red, but the bandage is more like a large band aid. Her face is puffy and scratched, but she looks pretty, almost radiant. To Jake, she could never be ugly, no matter how much damage the fire inflicted upon her. He clears his throat and she opens her eyes.

"Hi stranger," he whispers with an empathetic grin.

"Hi," she mumbles.

"Please don't try to talk. Do you know me?" She nods and forces a slight smirk. Of course she knows him. Her brain is still functioning. She must look awful and she hates for him to see her like this.

They sit quietly. He knows she doesn't like to be touched and her hands are wrapped in gauze. But he touches her shoulder gently and tells her he never stops thinking about her. She smiles with her eyes and he knows she cares for him.

"Is the pain bad?" he asks and she shakes her head. He can see the morphine drip. He knows she is heavily medicated. "They told me your husband is upstairs. He is just here overnight. He wasn't injured badly. Was he downstairs and you were upstairs?" She nods.

"He…tried…tried…to…save…me. Fire…too…bad."

"Don't talk." Her voice is a raspy whisper and each word is a struggle. He thinks about Arty trying to climb the stairs, but finally giving up on her…deserting her. His muscles tense and he cannot suppress his disgust. He mumbles under his breath. "I would have walked through fire for you…I would have stepped into the flames." He knows he should not have said it, but it is the truth.

She stares at him as if he is her hero. Her eyes widen with reverence and adoration. She knows he would have saved her…or died trying. A lone tear slides down her left cheek and he slowly moves his index finger towards her face. She does not flinch as he delicately scoops up the tear and places his wet fingertip to his lips. His mouth absorbs her tear just as his heart begs to absorb her pain. There are no words between them. Tears fill his own eyes, but he fights them, refusing to allow them to fog up his thoughts with sadness. He is filled with joy because she is alive and he has never been more certain that she is the great love of his life.

Thoughts of the farmer's porch race through the back of his mind. The second rocker can only be reserved for one person, only for Pia. Without her, it would all seem so meaningless, so empty. He continues to watch her face, to snatch away more of her tears, but she no longer weeps. The lone tear was not a reflection of her pain, but a mere signal of how much he moves her heart. She has no doubt Jake would have raced through the fire to save her for she has never witnessed such devotion in her life. Not even in the cinema where happy endings are often the norm and lovers proclaim their passion for one another in the spirit of *Romeo and Juliet*.

When their eyes first met over a cantaloupe over nine months earlier, Jake was instantly smitten. But he had seen pretty girls before, watched and admired them from afar, often never daring to speak or stare like a child on Christmas morning. But when their eyes inadvertently met in that smaller market, in the limited produce aisle, something inside of him woke. It was as if he never knew what he wanted in life, in love, not until that very moment in time. In an instant, he knew. He knew she was the one, the woman he had been searching for, his soulmate, the person who would complete him.

He thought of her often after that first chance encounter, on the basketball court, in the car lot, and lying on his bed alone each night. He had told himself she was a fantasy, a mirage, a phantom of his imagination, but after the third chance encounter, he had to pursue her, he had to win her heart.

When she appeared in a second produce aisle, in a second market, a larger store with an abundance of melons and miscellaneous berries and bananas, he saw it as a sign from the universe. That's when he knew they were meant to be and he asked her to dinner, but she shot him down. He searched for her for weeks and weeks to no avail and then finally, while indulging a whim one day after his 23rd birthday, she nearly fell into his lap.

Claire had been merely a silly impulse, but his decision to dine with her led him back to Pia. Sure, Claire was sexy, but he tried to avoid women like Claire who were just a little too confident, too sure of themselves as they batted their eyelashes as if they were a lion tamer and he was their prey. Claire reminded him of a dominatrix he had seen in an old film, a woman of mystery, who would use men and then spit them back out like a bad oyster on a hot summer night.

He knew Claire wanted a quick roll in the hay, but he was determined to preserve his virginity while he searched for Pia. Yet he had capitulated to the reality that he might never cross paths with Pia again and he agreed to the dinner date out of boredom and a bit of self-pity.

It turned out to be the best decision he had ever made when Pia nearly dropped into his lap like a penny from heaven and from that moment on, he was determined to keep her close. He dropped Claire off that night with a peck on the cheek as he dashed back to the restaurant to comb the streets in search of her. Finally, having given up for the moment, he went back to Silver Spring to shower and sleep for a few hours before returning to her neighborhood with the dawn so that he could plop his bones on a nearby bench and watch for her.

When she appeared, biting into a red apple, dressed like a tomboy on a lazy Saturday morn, his heart skipped a beat and the world opened up to him. Much happened over the subsequent days and he was encouraged by her smiles and laughter until the emergence of her husband that complicated his vision of their future on that farmer's porch. Arty took away the dream, but Jake was determined to fight for her. He knows her husband does not love her, not like he loves her. Jake will do almost anything, shy of murder, to win her heart and vanquish Arty from her life.

"I'm sorry, but you have to go now," the nurse whispers, waking Jake from his thoughts, from his dreams of farmer's porches, rocking chairs, and children, lots of youngsters dashing about. Jake nods and stands. There are no more tears on Pia's face, but he takes his finger and follows the trail of that lone tear that is now part of him. He gently rubs her cheek and tells her he loves her and that he will be back in the morning. She nods and attempts to smile. Her heart is warmed by his very presence. But how could he know? How could he know that she loves him too?

The nurse smiles when she hears him tell Pia that he loves her. She is touched by the affection she believes exists between two siblings. She does not know the truth that they share no parent, no bloodline, but yet, they share one heart, for Jake carries Pia is his own heart and he prays she will one day feel the same.

He wanders around on the floor above and asks for Arthur Thompson's room, but he is mistaken. A kind nurse makes an inquiry and sends him up another floor. When he arrives at Arty's room, he recognizes him from the July 4th encounter and he enters.

"Hello Arty," he mutters as if they are well acquainted.

"Do I know you?" Arty asks as he turns down the volume on an old TV western.

"We met in DC on July 4th, well we weren't exactly introduced."

"You're one of Pia's Maryland friends?" he asks.

"Yes, you could say that. I'm in love with your wife, man, head over heels in love with her."

"Fuck you, asshole. She's married to *me*."

"I know, but when I met her, she didn't tell me she was married and I just fell for her."

"Well, now you know, so beat it."

"I came when I heard about the fire. I thought she was dead. I was devastated."

"Well, you were wrong," Arty snaps. "So go back home and leave us alone."

"I came to see if you needed anything."

"Why do you care?"

"I care very much about Pia."

"You got fifty grand?"

"No."

"Then get lost."

"Listen, I saw Pia. She looks good, but I know she is hurting, not just from her burns and the smoke inhalation. You know how much she fears fire. I'm afraid she has regressed. I can get you the number of her psychologist in Maryland."

"Fine, just give it to the nurse at the station and go back to where you came from."

"She may need a lot of care. Where will you live?"

"That's none of your fucking business."

"I want to help."

"Why? Because you're still trying to get into my wife's pants?"

"It's not like that. I have never touched her, well not until today."

"You touched my wife?" Arty screams with clenched fists. The nurse comes running to see what all the commotion is about.

"Everything is fine," Jake assures the nurse. Arty nods.

"She barely lets me give her a hug. You know the bitch is frigid!" Arty mumbles with a threatening glare.

"I merely touched her cheek to wipe away a tear. She was crying and I don't think it's from the burns. I think she is lost again from the trauma. She needs help."

"Fine, I told you to leave the fucking shrink's phone number with the nurse. Now go away."

"You need help man. You can't do this alone. Your house burned down. I assume you have insurance, but it will take time to rebuild."

"I don't get your angle, why do you give a damn?"

"I told you I love her. Even if I can't have her, I still want to help both of you. I want to help you pick up the pieces of your lives."

"Why do you want to help me? I wouldn't want to help you if the shoe was on the other freaking foot."

"Because…I care about her happiness. I don't have to be the man in her life, but I still want to know I helped her get back on her feet. She has to be having emotional issues on top of her injuries. The nurse said they are going to X-ray her chest again later. She's in ICU, man, she's in trouble."

"And what do you want me to do about it?"

"Anything, everything, whatever it takes. But let us help you."

"Who's us?" Arty demands with a scowl.

"Portia and Ben are downstairs. Do you know who Portia is?"

"Yeah, her friend from the freaking orphanage."

"Ben is her fiancé. They care about her too. Portia loves her like a sister. What can we do to help?"

"Like I said, I need fifty grand to rebuild my life."

"If I had it, it would be yours," Jake declares.

"I should just get out of this fucking bed and kick your ass right now," Arty says with contempt in his voice.

"If you think that will help Pia, go right ahead. But if you throw the first punch, don't expect me to lie down. I'll fight you."

"You think you're pretty tough, don't you?"

"I didn't come here to fight. I came to help, to help Pia."

"Like how?"

"I'm not sure. We need to put our heads together."

"Look, you and Portia and her man are all strangers to me."

"But Pia loves us."

"My wife loves *you*?" he screams as he attempts to get out of bed.

"She loves us all…as friends. I told you I have never touched her. But I do love her."

"As a friend?" he probes as he calms down.

"No, she's the love of my life, but she wants to be with you. I know I have to step aside and honor her wishes. Do you love her?"

"How dare you ask me that, she's my fucking wife, isn't she?"

"Lots of men don't love their wives. Do you truly love her?"

"None of your business, asshole."

"Because if you don't love her with all your heart, then let us take care of her. We'll take her back to Maryland as soon as she can travel. She can talk to her psychologist. We'll all take good care of her. And then when she is better, if she wants to resume the marriage, she'll come back to you. You'll have a chance to rebuild your house."

"There's no damn insurance, I didn't buy fire insurance. I'm ruined." Arty's eyes redden with tears, but he refuses to let them flow.

"Why didn't you have fire insurance?" Jake asks meekly with utter astonishment.

"It slipped my mind. Look, I was thinking about asking Portia to take her back while she's on the mend so I can figure things out. But now I have to worry about you trying to steal her away. How can I trust you to be around my wife when you'll do everything you can to turn her against me?"

"I swear I won't do that. I only want what Pia wants. You should feel the same way."

"Hey, I own her, I own the bitch. She's bought and paid for. She does what I say."

"She told Portia you had changed, but I think you're still the same jackass you ever were."

Arty leaps from the bed and lunges at Jake. They are rolling on the floor and Arty is on top with his hands around Jakes neck when the nurses pull him off. They tell Jake to leave at once before they are forced to call security.

One of the nurses actually winks at Jake as he departs. She seems to know Arty is a complete jerk. She probably wishes Jake had gotten in a few punches before they broke it up. Jake rides the elevator down as he attempts to calm himself. He is filled with rage and contempt. When the elevator doors open, he steps out and seeks out his comrades. He is still trembling with anger.

"Where were you?" Portia asks with a look of concern.

"I saw Pia. Then I tracked down Arty."

"You OK?" Ben asks. "Your hair is all messed up and your shirt tail is out."

"I tried to reason with Arty and he attacked me. He was like a raccoon with rabies. He tried to choke me. I could've rolled him off me easily enough. I was a varsity wrestler in high school. But the nurses ended it pretty quickly." Jake tucks in his shirt and then pushes down his thick head of hair with the flat of his palms while Ben laughs and Portia shakes her head.

"I wish you had punched his lights out," Ben mutters.

"The bastard ran to save his own life and left Pia to die," Portia admits with a look of disgust.

"I told Pia I would walk through fire for her, I would have stepped right into the flames to save her."

"I believe you, man," Ben says with a pat on the shoulder.

"I believe you too, Jake. You're a good man," Portia says.

"What am I? Chop suey?" Ben asks with a whimper.

"You're a good man, too, Ben. I love you with all my heart. Would you walk through fire for me?"

"Definitely," Ben declares.

"Listen guys," Jake says. "I was trying to convince Arty to let us take care of Pia. We could take her back to Maryland as soon as she can travel. She could start seeing the psychologist again. I'll pay for it."

"I take it Arty wouldn't go for it?" Portia asks.

"Nope. But he's in a jam. He didn't have fire insurance on the house."

"What?" Portia gasps. "That's insane."

"What a moron!" Ben adds.

"I asked him what we can do for him and he asked me for fifty grand."

"Jackass," Ben mumbles.

"So, the guy hates me, maybe you can talk some sense into him, Portia," Jake comments with a worried look.

"I'll try. I think he's leaving the hospital tomorrow. We'll come back early and see if he's in a better frame of mind before he's discharged."

"Where the hell will he go?" Ben asks.

"Search me, the guy's a bit of a loner," Portia responds.

"OK, let's go find a place to have an early dinner and then hit the hay early. We should get back here by nine," Ben says.

"I still can't believe Arty didn't buy fire insurance," Portia says as they exit the hospital.

"And I told the bastard I'm in love with his wife," Jake laughs.

"I'll bet that went over like a lead balloon," Ben chuckles.

"Yeah, most husbands don't want to hear shit like that," Jake adds. "I asked him if he loves her and that really pissed him off."

"Did he say he loves her?" Portia probes.

"He never answered the question," Jake replies.

"I don't think the creep knows the first thing about love," Portia says. "He's such a loser. Leopards don't change their spots. Arty will never change. I still don't understand how Pia can stand the guy. When she ran away, I thought she was done with him."

"I guess she got confused. He kept saying he changed," Ben says in Pia's defense.

"He didn't change," Portia declares. "The fire brought out his true colors."

"I have to admit…I really detest the guy," Jake adds as they head towards his sedan.

"He probably detests you too," Ben laughs.

Arty is sitting up in bed, sipping on an apple juice. He wants to kill Jake at the moment, but another part of him wants Portia to take Pia. The girl is a mess. She's injured and probably more frigid than ever. He needs to sell the Mustang to pick up some quick cash and Pia will not be happy about that.

He just wishes Jake wasn't in the picture. He's not sure he even wants Pia back, but that doesn't mean he wants Jake to have her. Still, if she's a basket case now, worse than ever, maybe the two of them deserve each other. He thinks about hiring a few more hot waitresses and banging a different chick every night of the week. Why the hell is he hitching his wagon to such a broken girl?

Maybe he'll send Pia back to Maryland. He'll tell the neighbors and his coworkers she is in a special rehab. That should help him milk them out of some serious dough. He just might raise fifty grand, enough to rebuild the house. At least the new bedroom set wasn't destroyed. He needs to call them and tell them to hold onto it. Maybe he can get a refund.

25

P ortia and Ben decide to make love after digesting their early dinner since Ben is feeling a bit neglected of late. Jake took a room on a different floor so that he doesn't risk hearing them bang the headboard against the wall. Jake envies them, they are in love and happily making wedding plans. In his fantasy world he and Pia will attend the wedding, dressed in their finest, as they dance the night away.

Then Pia and Jake will make love and start planning their future by buying a house together, one with a large farmer's porch. But it's merely a fantasy at the moment. Pia is injured physically, emotionally, and perhaps, mentally. She had her troubles before the fire, but she has to have regressed into an abyss of phobias with shattered nerves and a splintered spirit.

Jake knows how much she fears fire. Just the thought of a busboy lighting a candle on their first date sent her into a fright. Now she has endured her worst nightmare, but the silver lining is the fact that she survived, unlike her dear parents and her beloved Gaetano. He needs to help her climb back out of her fissure of fear and trauma and he refuses to allow Arty to stand in his way.

Arty is a bad person and Jake is certain that Pia knows this. She is trapped in a dreadful marriage and she is too good a person to refuse him a second chance after he practically begged her on bended knee. She must have been content over the past two months since she did stay. The guy taught her to drive and bought her a new car. Jake wanted to do those things for her. Jake still wants to do everything for her.

Jake is confident that he is the better man. He would cherish her and never call her names. Arty is what his Jewish friends would call a *first-class schmuck*. Pia is young and naïve and she is likely just starting to figure life out. But she knows her husband left her to die. She knows.

It is Tuesday morning, a few minutes past nine, and the ICU visiting hours do not begin until ten. They ate an early breakfast so they can pay a visit to Arty before he is discharged. Jake opts to wait in the lobby with a magazine since he knows Arty would sooner strangle him than have a second conversation with him.

Portia and Ben meander along the corridor until they find Arty's room. He is already dressed to leave, but he continues to wait for his discharge paperwork. Thankfully, he doesn't have a roommate and they can talk in private.

"Hi, Arty," Portia says as they enter. "I'm Pia's best friend from Maryland."

"I remember, from DC," he replies. "Pia talks about you all the time. Portia, right?"

"Yes, and this is my fiancé, Ben." The two men shake hands and Portia takes a seat in one of the two chairs. Ben joins her and Arty sits on the bed.

"Is that asshole, Jake, still around?" Arty asks with contempt.

"He's downstairs," Portia responds. "I guess you two didn't hit it off yesterday?"

"The guys tells me he's crazy about my wife. How am I supposed to hit it off with a guy who wants to steal my woman?"

"Jake's not like that. He's more of a friend," Portia argues. "When they met last January, she didn't tell Jake she is married. He had no way of knowing. He knows now and he's not trying to break up your marriage. But he does care what happens to her. Any word on yesterday's second chest X-ray?"

"Yeah, it wasn't as bad as they thought. She's going to be fine. She'll be hoarse for a while and her hands and feet are burned, but Pia will snap back."

"So, you're leaving the hospital?" Ben asks.

"As soon as these jerks give me my paperwork. I need to get to work. I just called the furniture store and told them to sit on our bedroom set. There's no house left to deliver it to."

"We are so sorry you lost your house," Portia says, sympathetically.

"I'll rebuild."

"Jake said there is no insurance," Portia mentions.

"I know. It was a boneheaded move on my part. But I have an idea. All the neighbors seem to like Pia. And my staff at the restaurant want to help. We're going to have a few fundraisers, you know, like in the old days when a barn burned and the neighbors all helped build a new one."

"Barn raising," Ben interjects. "The whole community would chip in lumber and labor, and the ladies would feed everyone. They also called them barn bees."

"Yeah, like that. Since most people think Pia is so sweet, I think they would want to help her. The neighbors thought she died and everyone on my street is rooting for her now. My neighbor, Bonnie, stopped by last night. She says everyone wants to do something."

"That's great, Arty, but what about in the meantime? Pia will need a place to live while you are raising money to rebuild. She'll need a lot of care."

"I'm trying to figure that out. I can crash at the restaurant and shower at my gym, but I don't know what do to about Pia," Arty mumbles.

"Let me bring her back to Maryland," Portia pleads. "She stayed with me when she first moved there. I have a guestroom and I can take some vacation time to take care of her. I'll even hire nurses. I can afford it. Let me help you both, Arty."

"I'd be OK with it, but I don't want that Jake guy hanging around her," Arty complains.

"Deal, I'll keep him away from Pia, I promise," Portia lies. She tells him what he wants to hear.

"How do I know I can trust you?"

"The two people I love more than anything else in this world are Ben and Pia. She's like a sister to me. We grew up together in the orphanage. I am not trying to break up your marriage. I want Pia to be happy."

"I'm not sure. That Jake guy has the hots for Pia."

"He cares about her. He drove us all here. Let us take her back with us as soon as she is discharged."

"It's a long trip," Arty mutters.

"We can drive half way back and stay in a nice hotel for a night so she can rest. Then we'll take her the rest of the way."

"The sooner she gets on her feet, the quicker she'll come back to you, man," Ben adds.

"And you swear you won't let that Jake try to split us up?"

"Hey, he didn't try to stop her when she went back to you in August. He's really a good guy. You two just got off on the wrong foot. Either way, you can trust me. I'll protect Pia."

"We both will. Jake's no friend of mine," Ben proclaims. "I hardly know the guy."

"I don't know him very well either," Portia admits. "Don't worry, we'll both protect her."

"Well, in the end, I guess it will be up to Pia. But I'll encourage her to take you up on your offer. It would be a lot easier on me for the time being."

"Good, then it's settled. We'll talk to Pia and her doctors about it today. Do you have any idea when she might get discharged?"

"I saw one of her doctors last night. Since the X-ray looked pretty good, he thought she could leave by this weekend, probably on Sunday. But he told me she'll need some home nursing for a while and I am worried about her mental stability. You know what's she's like." Arty twirls his index finger in circles near his own head to indicate that Pia is a nut job and Portia silently fumes. But she will humor him to get Pia away from this man.

"Her psychologist in Maryland is great," Portia adds. "She will probably lose her insurance now that she can't work for a while. She told me it just kicked in from her new job."

"I spoke to her boss," Arty responds. "She is on a medical leave and she is covered for the next six months. They're hoping she can get back to work much sooner than that of course. Then she'll be fully covered for as long as she continues working."

"Well, just in case her insurance doesn't cover Dr. Forte, I'll pay whatever it takes. She is my family, which makes you family too, Arty," Portia lies. She does not consider him family, but she would do anything for Pia.

"OK, talk to Pia and the doctors and see what they think. You have my approval. Tell Pia I'll see her tomorrow or Thursday at the latest."

"Thanks Arty. You are a good man," Portia lies again. She knows he is far from a good man. Ben is a good man. Jake is a good man. She knows what a good man looks like.

The nurse comes in with his discharge papers and Arty yells out "Finally!" Ben and Portia say goodbye and return to find Jake to tell him the good news about the X-ray. Jake will be thrilled to know Pia is coming with them, back to Maryland.

As they ride the elevator back to the lobby, Ben takes Portia by the hand and both of them smile. They convinced Arty to trust them, but they have no intentions of keeping Jake away from Pia. That will be Pia's choice.

The elevator doors open and Jake is standing there, looking worried and anxious. Ben chuckles when he sees the forlorn expression on Jake's face.

"How'd it go?" Jake mutters.

"The dude does not like you one bit," Ben laughs.

"The feeling is mutual," Jake replies.

"We have good news, Jake. Arty agreed to let us take Pia home with us. She can sleep in my guestroom again until she is well. And the second chest X-ray wasn't as bad as they feared. The doctor told Arty Pia can leave the hospital this weekend."

"That's great news," Jake declares with a grin.

"There is a condition," Ben adds. "We promised Arty we would keep you away from Pia. He thinks you are a threat to his marriage." Jake's expression turns sour and Portia laughs.

"But we both had our fingers crossed," Portia whispers.

"And we sometimes break our promises," Ben adds. Jake smiles and takes a deep breath.

"I can't wait to get back to Maryland," Jake comments. "Listen, I already talked to the desk. They will allow all three of us to visit Pia in a few minutes. We just have to keep the visit short. I thought we could hang out with her until they kick us out and then go grab lunch and figure out a plan. I don't know about you guys, but my boss isn't going to be happy with me, but I'm staying right here until Pia is well enough to travel."

"My boss is cool. I haven't used a sick day in two years," Ben says. "I'm counting this as a family leave."

"My employer will be OK. I'm taking a two week vacation starting today. Pia will need me when we get back. I have a little experience since I took care of my cousin for a long time. I'll hire people to take care of her too. Whatever she needs."

"I'll chip in," Jake adds.

"And we have to get her back to Dr. Forte as soon as possible," Portia insists. "I'm more worried about her emotional state right now. Her precarious mental health may be her biggest challenge."

They go retrieve their paper badges and head upstairs. Jake is fidgeting in the elevator. Portia tells him he looks like he is starting to unravel and Jake says he is concerned about Pia's reaction to their plan.

"Suppose she doesn't want to go with us?" he asks.

"Hey, her house burned down. Arty has no plan. She'll be happy to be with me while she recovers," Portia states with confidence.

When they arrive at the nurses' station, they are told the doctor is in with Pia. Portia really wants to speak to a doctor and she asks to join the conversation. The nurse insists the two men wait outside, but she allows Pia's "sister" to enter the room.

"Morning," Portia says with a cheerful tone. "Hi, I'm Pia's sister, Portia."

"Dr. Swanson, I'm pleased to meet you. Pia is doing better this morning. She is reacting to the medications quite well. She's a medical marvel."

"I just spoke to her husband. He told me the last X-ray was better than expected," Portia comments to show the doctor she is an involved relative.

"Yes, no serious lung damage. There is some swelling in the esophagus and she is still struggling to breathe properly. But by the time we discharge her, I don't anticipate she'll need oxygen at home."

"Arty said you can come home this weekend," Portia whispers to Pia while the doctor writes something in her chart. Pia smiles.

"I'm hoping we can discharge her on Saturday morning. We'll be watching her blood count and tending to her burns for a few more days. I want to keep her in ICU at least another day. Then we can transition her to a regular room."

"Where...where...will...I...go?" Pia whispers in a hoarse tone.

"To my house. You can have your old room back while I nurse you. You know I have all that experience taking care of my cousin."

"Are you a nurse?" the doctor asks Portia.

"No, but I learned a lot. I took care of a terminal, elderly relative 24/7 for over a year. I'll hire professionals too. Nothing but the best for my sister," Portia declares.

"Well, if Pia continues to improve, she will be on her way in a few days. I'm glad to see so much improvement in such a short time. She was very lucky. She could have died in that fire." Pia's eyes widen with fright due to the doctor's last comment and Portia quickly changes the subject.

"Did anyone ever tell you, Doctor, you could be a dead ringer for Charlton Heston?"

"That's funny. *Ben-Hur* is my favorite movie," the doctor laughs.

"Doesn't he look like Charlton Heston, Pia?" Portia continues and Pia nods with a small grin.

The doctor moves on with his rounds and Ben and Jake scurry to join the women. They were standing by a window at the end of the hallway, watching and waiting for a white coat to exit the room.

"Hi Pia, how are you feeling?" Ben asks.

"Don't talk, just nod," Portia reminds her. "Are you feeling a little better?" Pia nods.

"Morning beautiful," Jake whispers as he gets close to the bed. He lays his index finger once again on her cheek for a moment and she smiles. It is the only touching they have shared and it has become Jake's signature greeting until she invites him to do more by opening her arms to him. He adores her. He doesn't know why his passion for Pia is so strong, but it is undeniable. He is smitten as if God has waved a magic wand and dubbed her as his other half. He is starting to believe in Cupid and he can feel one of his incredible arrows poking out from his stolen heart.

Portia tells Pia their plan and Pia continues to nod. She wants to return to Maryland. She knows the house is gone and she fears she will be homeless or left to fend for herself in a cheap motel. As much as Arty claims to have changed, Pia knows he abandoned her during the fire, allowing her to confront her worst nightmare.

"I…was…so…scared," Pia mumbles.

"When you realized the house was on fire?" Portia whispers. Pia nods.

"You were so brave, going out the window," Ben comments with a warm expression of admiration.

"We are all so proud of you, Pia," Jake adds. "You refused to let that fire take you. I know how much you fear it after what happened to your family. But you fought to survive. You did good, kid. You're my hero, for sure." The others nod in agreement.

Pia knows she is lucky, not just because she survived the flames, but because, unlike her parents, she didn't have to crawl through the smoke to attempt to rescue a toddler in his crib. Her parents both perished because they refused to leave Gaetano behind. They could have jumped out a window too, but not without their baby boy. Pia knows her parents would have done the same for her had she been there. Arty did not try to save her. She knows this. He claims he tried, but she feels abandoned and betrayed.

She is getting sleepy and as her eyes close, they all tiptoe out of the room before the nurse exerts her authority and asks them to allow the patient to get some rest. They will be back later. It is time to call their employers and explain the situation. Portia thought about returning to Maryland for a few days and then coming back for Pia on Saturday, but she has a feeling in her gut that they should stick around. Jake agrees and it's his car.

26

Portia, Ben and Jake spent hours with Pia over the next few days. Arty would stop in to check on her, but he never stayed long. They had a system set up. Jake gave the volunteer in the lobby a ten-spot each morning and asked the sweet woman to alert the nurses' station whenever Arty was on his way up. Jake also brought the nurses a wicker basket that was filled with both fruit and chocolate goodies. The nurses were quick to pick up on the situation. They still thought Jake was Pia's brother, but they also understood there was bad blood between Jake and his so-called brother-in-law. And since every nurse probably had a slight crush on Jake McGuire, they all assumed the *husband* was not a very nice guy.

Whenever they got word that Arty was on his way up, Jake took the backstairs and vanished. He didn't need to confront Arty in front of Pia. Portia didn't want Arty to change his mind either. Ben would go find Jake when the coast was clear. He often found him staring through the glass wall on the fifth floor where all the newborns were snuggled in warm blankets and lying in individual acrylic bassinets. It was apparent to Ben that Jake loves kids.

On Saturday morning, Portia is helping Pia dress and the men are in the waiting room. Pia has a roommate now that she is no longer in ICU and the elderly woman gave Pia a small parting gift. It is a broach with a pair of penguins holding hands. The woman is 88 years old and she asked her granddaughter to find it at the bottom of her jewelry box that sits on her antique dresser at home. She wants Pia to have it.

"My husband gave this to me decades ago. He passed away five years ago and I suppose I'll be joining him soon enough. I want you to have this, Pia. It will remind you of our time together." Pia had mentioned that she thought penguins were cute while the woman was watching a documentary on the television. Pia's voice is returning and she enjoyed the warmth and companionship that the woman has happily provided.

"I will…treasure it," Pia whispers. The doctors told her not to strain her voice for a while and she tends to speak in short sentences. Portia continues to be boisterous and overly cheerful. The woman assumes Portia is Pia's big sister since everyone in the hospital had become a victim of Portia's deceit. Of course, Arty knows, but he is hardly around.

Arty has been busy running a restaurant and begging for charity. He raised over $11,000 from corporate, well-to-do customers, and the generosity of waitresses, bartenders and cooks. Arty isn't especially well-liked at work, but most of the staff feel sorry for poor Pia, who is still lying in the hospital with second degree burns.

Next Arty convinced his neighbor, Bonnie, to hold a neighborhood fundraiser in the weeks ahead. Arty has a shell of a house that is still sitting on a nice piece of land. He got two estimates to bring the house back to life again. One contractor said he could do it for $47,000 and the second guy offered to complete the job for $45,900. Arty decided to get a few more bids since he still doesn't know how he is going to pay for it. He still has some money in the bank, but he refuses to part with every penny since he needs a new wardrobe and basic necessities.

In the meantime, he has been sleeping in his office at work and cleaning up at the gym around the corner. One of the waitresses has begun providing him with some sexual release again and he feels he has it coming. Pia will be living in Maryland and she will hopefully never find out.

His car was miraculously salvageable, but it required $1,350 worth of work to make it drivable. At least he does have car insurance and even though he had neglected to call Frank, the policy covered most of the repairs after he paid the $200 deductible. He decided to sell the Mustang to help pay for the renovations on the house. He still needs to find another twenty-five grand and he began calling distant relatives with a sob story. A few turned him down, but most of them promised to mail checks to the restaurant.

He has accomplished a lot in a short time and he is quite proud of himself. On Thursday, he ran into his old landlord and he found out his old apartment is vacant. The previous tenant skipped town without paying the last two month's rent. He left behind a bunch of crappy furniture along with pots and pans. The landlord took pity on Arty and offered him the place for free for two months if Arty would clean up the joint and paint each room. Then they could negotiate from there.

So Arty decided to move into the old apartment on Friday morning. He got someone to cover the lunch shift and he was pretty settled in by the dinner hour. He figured Pia would be excited to move back to their old honeymoon love nest. Arty never did understand women. Pia boarded a Greyhound a year ago to escape the memories of that place.

Pia will be discharged within the hour. She looks so much better. Portia hired a hairdresser to trim her burnt, split ends and reshape her hair. The woman washed Pia's locks in the bathroom sink and trimmed them in the hospital room. Pia looks adorable with her shorter hairdo and the woman even added a few highlights. It was a gift from Portia. Portia also bought Pia a few new clothes for the trip south. She reminded her friend that Pia had left some clothes in her guestroom closet, having forgotten all about them. Pia also left some clothing behind in her own apartment. Pia's entire wardrobe didn't perish in the flames.

A nurse steps in and alerts Jake that Arty is on his way up. Jake wrinkles his nose and dashes off to visit the babies. Ben decides to accompany him. Portia was hoping they could get out of town without running into Arty since he said goodbye to Pia on Thursday, telling her he would be too busy to visit again before she was discharged.

"I guess he wants to say goodbye one more time," Portia comments while they wait. Pia nods, but she has an odd fear in her eyes.

The doctor walks in to say goodbye and compliment Pia on her progress and determination. It's the same doctor who Portia thought stepped right out of *Ben-Hur*.

"I want to wish you the best, Pia," the doctor says, warmly. He does not shake her bandaged hand, but he touches her shoulder in a comforting manner and Pia flinches just a bit.

"Thank you from both of us, Doctor," Portia says. "Everyone has been so kind to our Pia."

"I know she will be in good hands with you," Dr. Swanson responds warmly.

"Hey, hey," Arty proclaims as he interrupts the conversation.

"Hello, Mr. Thompson. I'm told Pia will be traveling to Delaware today and then she'll rest up before heading to Maryland on Sunday."

"That *was* the plan, Doc, but new plan. Pia, I got us our old apartment. Isn't that great?" Arty exclaims as if he assumes Pia will be thrilled with his news.

"I thought you were saving money to rebuild the house?" Portia asks in a panic.

"My old landlord gave me the place for free for two months. It's furnished too. I just have to clean up the dump because the previous tenant skipped town and left the place a mess. I promised to paint the place little by little over two months. It's a miracle. It's where Pia and I first lived together after our honeymoon."

"Doctor, I really feel she needs to be with me right now," Portia demands as she looks for his support.

"Mr. Thompson, will you be able to care for your wife?" the doctor asks as he sees the desperation in Portia's eyes and the confusion in Pia's face.

"A couple of my waitresses will look in on her. I figure she'll be whipping up dinner in no time. My girl is resourceful."

"Your wife will not be able to cook or do dishes for at least another month. Her hands and feet were badly burned."

"Oh, she'll probably surprise you, Doc," Arty insists. "You don't expect me to do women's work, do you?" Arty laughs. But no one else is finding any humor in his comments. "I mean real men don't wash dishes, Doc. I have to earn a living out there."

"I'm not sure you understand the full extent of your wife's injuries, Mr. Thompson. She still has a long way to go."

"Well, I think I know what's best for my wife, Doc. No offense, intended."

"Mr. Thompson, can I ask you a personal question?" the doctor responds.

"Sure."

"When you woke up and realized your home was on fire, you said you were downstairs and your wife was trapped upstairs. What did you do to help her?"

"I called out and told her to wet some towels like I was doing."

"And then what happened?"

"The fire got hotter and the smoke was really bad. I had to get out of there."

"Did you even attempt to climb the stairs…to help your wife?"

"Come on, Doc, don't make me out to be the bad guy here," Arty laughs. "You don't expect a guy to just walk through fire, do you? I mean I'm not Superman."

"I think I would have tried in your shoes. There were no burns on your hands or feet. You didn't even try. I'm not getting the feeling you appreciate how much your wife is going to be relying on you over the coming months."

"Well, you might walk into fire to save your wife, but if I was that stupid, neither one of us would be able to earn a paycheck right now. It's bad enough I have to support her now that she can't work, but at least I saved myself so I can keep working at my job. But I'm sure Pia will be back on the job in a few weeks."

Dr. Swanson senses the despair in Pia's eyes. He makes a decision. He tells Arty he wants to run another blood test before signing the discharge papers. He suggests that Arty should plan to bring Pia home around 3pm. Arty nods and tells Pia he'll see her later.

As he leaves, Ben is watching from down the hall. He goes to get Jake. Meanwhile, the roommate, 88-year-old Mabel Morrison, has heard the entire conversation while she lay quietly in the next bed.

"I am so sorry to stick my nose in where it doesn't belong," Mabel begins. "But I was married to a wonderful man for over a half a century and I know what a good man looks like. I have serious doubts dear about your going home with that man."

"Mrs. Morrison has a point, Pia," Dr. Swanson interjects. "I don't think your husband is prepared to take care of you right now. Perhaps he is still in shock himself. It has been a difficult week for you both."

"Oh, he's not in shock. That's just Arty being Arty," Portia mumbles.

"I need...blood...test?" Pia asks.

"No, I can sign you out now," the doctor responds. I just wanted to buy you a few hours to reconsider your situation. In my medical opinion, you would be better served going with your sister to Maryland right now. I can't make this decision for you, but I am worried about you going home with a man who seems to be very confused about your medical condition."

Jake and Ben walk in and quickly get the gist of what has just transpired. Portia is angry, but she is attempting to keep her cool in front of the doctor. She and Pia keep shooting each other looks with the same silent code they have used for years. Living in the orphanage bonded them and in many ways they *are* sisters.

"What do you want to do?" Jake asks Pia. He is gentle with his tone, but his eyes are pleading with her to go with him.

"Arty...said...he...not...stupid...Said...stupid...man... walks...through...fire." She seems exhausted from her comment and she lies back against the pillow and begins to weep. She curls into a fetal position and trembles and Portia instinctively covers her with the blanket.

"I'm very concerned about this situation," the doctor says with a wrinkled brow. He can see Pia is emotionally regressing. He has been told about her phobias. He knows she needs psychological counseling which Portia has promised to provide for Pia. He also knows she needs wound treatments for her burns and tender loving care. The thought of Pia going home to her husband seems utterly unthinkable.

"Don't discharge her, Doc," Mabel demands. "Keep her here a few more days."

"Pia, would you like me to drive you back to Maryland?" Jake whispers as he gets close to the bed. "We'll spend the night in a hotel in Delaware so you don't have to make the trip in one day."

"We'll take care of you, Pia," Portia insists in a comforting, nurturing tone.

"I'll help take care of you too, Pia," Ben adds.

Pia continues to rock and the doctor believes she is shutting down emotionally. She appears to be overwhelmed and conflicted and he needs to see other patients. But he cannot leave her like this. He is not a psychologist, but he knows trauma and Pia is slipping away, regressing into a childlike confusion as she continues to rock in silence.

"Stay here, Pia. Stay with me for a little longer," Mabel offers.

"I wish it was that simple," the doctor utters. "The hospitalist has already signed off on her discharge. I could try to get her a bed in a rehabilitation facility. I could have the nurse contact social services and put a rush on it. I could certainly make an excuse to keep Pia here one more night."

"I don't think she has the financial resources for that," Portia insists, assuming Pia's work insurance may not pay for a rehabilitation facility, hoping Pia will still opt to return to Maryland.

"I'll order some tests to delay her release another day, that's the best I can do," the doctor proclaims. "I'll also have social services check on her insurance and see if there's a bed in a facility in the area."

"Wait…wait…wait," Pia begins to chant in a hoarse whisper. Jake falls to his knees and puts his face close to her. Their noses are nearly touching like Eskimos in love.

"What do you want to say, Pia?" Jake whispers as he plants his index finger on her cheek once again and wipes away a tear.

There is an eerie silence in the room as Mabel and Dr. Swanson continue to stare at the small figure under the blanket who is trembling with despair. Ben places an arm around Portia's shoulder to comfort her. Pia finally speaks.

"Jake…not stupid…Jake not stupid…Jake not stupid."

Everyone stares at Pia and then at one another in confusion. But Jake understands. He knows he told her he would walk through fire for her…step into the flames for her. Pia continues to babble as the others attempt to make some sense out of what she is trying to say.

"Jake…not stupid…Jake…would…step…into…flames. Jake…would…save…me." Then she goes silent again and continues to rock with bent knees and a slight whimper.

"She knows that moron of a husband didn't try to save her," Mabel exclaims. "She knows her brother would have tried."

"I'm not actually her brother," Jake finally admits.

"Then who are you?" the doctor asks with a perplexed look.

"I'm her friend. I'm in love with her. And I *would* step into the flames for her. I wouldn't think twice."

"It's a long story," Portia mumbles.

"And are you really her sister?" the doctor demands.

"Not exactly, but we are like sisters," Portia admits, sheepishly. "We grew up in an orphanage together."

"And I'm *her* fiancé," Ben adds with a goofy grin.

"I don't know what to say," the doctor mutters.

"Well, it's obvious they all care about Pia a great deal more than that idiot of a husband cares about her," Mabel insists as she claps her hands together. This is better than her favorite soap opera.

"I fell in love with Pia before I knew she was married. She had left him and was living in Maryland," Jake admits. "We have never even kissed. But I love her, Doc, with all my heart. I've never felt this way about anyone before. I would have run though the fire to save her."

"I believe you, son, I actually believe you," the doctor says with a nod. It has been quite a morning. He watches Jake use a single finger to continue to wipe Pia's tears. He is overwhelmed by the love he sees in Jake's eyes.

"Take her to Maryland. I'll deal with the husband when he comes for her. Take her with you if she'll agree. It's best for her. She'll get the love and care she needs there. She has a psychologist there who knows here. Take her. I'll sign the discharge now. Pia, do you hear me? I am advising you to go with these nice people. They may not be your blood relatives, but I can see they are your family. I can see they care about you very much."

"They love her," Mabel proclaims with glee. "And don't forget the penguins. They will bring the two of you luck, Jake. They're like a pair of lovebirds."

"Pia, Pia, will you come with us?" Jake whispers. Everyone freezes. They barely breathe in anticipation as they all await her response. "Pia, will you come stay with Portia?" Jake asks again.

"I'll make you spaghetti and meatballs," Ben calls out to break the silence.

Pia opens her closed eyelids and looks up at Ben. "I…prefer…linguini."

"You got it, linguini it is, smothered in marinara sauce, just like your grandmother used to make for you," Ben proclaims with a laugh.

"OK…let's…get…the…hell…out…of…here," Pia whispers.

The room erupts with laughter. Portia nods and mumbles to herself. "That's my girl, that's my girl."

"I'll miss you, Pia," Mabel calls out.

"Miss…you…too." She sits up and Jake helps her to stand by supporting her elbow. She doesn't flinch. Instead she allows him to touch her as she turns and shoots him a hidden smile. She trusts him with her life. The doctor goes to complete the paperwork. He promises they will be on their way within twenty minutes.

"Nurse, order a wheelchair. Pia Thompson is being discharged," Dr. Swanson demands with a smile.

"I'm…going…home," Pia whispers to Portia.

"Yes you are, sweetheart. You are going home."

Jake wants to draw her injured body into his arms and fill her with his strength, but he knows he cannot. She is fragile, but he believes in her. He believes in that farmer's porch and he refuses to give up on his dream. He can only see one person sitting beside him in his old age. And that person is Pia, the girl who helped him find a ripe cantaloupe.

27

P ortia sits in the backseat with Pia as they arrive at the hotel in Delaware. Pia slept most of the way and she is grateful that her friend got some rest. Jake has two rooms reserved. He and Ben will bunk together tonight, much to Ben's obvious disappointment, and Portia will stay with Pia. The road to recovery is going to be riddled with challenges, but the three of them are up to the task. Jake would do anything for Pia. As would Portia. And Ben will do anything for Portia. She teased him about the marinara sauce and he admitted he planned to buy store-bought jar sauce, but he would doctor it up with fresh garlic and basil.

After they settle into their rooms, Jake goes out for takeout and quickly returns with a feast, enough to feed the entire sixth floor of the hotel. Ben salivates with hunger and Portia laughs when she sees Pia's eyes open wide with wonder. She still only eats soft foods and Jake bought plenty of mashed potatoes and apple sauce.

"Can you eat something?" Portia asks Pia. Pia nods. They set up a makeshift tray table so Pia can eat in bed and the others crowd around the desk in the women's hotel room. Jake dragged in a chair from his room.

"I could eat a horse," Ben mutters as he dives in.

"There's enough food here to feed two horses," Portia laughs. Then she looks up after serving herself and notices Jake is on the bed next to Pia. He is sitting up, cross-legged, feeding her as if she is his child, his fragile, young child. She wipes a tear of joy from her cheek as she witnesses such utter devotion with a lump in her throat and a warmth in her heart.

"He adores her," she whispers to Ben.

"Yup," he mumbles with a mouthful of steak.

"I love this guy," Portia murmurs very softly.

"As much as you love me?" Ben prompts as he gulps down his meat.

"No, sweetie, you're my man, but he is pretty great, isn't he?"

"Yeah, if I was gay, I'd go for him," Ben jests.

"So that's what you meant by an open relationship?" she jokes.

"No, that open thing is closed shut. I only have eyes for you, babe."

"And Jake only has eyes for Pia," Portia whispers as she picks at her broccoli. She says a silent prayer to the universe that Arty will divorce her quickly and move on. Pia's future is in the hands of Jake McGuire now in her humble opinion. As she watches him gently feeding her friend, carefully dabbing her chin clean with a paper napkin, she takes a deep breath. Pia is wearing the penguin broach from Mabel. She hopes it will bring Pia and Jake good luck.

The next morning, Pia seems to have suffered an emotional setback. It was a rough night of tormented dreams and restless tossing and turning. Portia didn't sleep well either since Pia's suffering became her own. Twice during the night, Portia rose from her bed and fetched a cool washcloth to place on Pia's forehead while the younger woman mumbled words of terror in her sleep. Portia feared Pia was running a fever, but by morning, her temperature appeared to be stable.

"You had a hard night," Portia mutters as she helps Pia dress. Jake is already out picking up some breakfast for everyone while Ben showers.

"I know…dreaming…about…fire. Crawling…through… smoke…trying to…find Gaetano. Crib…miles…away. Reaching …for me…crying…moaning…so…awful…"

"I'm so sorry, baby," Portia whispers as she places a hand on Pia's shoulder to comfort her. "Is it OK if I touch your shoulder?" Pia nods and forces a slight smile of appreciation.

Jake is at the door with a knock and Portia stands to let him in. She can smell the coffee as the door opens to reveal a gleaming smile and a look of boyish charm in his eyes.

"Looks like you got a good night's sleep," she comments as she opens the door wider so he can carry in the two large bags.

"I took your advice and didn't go overboard on the food," he exclaims as his eyes scan the room to find her fully clothed, but still in bed. "Good morning gorgeous," he calls to her and she smiles as much as she is able. Her face still hurts from the burns, but not nearly as badly as her feet and hands. The neck bandage has been removed and her burn looks more like a mark left by an aggressive lover.

"Hi," Pia whispers as their eyes meet.

"I'll go check on my roomie," Jake says as he drops the food on the desk.

Portia shuts the door, but leaves it open a crack before unwrapping breakfast sandwiches and finally discovering a container of soft scrambled eggs. She tests them to see if they are too hot for Pia and then she attempts to get her friend to eat a bite. Pia cannot tolerate anything too hot just yet, but Jake brought bottles of orange and apple juice with straws for Pia.

As Portia helps Pia take a few sips of apple juice and eat a couple of bites of soft eggs, Ben arrives with Jake on his heels. The boys are rowdy and wide awake at such an early hour. They hope to be on the road by half past nine. Jake wants to get to Portia's place well before rush hour as the beltway will be crammed with cars by four.

"Morning everyone," Ben says with a smile. "I'm starved."

"After all the food you ate last night, I would think your tummy would still be full," Portia teases.

"Hey, I'm still a growing boy. Last night's dinner is either gone or it's in my lower intestines. My stomach is empty."

"OK, far too much information for me," Jake laughs as he sips on caffeine and grabs a sandwich.

"How did you ladies sleep?" Ben asks, but Portia doesn't need to answer. He can see the fatigue in her face with her tired eyes and her look of sheer exhaustion. Ben nods and begins to eat. There is little to be said. They all know it will be rough sailing ahead for Pia, but they continue to be consumed with optimism.

They check out of the hotel at 9:20am and are soon on their way back to Maryland. Delaware is a small state and the welcome sign soon greets them. Traffic will start to get heavier as they approach the Capital Region, but Jake knows the roads and Pia seems to be more herself as Portia continues to entertain her in the backseat.

When they finally arrive at Portia's place, the men help Pia navigate the front steps. They do not dare touch her arms due to her phobia and her burns, but they hold doors, carry stuff, and make sure her path is clear. Portia gets Pia into bed so she can get some sleep. The pain meds make her sleepy, but they also ease her suffering, and for that, they are all grateful.

"Is she asleep?" Ben asks as he sits perched on the sofa with a beer in his right hand.

"Out like a light. She seems calm now, perfectly still, like watching a baby take a nap. She looks so pretty."

"She's still gorgeous," Jake pronounces, "she just doesn't know it."

"Arty said something to the doctor," Portia whispers, "about not being stupid enough to face the flames and attempt to rescue her on that awful night. You told Pia you would have run through the flames to save her, didn't you Jake?" Portia asks. Jake nods. She knows he meant it.

"Jake would do anything for Pia," Ben agrees as he takes another gulp of his cold beer.

"And would you do the same for me?" Portia teases.

"You know I would sweet girl," Ben declares. "I'm the luckiest guy on the planet. I can't wait for our wedding day."

"So what's the plan with regard to Pia's apartment?" Jake asks.

"She will stay here until she is much better. When she's ready, I hope she'll move back in and never go back to New York."

"And Ben?"

"He'll move in here. We will be looking for a bigger place in a few months. I want us settled well before the big day."

"Did you guys pick a date for the wedding?" Jake asks.

"August 4th. Pia will be my matron of honor. If she's divorced by then, I guess she'll be my maid of honor."

"And how would you like to be my best man?" Ben asks Jake.

"I thought you asked your brother?" Portia interrupts.

"He chickened out. He's afraid to make the toast, the guy's got stage fright. And he doesn't want to plan a bachelor party. He's kind of reserved."

"Like you?" Portia teases.

"We're complete opposites. He'll be one of the groomsmen along with my two cousins."

"So you are in need of a best man?" Jake asks with a sly grin.

"Yeah, and since we slept together last night, I figure we've bonded a bit."

"We slept in separate beds," Jake declares with a defensive grin as he glances over at Portia.

"Oh, me thinks my fiancé has a man crush," she jokes.

"Well we did spend nearly a week together in New York. Jake's my buddy now."

"And I would be honored to be your best man, bro," Jake says as they high-five each other as if they are on the basketball court and their team just scored.

"Which means you would be partners with Pia in the wedding party," Portia mentions with a serendipitous smile.

"Exactly," Jake agrees with a shrewd grin.

"Now we just have to make sure Arty doesn't attend the wedding," Ben laughs.

"Well, we're certainly not adding him to the guest list, he'll only be there if Pia brings him."

"Can I ask you a serious question?" Jake asks Portia.

"Shoot," she says. "I'm all ears."

"Do you think she'll go back to him?"

"I really don't know. If she does, it's not because she's crazy about the creep."

"Then why?"

"Pia's funny. When she left him, she was determined to never see him again. But in some ways, he has become her family too and she yearns for family, for familiarity. She also feels obligated now that he has proclaimed himself a changed man."

"But did he really change?" Jake prompts.

"I doubt it. I think he runs around on her, especially because of her fear of being touched."

"And he physically attacked Jake," Ben adds. "It's not like Jake was such a threat to him. I think the guy is possessive for sure."

"But does he really love her?" Jake challenges.

"I doubt he is capable of loving anyone. He's such a jerk. I think Pia knows that. She is so torn."

"One more question. I know you guys like me, but how much do you think Pia likes me?" Jake asks with an anxious look like a schoolboy who so wants to hang out with the popular kids.

"I think she likes you a lot," Ben says.

"I think she likes you more than ever, Jake," Portia adds. "When you were feeding her dinner last night, she looked so fragile, but her eyes followed your every movement with a look of true appreciation. She was really looking at you with adoration in her eyes, Jake. I think she is falling in love with you, but she is so conflicted between her marriage to that controlling jerk in New York, her phobia about being touched, and now her traumatic experience where she nearly died in the fire. All her fears must have come to a head when she sensed the house was burning. I can't imagine what's she's feeling. She's still in pain from her injuries, but she is suffering emotionally as well. She had an awful night and I hardly slept either. I'm hoping to get some real sleep tonight. You should stay over, Ben. We can take shifts keeping an eye on her."

"Will you hire a nurse?" Jake asks.

"Yes, I'm calling on Monday morning, first thing."

"And you really think I'm still a six and a half in Pia's eyes?" Jake asks, sheepishly.

"I think you're closer to a nine, bro," Ben interrupts. "We can't all be tens," he laughs.

"I think Ben's right, even if he is teasing you. You're up there Jake. She adores you. She's just fighting all her feelings because Arty has her confused and after all she's been through."

"I can't believe that jerk buys Pia a car and now he plans to sell it on her," Ben adds. "Can he sell it without her approval, Jake?"

"He'll just forge the paperwork," Jake mutters. "It's not that hard to pull off."

"She won't be needing a car for a long time," Portia comments.

"And I'll buy her another one," Jake insists. "I'll keep an eye out for the perfect used car with low mileage. I'm also happy to chauffer her anywhere she needs to go."

"You're really a good guy, Jake," Ben says. "I'm really glad you're going to be my best man."

"Well, no strippers at the bachelor party," Portia demands with a smirk.

"Oh, man…" Ben teases.

"Who needs strippers when you have such a beautiful fiancé," Jake says to Ben.

"Oh, you just became a ten in my book," Portia declares with a broad smile.

"I thought I was your only ten?" Ben protests.

"You're a ten and a half, babe, but no strippers."

"OK," Ben agrees with an exaggerated frown as he feigns a little mock disappointment.

"I hope I can become a ten in Pia's eyes," Jake mumbles to himself. "I didn't want to wreck her marriage, but that guy is all wrong for her. Even if I can't have her, I still can't see her with him."

"Amen, Brother," Ben says as he finishes his beer.

"I'll call Dr. Forte on Monday right after I hire a nurse," Portia says. "As soon as Pia is up to it, I'll take her to see her former psychologist. Pia has a lot of healing to do on the outside, but especially on the inside."

"Thank heavens for Dr. Forte," Ben agrees with a nod.

"Pia is really lucky to have you guys too," Jake says.

"And you, Jake," Portia adds. "She's smitten with you, I know she is. Just hang in there. You're the guy who said he would walk through fire for her."

"And I meant it," Jake adds.

"I have no doubt," Portia agrees with a comforting look. Jake is a keeper in her eyes and she is confident Pia will soon concur.

28

Portia is driving Pia to meet with Dr. Forte. It is early December and Pia's primary physician is quite pleased with her progress. Her voice has returned and she is able to walk in soft slippers now without the aid of a walker. The nurses stopped coming before Thanksgiving. Portia gave her an early Christmas present last night, a pair of camel-colored UGG boots. Pia decided to wear them this morning. It is her first time wearing something other than slippers since the fire.

"How do the boots feel?" Portia asks as she navigates DC traffic like a pro.

"They feel OK, just a little weird after not wearing shoes for so long."

"Well, I have your slippers in my bag if you want to switch."

"Thanks, you take such good care of me."

"I know you would do the same for me," Portia comments, sweetly.

"You know I would."

"I'm just thrilled with your progress," Portia says.

They arrive at the appointment a few minutes early. Portia brought one of her romance novels to read. It is Pia's first appointment since the fire and Portia hopes she will stick around long enough to face her fears. Pia has not said a word about returning to New York.

Arty calls about once a week to check on his wife. If Jake were Pia's husband, Portia believes he would be calling three for four times a day…every day. Arty usually drones on about work and the house renovations.

"Pia, it's wonderful to see you," Dr. Forte exclaims with a warm smile. Pia introduces Portia to her doctor.

"I'm so pleased to finally meet you, Portia," the psychologist says with a firm handshake. She knows better than to attempt to touch Pia. They did shake hands a few times in the past, but much has changed. Dr. Forte notices the burns on Pia's hands and she winces. The bandages have been removed, but the scarring and blistering are apparent, especially on her right hand. But she says nothing.

"I'll be right here when you are finished, Pia," Portia says as she opens her book. It's a story about an abusive husband and Portia already has an image of the creep in her head. He looks just like Arty.

"So, Pia, I like your boots."

"They're new, an early Christmas present from Portia and Ben. I haven't worn anything but slippers since the fire. This is my first venture into footwear."

"Are the burns on your feet still painful?" she asks.

"Yes, but not nearly as much as before."

"Can you talk about the fire?"

"I suppose. I woke up thinking it was one of my nightmares. I almost just went back to sleep, thinking it was not real. But then reality set in fast as smoke began to fill the guestroom. We were waiting for a delivery in a few days, a new bedroom set for the master. Arty had been sleeping downstairs on the sofa. We never did anything but hug during the time I was back in New York, and only a couple of times. He bought me a new Mustang and I hugged him for that. But now he has sold the car to pay for house repairs. He never bought fire insurance."

"Well, that's a lot to digest. I'm sorry there's no insurance."

"Arty has been raising money. Relatives, neighbors, coworkers...that's helping."

"How do you feel about him selling your new car? I didn't even know you finally got your license."

"Arty taught me. I don't care about the car. I have other things to worry about that are far more important."

"So back to the fire, once you realized you were trapped, what happened next?"

"I thought about wetting some towels, but I couldn't get to the hall bathroom. The guestroom doorknob was hot. I stuffed a blanket under the door, but smoke was still getting in from the top and sides. I just tore the sheets off the bed and made a rope. I tied it to the bedframe and threw it out the window. I didn't bother to grab anything. I was in a nightgown. So I just hung out the window and then grabbed the sheets and tried to lower myself. I remember coughing a lot and then I slipped and fell into the bushes."

"How did you get so burned?"

"The fire seemed to come out of nowhere. I guess I got out of there in the nick of time. As I was making the rope, it came through the door, through the walls. The curtains around the window were on fire when I escaped. It's weird. I don't remember the fire hurting while I was trying to climb out the window. The only memory I have is struggling to open the window. It was stuck. I was going to try to break the glass, when it finally budged. I think it was painted shut. I usually used a window on the other wall. I had never opened this window before, but the drop from the other window would have been much harder. I would have fallen on the driveway. The bushes and grass seemed like the better choice."

"So then what happened?"

"I think I started crawling towards the woods and then I woke up in the hospital."

"And your husband?"

"He said he screamed to wake me, yelling for me to wet some towels, but I never heard him. He finally ran outside because the fire was so bad. He said our neighbors called the fire department and the nice man tried to put out the fire on the porch with a regular hose."

"I assume the damage to the house was extensive?"

"Yes, I lost everything. I did leave some clothes behind at my old apartment and at Portia's. She also bought me some new stuff."

"So, you're back living with Portia?"

"For now. Ben has been subletting my place. He and Portia are getting married in August."

"And what are your plans for 1984?"

"Portia thinks I should move back to my apartment when I am better and then Ben will move in with her. They'll be looking for a bigger place when her lease expires. She wants to fix a new place up before they get married. I'm supposed to be her maid of honor or matron of honor, whatever I am."

"Matron of honor if you stay married," Dr. Forte comments.

"And Jake is going to be Ben's best man."

"Tell me more about Jake."

"Well, you know how I met him in grocery stores and then we went out a few times?"

"I remember."

"He drove Portia and Ben to New York. They all stayed almost a week until I was discharged from the hospital. Then they drove me back. Jake stopped in Delaware for a night to make the trip easier on me. I was a mess, but I am so much better. I could barely even talk and I was on major painkillers. But I'm done with the pills and my skin is healing."

"What about your fear of fire?"

"You know, Dr. Forte, I still have nightmares. But I think I'm starting to be less afraid. I keep dreaming about trying to save my brother, crawling through the smoke. If I had to save a child when our house burned, I probably would have died just like my mother. But I only had to save myself. I think I have been haunted with the notion that the fire was still trying to get me. I escaped the flames because I was at Nonna's house, but I have lived in fear that the fire was still looking for me."

"You talk about fire as if it is a living thing, like a demon or a devil that is stalking you."

"That's how I think I have been feeling for years. Every time I saw a flame, even a candle, it scared me. I thought the flame was trying to get me."

"And now you feel like you are facing your fears?"

"Well, I certainly didn't plan it that way. But when the curtains started to burn, I didn't panic. I just saved myself."

"And your husband never climbed the stairs to help you?"

"No, he told the doctor in the hospital that only a stupid person would have done that. He said he saved himself so he could work and rebuild the house."

"Did he think you died in the fire?"

"At first, I guess. The firemen found me out behind the house."

"How do you feel about his not trying harder to help you?"

"I don't know. I'm sure he was a little drunk and not thinking straight."

"Any idea on how the fire started?"

"I think he was smoking and fell asleep."

"Do you blame him for the fire?"

"It was a stupid accident. I do blame him for not buying a fire extinguisher. He was supposed to pick one up at the restaurant supply store. He goes there all the time. But he kept forgetting. He also never bought fire insurance. He said he kept forgetting to call Frank."

"Who?"

"His insurance agent. At one point he bragged about all the money he saved us by having no insurance."

"What did you say?"

"I told him to stop pushing his luck."

"Jake must care about you."

"He does. He didn't even know I was married at first, and then I told him I was saving for a divorce."

"So before the fire, how *were* things in New York?"

"I started a new job. That was OK, I guess. I figured out Arty was cheating on me. He claimed he was having sex with three different waitresses. But he said it was just sex. I made him promise to stop. But then I did something that is totally out of character for me."

"What did you do?"

"I went to the restaurant for lunch. Then I told Arty I wanted to use his office to speak to all three waitresses one at a time."

"How did he react?"

"He wasn't happy, but he didn't want a scene."

"And how did that go?"

"The first two apologized and promised it was over. The third one was unapologetic and rude," Pia says with a hint of anger.

"What did you do?"

I told the first two I hoped I wouldn't have to come back to discuss this again. I told them I wouldn't be nearly as nice the next time. Then I told Arty to fire the third one."

"Did he?"

"He said he was afraid of being sued for harassment."

"So he kept her on?"

"I made him promise to keep cutting her hours back until she quit."

"Good for you."

"I still don't trust him. He's probably back to his old ways as we speak."

"How does that make you feel?"

"A part of me understands. I wasn't letting him touch me. Just before the fire, he asked me if we could sleep together when the new bedroom set arrived, at least for one night. He promised to do nothing but cuddle."

"What did you say?"

"I said maybe. Of course the set never arrived. At least we didn't lose that in the fire."

"Will you give him another chance when you fully recover?"

"I don't know. I guess that's part of the reason I'm here with you."

"Tell me more about Jake."

"He's fantastic. I told him Arty was never more than a three or four out of ten in terms of his character and my attraction to him. Maybe when he bought me the Mustang, he rose to a five for a few hours. But then he admitted to having sex with three other women."

"And his number plunged?" Dr. Forte suggests.

"To a zero."

"Did you ever rate Jake?"

"It was actually his idea to rate Arty. It was kind of a game. Then I rated him as a six. Later, he rose to a six and a half."

"And now?"

"I guess he's a seven and a half, but only because I'm married and I keep suppressing my romantic interest in him."

"Let's pretend that Arty is no longer in the picture. He divorces you and marries one of those waitresses. Could you get more involved with Jake?"

"I'm still afraid of sex, I haven't even hugged Jake."

"You haven't touched at all?"

"He wiped away a tear on my cheek in the hospital, just with one finger. Then you know what he did?"

"What?"

"He licked his finger to swallow my tear."

"Oh, he cares for you a great deal," Dr. Forte laughs.

"I know, he doesn't hide it very well. And he is so patient. He fed me my dinner in Delaware, at the hotel. He was so nurturing, so sweet."

"I like this man."

"I do too. I guess he's really a solid eight in my mind. He could be a ten if Arty was out of the picture and I allow myself to touch and be touched."

"Which is what you and I are working on. You'll get there. I have no doubt. And Jake seems like he is willing to give you all the time you need."

"He says he's still a virgin, saving himself."

"And you still believe him."

"Definitely. I just don't know if I'm the right girl for him."

"Suppose he found a wonderful girl, how would that make you feel?"

"I would be happy for him. I care about him. But…I would miss him…terribly."

"That says a lot. I suspect you are falling in love with Jake. You're not the teenager you once were. You have grown a lot, Pia."

"I'm almost 22 now."

"And you confronted the fire and refused to allow it to take you."

"I guess."

"I advise you not to make any rash decisions. Heal your body. Heal your mind and you will know what you want. Just don't feel obligated to stay in a marriage where the guy is vacillating between a zero and a five."

"Oh, Arty has been a negative number too," she laughs.

"And don't feel some kind of misplaced loyalty to a guy who abandoned you and didn't try to save your from the flames."

"You know what Jake said?"

"What?"

"He said he would have stepped into the flames to save me. He said he would walk through fire for me."

"OK, he is either a player with a great line, or he is a definite ten."

"He's not player. He's a ten, at least for some lucky girl."

"You may be that girl."

"Then why can't I let him hug me?"

"Try, just a short hug. I want you to try something. Stay seated. I want you to give me a short hug. Will you try?"

"OK."

Dr. Forte rises from her chair and steps closer. She opens her arms slowly and waits for Pia to do the same. The hug is brief, but Pia doesn't flinch. Then Dr. Forte sits back down.

"Was it terrible?" she laughs.

"No, it was fine. It was nice. I trust you."

"Do you trust Arty?"

"No, the time I hugged him for buying me the car, he grabbed my breast."

"Do you trust Jake?"

"With my life. I think I would walk through fire for him."

"That pretty much says it all."

"I still feel like I killed my parents…and Gaetano. I still live with that guilt."

"I want to try something else. Have I ever said anything to you about *telescoping*?"

"I think you mentioned it once."

"In cognitive psychology, there is a theory that refers to the temporal displacement of events. People sometimes perceive recent events as being more remote than they are and distant events as being more recent. You were in the orphanage a little over three years ago. Backwards telescoping or time expansion may be causing you to think the orphanage was a very long time ago. Your mind may have blurred out many of the sad memories at the orphanage, which is fine. Forward expansion causes you to continually relive that moment when you stuck the knife into the toaster, the moment that haunts your dreams."

"So I keep thinking about the day of the fire, when I was only four, as if it happened more recently?"

"Precisely. Do you remember what you had for breakfast on the day Arty bought you the car?"

"No, I barely remember what I had for breakfast today," Pia laughs.

"But you remember sticking the knife in the toaster as if it just occurred?"

"Yes."

"I want you to close your eyes. I'm not going to try to hypnotize you, I'm just going to relax your mind a bit and bring back that day."

"I trust you." Pia closes her eyes and the doctor continues speaking to her in a soft, lulling voice. Had she taken a pain pill with breakfast, she would likely doze right off. As Pia becomes more relaxed, Dr. Forte lowers the lights. She keeps talking to her, repeating certain phrases. Finally, after about ten minutes, she asks Pia a question.

"Think about the day you stuck the knife in the toaster, were there sparks?"

"I   think   so."
"Were the lights flickering?"
"I think so."
"Try to remember what you were wearing. Smell the burnt toast. Can you smell it.?"
"Yes."
"The toast is stuck. What is the first thing you do? Do you unplug the toaster?"
"No…I pick up my little paper plate. I pick up my little knife…"
"Why is the knife so little?"
"I'm not sure."
"Is it a child's knife?"
"I think it's pink?"
"Is it made of plastic?"
"I think so. Yes, it's a pink, plastic knife."
"What happens next?"
"I stick the pink knife in the toaster."
"And there are sparks then?"
"No, but the toast is still stuck."
"What happens next?"
"I unplug the toaster."
"Then what happens?"
"The toaster falls off the counter and my father comes rushing in and helps me."
"Are the lights flickering?"
"No, the lights were off…but my daddy turns them on when he runs into the kitchen."
"What happens next?"
"He hugs me to see if I'm injured."
"Then what?"
"I'm crying. I made a mess on the floor. There are crumbs all over the floor."
"Then what happens."
"My daddy picks up the toaster. He sits me down and fixes me some cereal. He is not mad at me. I am eating corn flakes now. He adds some sugar and I laugh. I don't like too much milk. It makes them too soggy."
"Are you eating?"
"Yes, I'm eating with my pink spoon, my plastic spoon."
"What is your daddy doing?"
"Cleaning my mess and telling me everything is OK."

"What happens next?"

"My mommy and Gaetano come in the kitchen. Gaetano just had his bath. Mommy is carrying him…he is playing with the light switch. The lights keep going on and off. Mommy puts him in his highchair. The lights are on again."

"What happens next?"

"Mommy and Daddy are laughing. Gaetano is eating some dry Cheerios. He is throwing the broken ones on the floor. Daddy is sweeping them up. I'm laughing. Gaetano is laughing. Mommy is laughing."

"What happens next?"

"I'm with Nonna. We're at her house…dancing…dancing in her kitchen."

"What happens next?"

"I'm crying. I'm in bed. Nonna is holding me. She is rocking me. I keep crying."

"Now what happens?"

"We are at the cemetery. Nonna is crying. Other people are talking. Some are crying."

"What are you doing?"

"Staring…staring at the holes in the ground."

"Now what happens?"

"Nonna and I are singing in her kitchen. I'm bigger. I'm holding a breadstick…like it's a microphone."

"So, you aren't four anymore?"

"No, I'm older…older…older." Pia stops talking. Dr. Forte stops asking questions. She brings up the lights and waits for a bit. Pia is silent. Finally, she tells Pia to open her eyes.

"How are you feeling?"

"Confused," Pia says.

"Why?"

"The flickering of the lights…it was Gaetano…he was playing with the light switch…I was eating corn flakes. I didn't like Cheerios. Gaetano liked Cheerios. He was playing with them, throwing the broken one on the floor. Daddy kept sweeping…sweeping up the crumbs from the toast….sweeping up Cheerios…"

"Tell me about the spoon."

"It was my favorite spoon. It was pink, my pink, plastic spoon. I brought it to Nonna's after that. It didn't burn in the fire. I still have it. It is one of the few things I saved. I hid it in the orphanage so other girls didn't steal it. I still have it. I think it's at my old apartment. I have to find it. I'll ask Ben to look for it."

"And the spoon came with a fork and a knife?"

"Yes, it was a set, but I don't have the knife or fork. I think they must have burned up in the fire."

"But you used the knife to free the toast that was stuck?"

"Yes, I used my pink knife."

"So, there were no sparks?"

"I guess not. I thought there were sparks. I remembering the lights were flickering."

"Gaetano was playing with the lights?"

"Yes, but that was after Daddy picked up the toaster and gave me my cereal. Then he swept up the burnt toast crumbs. Then he swept up the broken Cheerios."

"So the knife couldn't have caused the toaster to spark. Not if it was plastic."

"I guess not. Why do I remember sparks?"

"Do you have any ideas?"

"No, it's too blurry. I was so young. But I remember the plastic knife….and the plastic spoon. I don't know where the fork was. Gaetano was playing with a toy…Daddy bought him a toy that you wind up."

"What kind of toy?"

"I think it made noise and…and…it…made….some kind of sparks. I think the toy made sparks….but not real sparks….just fake sparks."

"So your memory of the sparks and the flickering lights was one of your last memories of Gaetano. It had nothing to do with the toaster?"

"I guess not."

"How do you feel?"

"Better…I don't think I caused the fire."

"I don't think the fire had anything to do with you, Pia."

"So why do I still feel guilty?"

"Because you survived by going to Nonna's house. You weren't there to try to help them?"

"How could I save them? I was only four?"

"There is a silver lining, Pia. One of your family survived. Think about Nonna. Think about her life had you died in the fire with your parents and Gaetano. How would Nonna have gone on without you?"

"She would have been so sad…"

"A part of Gaetano and your mother and father lives on in your memories. Your life is an extension of their lives. Don't you think they would want you to live?"

"Yes, I guess."

"Did you and Nonna have happy times over the years?"

"So many, so many happy times. I was twelve and a half when I lost her. I'll never forget Nonna."

"Do you have any happy memories about your parents and your brother?"

"I remember Mommy was fat just before Gaetano came home from the hospital. I remember she looked very happy."

"Can you pull their faces from your memory?"

"I looked at photographs of them so many times. I lost most of them when they took me to the orphanage. I don't know what happened to Nonna's picture albums. Mommy's pictures burned in the fire. Where are all of Nonna's albums?"

"Do you have any of her pictures?"

"Just a few. I saved them with my spoon. I hid them in a box under my bed at the orphanage."

"Could you bring me the pictures the next time you come see me? I would like to see photographs of your family."

"I'll bring the pink spoon too."

"That would be fine."

"I don't think I caused the fire."

"Neither do I, Pia, neither do I."

"I didn't kill my parents?"

"No, Pia, it was just a terrible accident."

"I didn't kill Gaetano?"

"No, Pia, you didn't kill anyone."

"I survived…because I was with Nonna. Nonna needed me. I needed her. We needed each other."

"You did. And you were lucky to have one another for all those years."

"But then she died and I became so sad."

"That's perfectly natural."

"But when I think of Nonna, it no longer makes me sad. It makes me smile. Ben made me linguini and meatballs like my grandmother used to do. His sauce wasn't very good, but I lied. I told him it was just like Nonna's sauce."

"That was very nice of you to spare his feelings."

"I'll teach him how to make sauce when I feel better. I still remember how to do it."

"Did you make sauce for Arty?"

"No, he hated Italian food. Arty is a meat and potatoes kind of guy."

"And Jake?"

"He took me to a great Italian restaurant. Jake loves red sauce."

"What else does Jake love?"

"He loves kids and animals. He wants to buy a house with a big porch, a farmer's porch, with two big rocking chairs…for when he gets old."

"Who's the second rocking chair for?" Dr. Forte asks, calmly.

"For his wife…maybe…for me. Oh, Doctor, why does he want me…a girl who is afraid to be hugged?"

"You hugged me a little while ago."

"I did…that's the first time we hugged, I think."

"You shook my hand when we first met."

"I forgot about that."

"I want you to try to wish Jake a Merry Christmas with a short hug, like the one you gave me. Will you think about it?"

"I will…I trust Jake, I really do trust him."

"Would he reach for your breast like Arty did?"

"Never, Jake is a gentleman."

"Start with brief hugs…and then try handholding if you are so inclined. Small steps, Pia, remember, small steps."

"Jake said he would step into the fire to save me."

"So you said."

"I think…I think I'm less afraid."

"Afraid of what?"

"I'm not as afraid of fire."

"Try having Portia light a candle and see how it makes you feel. Try blowing out that candle. Small steps, Pia. Fire is dangerous when it gets out of control. But we humans are able to control fire."

"Except for men like Arty who probably fell asleep with a lit cigarette."

"But you don't seem angry about that."

"No, it was just an accident."

"So was the fire that took away your family."

"How do I stop the nightmares, Dr. Forte?" she asks.

"Try thinking about happy memories as you drift into sleep. If you wake from a nightmare, wash your face to wake yourself up.

Then try to sleep, but focus on happy times with your family, with Nonna, with Portia, with Jake."

"I don't have many happy memories with Arty."

"Do you want to create new memories with him?"

"Not really."

"Well, as I said, take your time before making any life changing decisions. Just take your time, Pia."

"My hands are ugly now," Pia mumbles as she stares at her scars.

"Would Arty say they were ugly?" Dr. Forte prompts.

"Probably."

"What would Jake say?"

"He thinks I'm beautiful. It's like he's blind to all my imperfections."

"I think he loves you."

"I think so too."

"Do you love Arty?"

"No."

"Do you love Jake?"

"I...I...I guess I do. I do love him. I just can't let myself love him, not while I'm still married, not while I'm still so frigid."

"If you divorce Arty and we continue to make progress, could you love Jake?"

"I think so. Yes. He's wonderful."

"And he seems to adore you. Just give yourself time, Pia. You're still 21 years old."

"I will Dr. Forte. I think we made real progress today."

"You made progress, Pia. I mostly just listened."

"Well, you're a great listener," Pia says, sweetly.

"Thank you. Our session is up, Pia. You said you don't have any insurance right now?"

"No, it's $60, right? Portia will write you a check."

"Please tell Portia today's session is my welcome back gift to you. I am so happy you survived your ordeal."

"Me too. That is so generous of you."

"It is my pleasure, Pia. And you'll be getting a cash discount in the future. Instead of $60, just tell Portia the sessions will be $40 until you are insured."

"I'm speechless, Dr. Forte."

"I think you may not need to see me on a regular basis in a few months. But I hope you will keep coming back each week for now. Don't rush back to New York just yet."

"I may never go back to New York. I think I know where I belong now."

"Small steps, Pia. No rash decisions. I'll see you next week."

"Thank you so much for everything."

"I think you did 99% of the work, Pia. And I'm very proud of you."

"I think I'm proud of me too."

"You are a very brave person. You have endured far more than most women your age."

"Can I hug you goodbye?"

"If you must," she laughs.

29

Pia saw Dr. Forte two more times before Christmas and they continued to make progress. She showed the doctor her precious family photographs and her pink plastic spoon. Dr. Forte will be away for the month of January, but Pia is only a phone call away. She'll be checking up on her favorite patient. The lifesaver psychologist only works nine months out of the year. She spends January with her elderly mother in Switzerland and then she returns for the summer.

Dr. Forte's mother is 89 years old, but she comes from a long line of centenarians. Danielle Forte appreciates her mother and she needs to spend quality time with her. Pia understands. She envies the relationship between mother and daughter. But Dr. Forte will be calling her in January and the conversations won't cost Pia a dime.

Pia is starting to understand her phobia about touching. The fear of fire is no mystery to her, but after what she has endured, she no longer lives in fear of surviving such an ordeal. The flames tried to consume her, but she refused, she fought back and defeated the monster by surviving the blaze.

She thinks her phobia about touching began after Nonna died and the social worker embraced her with a sympathetic hug. Pia pulled away as the hug gave her no comfort. The arms of a stranger could not ease her pain. No one dared to touch her in the sterile orphanage where people kept their distance with little eye contact.

When Portia befriended her, she did not touch Pia at first, but eventually they held hands and sometimes hugged one another goodnight. In time Portia was the only person whom she was comfortable touching or indulging in deep conversations.

When Portia aged out, Pia became withdrawn, almost *feral,* and she remained that way after she left the orphanage. The halfway house was lonely and hostile at times and she had no desire to spend time with the other residents.

Then Arty wormed his way into her life and she tried to enjoy holding his hand, but it was difficult for her. She would tell herself that she was an adult now and touching was all part of being grown up. But she never enjoyed his touch.

She did agree to marry him and he was very patient until the honeymoon. Pia hated the sex, it was painful and unsatisfying, but at least Arty would get it over with quickly and fall into a deep sleep. She had hoped his hugs would eventually become natural and that she might enjoy the closeness, much as she had enjoyed hugging Portia at times. But things only got worse.

After running away to Maryland, she found herself yearning for the touch of another human being again and Portia was the only person she felt comfortable hugging. But as she watched Portia and Ben snuggle on the sofa and kiss passionately, she became more troubled and even Portia's hugs began to repulse her.

Living in the house with Arty changed little. She loved fixing up the home and the car was an unexpected thrill. Learning to drive gave her a newfound freedom. Yet, she continued to be sickened by the notion of ever making love to her husband again. She tried small steps, short hugs, a tiny ounce of affection when two of their body parts touched inadvertently. But Arty's body only reminded her of why she had left him in the first place.

She was hurt when she found out about Arty's other women and she was so proud of herself for confronting them. What they were doing was unethical and unforgivable. But she wasn't really jealous since she had no desire to lay with Arty. She wondered if she ever would and she knew she needed a new psychologist in New York if she was ever going to face her fears.

Now that she is back in Maryland, she wonders if she can heal. Dr. Forte has been such a godsend once again. She no longer blames herself for the death of her parents and her beloved Gaetano. She can even walk by a lit candle without flinching or tensing up. She hugged Portia recently and she has hugged Dr. Forte twice now. She thinks she is getting better.

Her hands and feet are healing along with her heart and she smiles when she recalls dancing in the kitchen with Nonna as Paul and John serenaded them with Ringo keeping the beat and George strumming his guitar as only musical geniuses can. The Beatles will always stir up happy memories for her and whenever she sees a breadstick, her thoughts run to Nonna who so often turned one into a microphone before taking that first nibble.

Nonna's death paralyzed her heart for years and threw her into a frenzy of the unknown as she lived with strangers in a cold, joyless dormitory. She is beginning to realize that when anyone hugs her, she finds herself reliving Nonna's death, once again experiencing the grief of finding her still body on the kitchen floor. If she is in someone's arms, why isn't it Nonna? Why did she have to die so young?

But now she can remember Nonna's hugs with fondness and warmth and perhaps she is ready to embrace others without tensing up as if she is about to be violated. Dr. Forte has opened her eyes and softened her defenses, causing her to wake with a morning smile as joyous birds sing their sunrise soliloquies to greet the new day. Colors are brighter now and strangers frighten her less for she is evolving, growing, changing…into the person Nonna would want her to be.

It's Christmas Eve and Jake is stopping by. He has a gift for Pia and she bought him something as well. It will be a humble gathering of the four of them, Ben, Portia, Jake and Pia. The festivities will end early since everyone has plans for later.

Ben and Portia are visiting friends and family before heading to midnight mass later and then they will be having a 1am breakfast with Ben's family. His clan opens gifts after their Christmas breakfast while youngsters are tucked away under blankets, awaiting Santa with restless joy. Jake has a late dinner engagement with his mother and grandmother. He wants Pia to attend, but she plans to stay home and cuddle up with a good book. She also expects to call Arty on Christmas Eve around 10pm since the restaurant closes early tonight and Arty should have Christmas Day off.

"Thank you guys," Portia and Ben exclaim in unison when they open their gift from Pia and Jake. Everyone knows Pia is still not working and Jake had to have paid for the gift certificate for one of his favorite Italian restaurants, the place where Jake took Pia on their first official date.

"Our pleasure, enjoy!" Jake responds with a smile as he winks at Pia.

"Open our gift, Jake," Portia returns.

"OK, let's see what we have here. I think it's a shirt…and a tie. Perfect, you guys know my taste. Thank you so much. A car salesman can't have enough of these since we continually spill soup on our ties."

"You like it?" Ben asks. "Portia picked out the shirt, but I chose the tie."

"I love it."

"And Pia is wearing our gift," Portia declares. Pia stands and spins around in her new red dress with a hunter-green sash and Jake applauds with glee and his usual devotion

"Open my gift, Jake," Pia demands as she hands him a small package. He tears off the paper and grins.

"It's a book, is it a book about how to be a better car salesman?" he teases.

"No," Pia laughs. "Check it out."

"How to Pick out Produce," Jake reads. "I love it. Thank you Pia." Of course the gift holds a special meaning to two people who first bonded in front of melons and grapes.

"There's another gift…here," Pia says with a silly grin.

"OK, it could be a soccer ball, kind of small to be a new basketball. Kind of heavy for a ball though. Oh, gosh, it's a cantaloupe!" He bursts into laughter. "Nowhere on the planet is someone else likely opening an orange Christmas cantaloupe."

"Nowhere but here," Ben jests.

"Thank you, Pia. Is it ripe?"

"Read the book," she teases.

"I will. And thank you from the bottom of my heart. Here Pia, this is for you," Jake whispers. Portia shoots a smile at Ben in anticipation.

"Let's see, it's very small…and light. Is it breakable?" she asks as she shakes the box and peels away the wrapping paper. It is a small white box. She slowly removes the cover. "Oh, gosh, it's beautiful, Jake."

"What is it?" Ben asks like a schoolboy.

"It's a silver charm bracelet, silly," Portia instructs her fiancé.

"Where are the charms?" Ben asks as Jake smiles and helps Pia with the clasp. Pia waves her slender wrist about and Portia cheers.

"There's more," Jake declares as he hands Pia a second small box.

"Must be a charm," Ben comments.

"Don't spoil the surprise," Portia whispers.

"Oh, wow, it's two charms, two matching charms," Pia utters with a blushing grin.

"They *are* identical," Ben agrees.

"Two little rocking chairs," Portia exclaims. Ben doesn't get it, but Portia understands. She knows Jake longs to grow old on a farmer's porch, rocking next to the love of his life. When Portia opened the gift certificate, she thought to herself, *this guy is a ten.* She hopes Pia is beginning agree.

"Thank you, Jake, thank you so much. I will treasure the bracelet and both charms."

"And now I know what I'm getting you for your birthday," Portia adds.

"A third charm?" Ben asks and Portia smiles at the obvious.

"I want to hug you, Jake, but I'm not ready," Pia admits.

"No problem. I'm a very patient man."

Pia is alone now. Jake is with his family and the others are with friends. They all urged Pia to join them, but she needs some alone time. Christmas Eve with Nonna was joyous and delicious. They would munch on fried dough and dance all over the house. *Jingle Bell Rock* was Nonna's favorite song during this magical time of year. Pia plays Christmas carols and dances around the apartment in her red dress until ten, sliding along in her soft slippers. Time to call Arty.

"Helloooo," a woman squeals.

"Is…is Arty there?" Pia asks in surprise.

"Hold on honey…Arty, telephone," she bellows.

"Hello," he says.

"Merry Christmas, Arty."

"Oh, Pia, hi, same to you."

"Arty, get your butt over here. I'm feeling lonely," the woman screeches from the sofa.

"You have company?" Pia asks meekly.

"Yeah, one of the new waitresses. She came over for a drink."

"Arty, I'm horny. I'm taking my clothes off…" the woman calls out.

"Arty," Pia begins, "I didn't want to tell you this until after New Year's, but I think I'm going back to my old job soon, in February."

"Huh? What about us?"

"And I'm moving back into my apartment next month. I want a divorce Arty. You keep the house, I don't want anything. Just pay for the divorce and send me the paperwork."

"Are you mad at me?"

"Not at all. I think I'm happier than I have been in a decade. Go have fun with your waitress friend. Happy holidays, Arty. It's over."

"Are you sure?" he pleads.

"I'm sure. Happy New Year and please call a lawyer next week. You're free, Arty. Go have fun without feeling guilty anymore."

"I never really feel guilty."

"I didn't think so. Goodbye Arty."

30

Pia wakes at nine. It's Christmas morning and she knows Ben and Portia are surely comatose in the other room. She heard them stumble in around 4am, but she was able to drift back into a sweet sleep. She has not slept so well in many years and she thinks the final closure with Arty is partly responsible for her mood. She slept with her silver bracelet and she dangles her wrist in the air as she lies in bed and smiles.

She fixes a light breakfast and then she calls Jake. She promised to call him at ten sharp. When she first hears his voice, her heart races as she stares at the two tiny charms, the two silver rockers.

"Merry Christmas," she whispers into the phone.

"Merry Christmas, Pia. Portia and Ben still out cold?"

"You guessed it," she giggles quietly.

"Have you changed your mind about joining my family for Christmas dinner?" he pleads with a smidgeon of hope. "It will just be us, my mother and grandmother."

"Actually, I have."

"You have?" he screams and his roommate stirs in his bed.

"I have. When will you pick me up?"

"I'll be at your place at 1pm. Dinner is at 2pm. Nana likes to eat early. She goes to bed at nine and gets up with the birds."

"I'll be ready. I better go take a bath."

"Pia, you just made me the happiest man on the planet."

"Oh, Jake, you are so dramatic. It's one of the things I adore about you."

"You adore stuff about me?"

"Lots of stuff. See you soon."

"Bye Pia. Merry Christmas."

"Wake up you guys," Pia yells as she bangs on their bedroom door at half past twelve.

"OK, we're up, we're up. Where's the fire?" Ben calls out.

"Don't say fire," Portia whispers.

"Oops sorry."

"No fire. But you said you need to be on the road by 2pm. You only have an hour and a half to wake up. Coffee is waiting for you in the kitchen. I'm getting dressed. Bathroom is free."

"Wait, are you going out?" Portia asks as she opens the door and sticks her head out.

"I'm naked in here," Ben reminds her.

"Oh, hush. No one cares," Portia laughs.

"Jake is picking me up in a half hour. I'm having dinner with his family."

"That's the best Christmas present you could have given me…or him," Portia laughs. "Merry Christmas, Pia."

"Merry Christmas, Portia. I have another surprise. I told Arty I want a divorce last night."

"What? That's fantastic news. So you're staying?"

"What's going on?" Ben calls out.

"Put on some clothes," Portia teases.

"And I'm moving into my apartment in January and Ben can move in here permanently while you guys find your next place."

"Do you feel ready to be alone?"

"I won't be alone. Jake will visit me a lot."

"I'm sure he will. And the old job?"

"Marie said I can come back after my birthday. I'll call her next week and tell her I'll be there."

"I'm so happy. You just made my Christmas."

"I think I made my own Christmas."

The dinner at Jake's mother's house is amazing. Nana and his mother are excellent cooks and Jake helped out in the kitchen and served the appetizers on a silver tray. Pia cannot get over it. His grandmother reminds her so much of Nonna. She has the same warmth, a similar spunk, the same smile.

"So, Pia, how are your burns?" Nana asks.

"Much better. I'm healing very fast."

"Will you be going back to New York soon?" his mother asks.

"Actually, no. I told my husband I want a divorce. We spoke last night."

"So you're staying in Maryland?" Nana asks. Jake is in the kitchen and he enters the dining room and asks what he missed.

"Pia is staying. She's divorcing her husband," Nana replies with a smile.

"What? You didn't say a word to me," Jake declares as he sits.

"It all just happened last night. I'm moving back to my apartment next month and starting work again in February."

"And you're free. You're done with Arty?"

"Completely. He had a date last night and I don't think he is too broken up about it. I told him he can have the house. All I want is for him to pay for the divorce."

"This is the best Christmas present you could have given me," Jake proclaims with a wide smile.

"Divorces are not Christmas presents," his mother teases. "But we are all glad you'll be staying, Pia."

"Can I court you?" Jake asks like a twelve-year-old boy with a huge crush.

"I think you already are," she laughs.

When it is time to leave, after the kitchen is once again spotless, Nana asks Pia if she can hug her goodnight. Pia nods. They embrace warmly for about ten seconds. Nana's arms feel good, she is back with Nonna again, transported through time. Then she holds open her arms and embraces Jake's mom for another long hug.

"I feel left out here," Jake complains as he stands with his arms at his sides. His grandmother laughs and gives him a bear hug. Then his mother hugs him. He is happy to hug them both for the millionth time, but then he glances at Pia. She looks away.

"Goodnight and thank you so much for a lovely day, Merry Christmas," Pia says warmly.

"You too and Happy New Year," Nana responds with a smile.

"Merry Christmas, Pia," Jake's mom says as Jake holds the door open.

They are back at Portia's apartment, sipping on a cup of herbal tea. He doesn't want to leave her and she doesn't seem to be in a hurry to go to bed. Portia and Ben won't be back for hours.

"I'm making progress, Jake. I have hugged four women in the past two months. Dr. Forte, Portia, and now your mom and grandmother."

"Yes, I am so glad."

"Of course they all have something in common."

"They're all females?" he asks.

"Yes, and I trust them."

"Do you trust me?"

"With my life. You know Jake, you are no longer a seven."

"I'm an eight now?"

"Nope."

"Nine?"

"Nope."

"Oh no, am I a two now?"

"You're going in the wrong direction, silly," she laughs as she points to the ceiling with her thumb like a hitchhiker with no sense of direction.

"I'm a ten?" he murmurs, his eyes bright, his jaw agape. She leans closer and whispers in his ear.

"At the very minimum. You are at *least* a ten."

"I want to hug you so badly," he pleads. His eyes are so penetrating, haunting, captivating.

"Then what are you waiting for?" she teases.

"Really?" he begs as he opens his arms. She does not answer, not with words. She falls into his waiting arms.

"I love you, Jake," she murmurs in his ear. They kiss, gently at first, and then they separate for an instant and kiss again, passionately. She feels the earth move. She is lost in pleasure.

"I love you too, Pia. I have loved you from the moment I first saw you," he says as they end the kiss. "I would do anything for you, you know that. I would walk through fire for you. I would *step* into the *flames*."

Epilogue

Four years after Portia and Ben's wedding...

A woman sits alone on a farmer's porch, rocking slowly, as a summer breeze wanders past and gently kisses her cheek. She squints up at the morning sun and smiles as she caresses her swollen belly with the flat of her hands.

"Morning," a stranger calls out from the end of her driveway.

"Morning, out taking a run?" the woman yells back. "Are you the new neighbor?"

"Yes, my husband and I just moved in. We're three houses down."

"There's an empty rocking chair if you'd like to rest a bit," the woman offers.

"Great," the jogger returns as she trots towards the porch.

"I'm Pia McGuire," the woman says with a smile as she extends her right arm. "Forgive me for not standing."

"No forgiveness warranted. When are you due?"

"Next month. My best friend and I are having babies around the same time. Of course it's her second. She has a little two-year-old girl named Francesca."

"Lovely name, Francesca," she says as she plops into the vacant rocking chair. "I'm Sarah James."

"Sounds like the name of an author," Pia laughs.

"I am an author, or at least I want to be. I'm working on my first novel."

"I can't wait to read it," Pia says warmly.

"My husband is Steve. He's a car mechanic."

"My husband sells cars, his name is Jake."

"We may be looking for a new car soon. You'll have to give me his card."

"Thanks, I will."

"Do you know the baby's gender?"

"I'm having a boy. Portia is having a boy too."

"Portia is your best friend?"

"Yes, she lives a mile from here."

"How long have you known her?"

"Forever."

"Do you work?"

"I did, I'm taking some time off. I worked in an office in DC. But Jake is doing well right now. His mom and grandmother helped us scrape up the down payment for the house. We moved in four months ago."

"It's a great house. I love the farmer's porch and the rocking chairs."

"Yes, we love them too. It was my husband's dream."

"Nice when dreams come true."

"I agree."

"Have you picked out a name for the baby?"

"Yes. We plan to name him Gaetano."

"Nice."

"We don't have a lot of family in Virginia. Jake's mom and his grandmother live in Maryland. Portia and Ben are our Virginia family. And Francesca of course."

"Ben is her husband?"

"Yes, he's a great guy. He and Jake shoot hoops on Sunday mornings."

"Steve loves basketball."

"I'll have Jake get in touch. What number is your house?"

"21."

"I like that number. I think I found my life around that age. My life as adult began when I went grocery shopping and a man asked me how to pick out a ripe cantaloupe."

"And that was Jake?"

"Yes."

"That's quite the meet-cute. Can I use it in my novel?"

"I don't see why not," she laughs. "It took me a while to realize my life was finally about to begin when I met Jake. I was pretty shy, but he never gave up on me. He was smitten from the start, although I couldn't figure out why."

"You *are* gorgeous. Any guy would turn his head to get a glimpse of those eyes, your beautiful face and hair."

"I'm too skinny, but I guess not so much anymore," she laughs as she gently massages her belly.

"How did you decide on the baby's name? Steve wants kids. We're trying, but I don't think we'll ever agree on a name. We are polar opposites on things like that," she laughs.

"I had a brother once. Gaetano. He died young, very young."

"I'm so sorry."

"Thank you."

"You must have loved him."

"I did…I do."

"Well, it's a beautiful name. So is Pia."

"Thanks. I like Sarah too."

"I never liked my name, very biblical."

"What baby names are you considering?"

"Actually, I like your friend's name…Portia."

"She's great. I love her name too."

"How did you two meet?"

"It's a long story."

"I have time, if you do."

"Go inside. There's a fresh pitcher of lemonade in the fridge. Grab a couple of glasses. There's a plate of cookies on the table too. You don't mind waiting on a very pregnant woman?"

"It would be my pleasure and my honor. Be right back."

As Sarah goes to fetch the refreshments, Pia ponder her story. How did she meet Portia? Where to begin? She decides to begin in the most logical of places…at the beginning.

www.ingramcontent.com/pod-product-compliance
Lightning Source LLC
Chambersburg PA
CBHW071600150726
48000CB00004B/1544